THE WEDDING CAPER

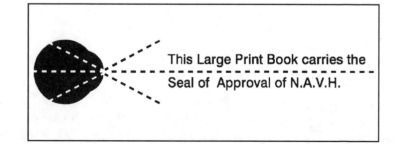

This Large Print Book carries the
Seal of Approval of N.A.V.H.

THE WEDDING CAPER

A COZY MYSTERY

JANICE A. THOMPSON

THORNDIKE PRESS
A part of Gale, Cengage Learning

Detroit • New York • San Francisco • New Haven, Conn • Waterville, Maine • London

GALE
CENGAGE Learning

LIBRARY OF CONGRESS CATALOGING-IN-PUBLICATION DATA

Thompson, Janice A.
  The wedding caper : a cozy mystery / By Janice A. Thompson. — Large print ed.
    p. cm. — (Thorndike Press large print Christian fiction)
  ISBN-13: 978-1-4104-1027-6 (hardcover : alk. paper)
  ISBN-10: 1-4104-1027-7 (hardcover : alk. paper)
  1. Large type books. I. Title.
PS3620.H6824W43 2008
813'.6—dc22   2008026288

Published in 2008 by arrangement with Barbour Publishing, Inc.

Printed in the United States of America
1 2 3 4 5 6 7 12 11 10 09 08

DEDICATION

To Kay, "Supersleuth extraordinaire!" Thanks for all the great ideas and for being the "real" Sheila in my life.

To Randi and Zach: Your February 2004 wedding was pure delight, and helping you prepare for the big day was more fun than I could have imagined. Your love story inspired me to write this fun-loving mystery. May the Lord richly bless your union — and that future grandbaby of mine!

To Courtney and Brandon: Your beautiful June wedding — just four months later — offered me plenty of incentive to stay on the ball. I've never had more fun. Your big day provided tons of inspiration for this happy story. I pray God's richest blessings on your marriage.

To Megan and Kevin: Just when I thought I could catch my breath — another wedding? I'm thrilled for you both! I thank you for being beacons of light in my life during the writing of this book. Your humor kept me going. Your big day is going to be deliriously beautiful. I know, because both of you are.

To Courtney Elizabeth: Honey, hang on. Mr. Right is coming. I can feel it.

To my amazing critique partners, Kathleen Y'Barbo, Martha Rogers, and Marian Merritt: Bless you for cruising through this story at warp speed. You made record time with this one, ladies. I can never thank you enough.

To my editors, Susan Downs and Becky Germany: Ladies, I don't know where to begin. I'm blessed beyond belief to be at such an amazing publishing house and to have two of the best in the business on my team. Thank you for believing in me, and thank you for giving me the privilege of "discovering my voice" through this new genre. I'm eternally grateful to you both.

To the Lord, Creator of all: You are my ever-present help in trouble and my inspiration in all I do. May this truly be a praise unto You.

PROLOGUE

I've had an aversion to Tuesdays ever since the day my husband robbed the Clark County Savings and Loan.

Okay, I can't prove it was my husband, at least not yet. And I guess you couldn't exactly call it a robbery, since no one witnessed the crime. But I'm fairly certain it happened on a Tuesday. My mind is a little clouded where the facts are concerned. That's what happens when you go into shock. Details slip right out of your head.

This much I do remember for certain: Warren arrived home from work at six thirty in the evening, as always. Loosened his navy blue tie. Grumbled about the unseasonably warm weather. Shrugged off his jacket. Scratched our dachshund behind the ear. Muttered a "How was your day, Annie?" Planted a kiss on my cheek.

Nothing unusual about any of those things. Nope, my suspicions didn't really

7

kick in until he pressed a 9 × 12 manila envelope stuffed full of cash into my unsuspecting palm.

"Enough to pay for both weddings," he said with a smile. A knowing smile. A suspicious smile. And the wink that followed did little to squelch the knot that suddenly gripped my belly.

Now, I've heard people talk about how your whole life flashes before your eyes right before you die, and I'm pretty sure I thought my small-town world had come crashing to a halt right then and there. But somehow I managed to muster up two words: "W–What?" and "H–How?"

He just shook his head and kept walking. Into the bedroom. Away from my questions. Away from my probing stare. Away from the envelope, which now vibrated in my outstretched hand like a pit viper waiting to be tossed into the fire.

I hurled the demon thing onto the kitchen counter and stared in disbelief. He'd done it. Sure, I'd heard him joke about robbing the bank for weeks, ever since our twin daughters, Brandi and Candy, both announced their engagements on the same night. With two weddings to pay for, who wouldn't have kidded about such a thing, especially with college loans to cover and a teenage son in football? But to actually do it? That was another thing altogether.

I stared at the envelope once again, the bills inside peeking out, tempting me — no, begging me — to count them. My palms sweated in anticipation as I reached to finger the first greenback, to make sure my imagination hadn't gotten the better of me.

It hadn't.

I began to count. One hundred. Two. Three. Four.

Ten minutes and still counting. By the time I reached twenty-five thousand dollars, my palms had completely dried out. Handling cash can do that to you. I guess that's why bankers always kept that little container of fingertip moistener available. Made sense to me now.

Ironically, my tongue seemed to have dried up, too. I wanted to call for Warren — wanted to ask him where in the world this cash had come from — but didn't dare.

I knew. In my gut, I knew. He was the one the police had been looking for ever since last Tuesday. And now I had the proof.

CHAPTER 01

Two days after I tucked the manila envelope into my underwear drawer, I paced the house and prayed. Pleaded with the Almighty to show my husband the error of his ways. Begged Him to give me peace if I'd somehow misinterpreted the situation.

Just ask him where the money came from.

How many times had those words flitted through my brain? A hundred? A thousand? A logical person would have done so, surely. And yet, every time I worked up the courage to approach Warren about the twenty-five thousand dollars, an image from the past flashed before my eyes. The third year of our marriage, I'd made a royal mess of our finances. With frustration mounting, I'd approached my husband with great dramatic flair. "You're the banker," I had announced with tears in my eyes. "And I'm not. It's just not my calling."

On that day, I passed my *Peterson Family*

Budget folder off to Warren, vowing to never pick it up again. Never. No matter what. He could have it — lock, stock, and barrel. I didn't want to know the whos, whats, whens, and wheres of budgeting or investing.

When it came to our family finances, I'd taken a hands-off approach. To be honest, my darling husband had handled things with such finesse over the years that I scarcely thought about money at all. Unless something big came up. Like two weddings, for example.

Even so, with twenty-five thousand dollars residing beneath my lingerie, I needed answers and I needed them quick. Where and when would I find them, though? With two bridal extravaganzas to coordinate, a new freelance editing business to expand, and a tight-lipped husband to absolve, I found my plate completely overloaded. How could I keep up with it all?

I settled down at the computer and signed on to the Internet. After deleting some unnecessary e-mails, I read through my morning devotional, focusing on the verse of the day, Philippians 4:6–7: *"Do not be anxious about anything, but in everything, by prayer and petition, with thanksgiving, present your requests to God. And the peace of God, which*

12

transcends all understanding, will guard your hearts and your minds in Christ Jesus."

I leaned back against the chair and spent a little time in prayer. I needed to rid myself of the anxiety, and I did my best to present my petition to God. I couldn't help but wonder how many other wives had prayed the *Dear-Lord-please-show-me-if-my-husband-robbed-the-bank* prayer like I now found myself doing. It did make me feel better to share my concerns with someone else, though. I no longer felt alone.

A wave of peace rushed over me, and with newfound determination, I set out on what I believed to be a God-ordained course of action — a sure-fire way to put an end to my anxiety.

I browsed the World Wide Web for information on crime solving.

When I stumbled across the site www .investigativeskills.com, I almost fell out of my chair. *Ah-ha.* Here, a world of information awaited me. Perhaps, with the help of the experts, I could determine my husband's guilt or innocence. And if proven innocent, maybe I could catch the real perpetrator in the process.

All for a small, one-time fee of one hundred and fifty dollars.

I read through the fine print, curious to

see what I'd get for my money.

"InvestigativeSkills.com is proud to offer this amazing course for professional and novice investigators alike. Increase your skills in crime solving with ten concise courses. For a small fee of $150, you will receive one e-mail lesson per day for ten days. Each day's teaching will bring you one step closer to solving crimes, large and small. Don't be fooled by other companies claiming to offer similar services. InvestigativeSkills.com can teach you everything you need to know — and more."

I whispered a quiet "Praise the Lord" as I reached for our credit card. What was $150.00 in the grand scheme of things? This money — albeit borrowed at 21 percent interest — would buy my husband's freedom.

I entered the required information and clicked the SEND button. Less than two minutes later, an e-mail arrived in my box with the first day's lesson. I glanced at the title and smiled. *"Lesson One: A Good Investigator Sticks to the Facts."* I skimmed the article, gleaning as much as I could from the teaching.

Stick to the facts, eh? Visions of Joe Friday danced through my brain as I took it all in. *Just the facts, ma'am.*

Alrighty then. Just the facts. And I would make note of every single one. I would purchase a new spiral notebook just for the occasion. And I would fill it with information that would eventually lead me to the truth — the whole truth, and nothing but the truth.

As a professional copy editor, I certainly knew how to come at things from a left-brained, logical approach. I'd go back through the details leading back to Tuesday — one by one. I'd contemplate every suspect, turn over every rock, and examine every motive.

In short, I would do this thing right.

Oh, and one more thing. I would do it all without raising suspicions. If my daughters learned their mother had taken on the task of crime fighting — even on the local level — they might think she didn't have time to devote to their weddings. My editing clients might be a little nervous, as well. And if my husband found out . . .

A shiver ran down my spine. What would I do if Warren discovered I suspected him of robbery?

Or was it burglary? I still hadn't quite

figured that one out.

Mental note: Check the Internet to find out if your husband will be tried as a first- or second-degree felon.

With new resolve, I made my daily trek to our local supercenter, anxious to find just the right notepad to house my newly discovered facts. Nothing too frilly — not for the wife of a vicious criminal. But nothing too ordinary, either. Heaven only knew who might stumble across my scatterbrained ramblings years from now. I wanted them to look sensible, with a decent cover and flowing handwriting. That way, when the folks from Hollywood decided to turn our story into a Movie of the Week, they wouldn't have any trouble deciphering my notes.

Naturally, I managed to select the only cart in the store with a broken wheel. I clack-clacked my way along, doing everything in my power to still my fractured nerves. As a temporary distraction, I glanced over my list. Laundry detergent — *Mental note: Get the new lavender scent;* toilet paper; three hundred bottles of wedding bubbles — the kind guests blow at the bride and groom; spaghetti sauce (there's clearly no better place to examine your husband's alter ego than over a bowl of steaming pasta).

Oh, and the notebook. I couldn't forget that.

With my supercenter know-how firmly in place, I raced about, gathering up most of the necessary items, then headed over to the school-supply aisle to select one last thing. My notebook. As I rounded the corner, I ran my basket headlong into another customer.

"Hey, why don't you watch where you're —" She stopped almost as soon as she started, and laughter rang out. I stared up in disbelief at my good friend, Sheila.

"Girl!" I exclaimed.

"Girl, nothing!" Sheila stammered. "You almost gave me a heart attack." She clutched her chest with dramatic flair — not an unusual move on her part. "And I'm too young to go. At least yet."

Now, truth be told, I had no clue as to Sheila's real age. She'd pressed forty-nine for so long, it was pleated.

"What's your hurry, anyway?" she asked. "House on fire?"

"No, I, uh —"

Sheila, perceptive gal that she was, must've grown suspicious from the hesitation in my voice. Her narrow eyebrows arched and she leaned in to whisper, "Whatever it is, you can tell me, Annie. I have no problem keeping secrets."

"Well, I —"

"It's only the people I tell."

She erupted in laughter and I couldn't help but chuckle. Leave it to Sheila to bring a smile to my face. However, it didn't take long for my facade to crack. She dove into a lengthy discussion focused on an article she'd read in today's *Clark County Gazette* about the "bank job" as she called it. Then she said the one thing I'd avoided for two days. "They took twenty-five thousand dollars, you know. Twenty-five thousand!"

I'd known the amount all along, of course. But hearing it spoken aloud made it even more real.

And my husband even guiltier, if that were possible.

"It's the strangest thing, isn't it?" she pondered. "Almost as if the money just got up and walked out of the bank on its own. And the police can't seem to get a handle on who's to blame."

I struggled to answer, "Oh? Didn't I read something about a drifter being arrested? Haven't they focused their investigation on him?"

"For now." She shrugged. "But I think —"

She lowered her voice and drew closer to share the rest. "It was an inside job."

I didn't mean to gasp but couldn't seem to help it. She clamped a hand over her mouth, realizing what she'd said.

"Oh, my goodness. I hope you don't think I'm saying . . . Well, of course I'm not. You know me better than that. And I know Warren better than that."

Clearly unnerved, Sheila turned her attention to the stack of spiral notebooks on the bottom row. She selected one with a lovely rose on top. "This is so pretty. I think I'll buy it for my grocery lists and new recipes. Not that I do much cooking these days. Now that the kids are grown, Orin and I have discovered the world of takeout." As she flashed a crooked grin, her perfectly sculpted eyebrows arched.

I reached down and came up with a black and white notebook with a puppy on the front. Dachshund. Ironic. "I'll take one, too. You just never know when the Lord will lay something on your heart."

Just the facts, ma'am.

We said our good-byes and I headed to the checkout. Afterward, I opted to drive through a nearby fast-food joint for chicken nuggets and a diet soda.

I arrived home at two fifteen, checked on

the package of hamburger meat I'd set out to thaw, took the puppy for a walk, and then settled down onto the sofa, notebook in hand.

"Just the facts, ma'am." I spoke the words to the dog, whose ears perked up, as if in response. "Just the facts." My Joe Friday impersonation improved with each rendition.

Sasha, ever my faithful companion, leaped into my lap, nearly knocking the notebook to the floor. I scooted over in the chair to accommodate her, then pulled the cap from my pen to begin my list.

Fact #1: Clark County Savings and Loan is missing a cash night deposit in the amount of twenty-five thousand dollars. Said depositor, Clarksborough Catering, telephoned the bank in advance to provide a heads-up of their plan. The owner of the catering company is said to be in a panic over the missing funds.

Fact #2: My husband, Warren J. Peterson, is a personal banker at the Clark County Savings and Loan, where he has been employed for twenty-three years. He often handles the night deposits.

Fact #3: Said husband has mysteriously turned up with twenty-five thousand dollars in cash to cover the cost of two weddings. Without explanation.

I gnawed at the end of my pen and did everything in my power to ignore the nausea that now ripped through my tummy. Was it the chicken nuggets, or had coming face-to-face with my husband's future behind bars caused this sudden rumbling? I pressed the feelings aside and focused on my list. More facts remained; facts that could not be ignored.

Fact #4: The police have already interrogated all bank employees, who came up clean as a whistle. Whew! Warren, I knew you were innocent!

Fact #5: The Clark County Electric Company has verified that a power surge on the night in question left the bank without electricity for several hours, thus disabling all cameras.

Fact #6: The police have turned their attentions to a male drifter from nearby Philadelphia, approximately twenty-four years of age, who had been seen hanging around outside the Savings and Loan at all hours of the day and night. *Mental note: Check date of arrest and question police regarding grounds.*

Fact #7:

Hmm. No Fact #7, at least not yet. Of course, there was that matter of the bank's new security guard, the pretty little blond who had sashayed into town just one month ago. Nikki. What kind of name was that for a security officer? And what kind of security guard spent her evenings doubling as a waitress at a diner? Sure, she was rumored to have come from the quaint town of Lancaster, just a little more than an hour away, but one could never tell. No — something about Nikki felt wrong.

Fact #7: New security guard raises suspicions.

Hmm. *Just the facts, ma'am.* I chewed the end of my pen as I contemplated what I'd written. Was a suspicion a fact? The editor in me opted to reword.

Fact #7: New security guard has arrived on the scene just prior to the bank's first-ever robbery. Or is it burglary?

Hmm. I still hadn't looked that up.
I did a quick Internet search using the words "Criminal Classification, State of Pennsylvania" and got my answer in a flash.

Fact #8: Said crime at Clark County Savings and Loan is considered a burglary, since no bodily injury or death took place. In the state of Pennsylvania, burglary is considered a second-degree felony.

Fact #9: Perpetrator of said felony could serve anywhere from two to twenty years in the state penitentiary.

Whoa. Two to twenty years. I tried to think of what my life would be like if Warren left for twenty years. What would the kids and I do?

I continued to chomp at the end of my pen until the goofy thing exploded in my mouth. As I sprang from the chair, the notebook slid down my shins and landed on the floor. Sasha tumbled to the floor, as well, letting out a yelp just as the phone rang. I stubbed my toe on the leg of the chair as I bounded toward the kitchen sink. The phone continued to ring as I scrubbed away at my hands and mouth. I managed to catch it on the last ring before the answering machine would pick up.

"H–Hello?"

"Honey, is everything okay?"

Warren. Tears sprang to my eyes right away. I tried to push the image of my husband in a bright orange prison jumpsuit from my mind.

"Oh, hi, baby." I tried to sound normal. "Yes, everything's fine. I just broke an ink pen and almost destroyed the armchair and the carpet all in one fell swoop."

"Ah. I thought you sounded a bit strange."

Hmm. I could've said the same thing about him. His voice sounded . . . odd. Off.

"Just wanted to let you know I'm going to be late for dinner." His sigh felt a bit forced. "O'Henry is here from the sheriff's office. Again. He needs to ask us a few more questions."

I stumbled my way through the rest of the conversation and hoped Warren hadn't picked up on the fear in my voice. As I hung up the phone, the words from today's devotional verse rang like church bells in my ears: *Do not be anxious about anything, but in everything, by prayer and petition, with thanksgiving, present your requests to God. And the peace of God, which transcends all understanding, will guard your hearts and your minds in Christ Jesus.*

With a heartfelt sigh, I reached for a new pen to write one last thing.

Fact #10: God is in control. He's already got this thing figured out.

With a sense of peace settling in, I turned my attention to preparing the best spaghetti-and-meatball dinner a steely-eyed burglar would ever eat.

CHAPTER 02

The following morning, I awoke with four words on the brain: *Just the facts, ma'am.* I scrambled from the bed, fixed breakfast for my husband and teenage son, kissed them both, and sent them on their merry way. Then I settled down with my laptop to read my daily Internet devotional.

Today's verse from John 8:32 caught me off-guard: " *'Then you will know the truth, and the truth will set you free.'* " Just a coincidence? I think not. Yes, indeed. I would know the truth — very soon — and my husband would be set free. Literally.

After spending some time in prayer, I showered, then dressed for the day. With fall making a rather sudden appearance, I opted for a spiffy pair of jeans and a brown turtleneck. It looked just right with my new choppy hairdo. Same color, too. A new over-the-top bead necklace in complementary reds and oranges fit right in with the ensemble. I glanced at myself in the mirror and whispered the words from lesson one: "A good investigator sticks to the facts."

With childlike energy, I bounded from the room and down the stairs, where I snatched up my new notebook. I sat in my favorite armchair, puppy at my side, to review what I'd written yesterday.

Hmm. In looking over my "facts" list, I had to conclude two things: Either my husband was guilty . . . or he wasn't. Not very profound, to be sure. But those were the facts, plain and simple. Knowing Warren the way I did, and knowing his love for the Lord, I found it difficult to believe he could actually have done such a thing.

Twenty-seven years of memories floated through my head as I pondered the possibilities. The birth of our twin daughters. The way Warren cradled them in his arms. The surprise arrival of our son, Devin, years later. Watching my two "boys" play football together in the front yard. The look of pride on my husband's face the day Devin made the football team. The tears in Warren's eyes the night the girls announced their engagements.

No. The more I thought about it, the more I knew he couldn't have done it. And I would do everything in my power to prove his innocence.

A plan erupted in my mind, one I could not ignore. I slipped on a light-weight jacket in a marvelous shade of coppery brown, put Sasha on a leash, and headed for the door. The neighbors might be thrown for a loop — seeing me out for a little walk this early in the day. But a brisk morning walk never did anyone any harm. And surely no one would be the wiser if I stopped off at the bank for a minute or two. After all, I did have a couple of checks to deposit.

As an afterthought, I grabbed my notepad and pen, shoved them into a bag, and slung it over my shoulder. Then I stepped outside to face a breezy autumn morning. Leaves whipped from the trees, which appeared to fuel Sasha's excitement. She pulled me along by her leash, and I found myself catapulted down the sidewalk, near breathless, at her command. I chugged along in a mad struggle to keep up. Dachshunds might be small, but they're fast as lightning.

We rounded the corner onto Wabash Street, and Sasha slowed a bit. I think I confused her by not turning back toward the house, but I had to move on, had to get to the bank to eye my suspects.

Now the obedient little pup, Sasha followed along at my heels, only veering every now and again to chase a squirrel or stray leaf. We hung a left off of Wabash onto Clarksborough and another left onto Main. There, directly in front of me, stood the Clark County Savings and Loan.

I stopped in awed silence as I took it in. How many times had I stood in this very spot, and yet I had never noticed the blue lettering in the sign, had I? And what about that landscaping? Had it escaped my notice in the past? Well, I certainly saw it now — it, and a host of other things — all through brand-new www.investigativeskills.com eyes. I resisted the urge to pat myself on the back when I realized just how far I'd already come.

But no time for that now, not with so much work left undone and my husband's fate hanging in the balance. When the traffic slowed, I crossed the street. I arrived at the side door of the bank with Sasha in tow and for the first time realized my dilemma.

Hmm. What was I thinking, bringing along a puppy? I couldn't take her inside, could I? Only service dogs allowed. I couldn't feign blindness, not with everyone inside knowing me so well. What to do? What to do?

With my keen observation skills intact, I noticed — for the first time, I might add —

a flagpole on the lawn of the bank. Sasha and I sprinted over and I secured her leash to the pole.

"Now, you be a good girl," I admonished. "And when we get home, I'll give you a treat." I leaned down to lift a floppy ear as I whispered the rest. "I might even give you two."

Her tail wagged in joyous response.

I turned back toward the savings and loan and drew in a deep breath. "Father, help me. If You really want me to solve this crime, then I'm going to need Your assistance every step of the way."

After a few courageous steps, I reached the door. To my surprise, it swung open, as if I'd been expected.

"Good morning, Mrs. Peterson."

Nikki, the *I'm-just-too-cute-to-be-working-in-a-bank* blond security guard met me with a broad smile. "How are you this morning?"

"I'm fine, honey. How are you?" *And what were you doing on the night of Tuesday, September 16?*

She let out a lingering sigh, and for the first time I noticed her bright blue eyes. Tinted contacts, no doubt. *Perhaps she's incognito, running from a former life of crime. Maybe she's . . .*

"I'm going through kind of a hard time

right now." She interrupted my thoughts with a pained whisper. "This investigation has really unnerved me."

Do tell.

"Having the police around so much has really put everyone on edge. Especially me."

No doubt.

"I was supposed to be protecting the bank from things like this, and look what happened. I wasn't even here when the burglary took place. Wasn't even here."

A woeful look crossed her face. A bit too woeful, if you ask me. Rehearsed. But, at least she knew the difference between a robbery and a burglary, which certainly gave her the upper hand, to my way of thinking.

"Oh? You weren't here?" I couldn't resist.

"No, my shift starts at seven in the morning," she explained. "And the money disappeared in the night, sometime before that. I feel just awful. I should have volunteered to drive the parking lot at night, but with no prior history of anything like this happening . . ."

Her voice faded a bit.

"And on top of all of that," she said, "my little girl is sick with the flu today. I had to keep her home from school. Wish I could've stayed home with her, but I have to work, you know? I'm a single mom."

Duly noted.

"Who's watching your daughter?"

Nikki's eyes lit up and her voice became more animated as she spoke. "I have a really great neighbor — an older woman named Katie."

Mental note: This girl knows how to change voices on a dime. She's clearly a skilled story-teller.

"Katie Stoltzfus?" I asked.

"Yes, do you know her?"

Know her? Katie Stoltzfus was my third-grade math teacher. *I've known her since you were in diapers.*

"Yes, I know her."

"Well, she's a wonderful woman. And she just adores Amber. But she's not in the best of health, and looking after a first-grader hasn't been easy on her. I'm grateful, of course. But I sure hope Amber is feeling better tomorrow."

Mental note: Nikki's cool blue eyes don't fool me one little bit. And I'll bet she doesn't even have a daughter.

Nikki grabbed my hand and gave it a squeeze as she finished her story: "I'm only telling you all of this because I know you'll pray. Mr. Peterson talks about you all the time. He says you're a —" Her lips pursed as she tried to think of the words. "What

32

does he call it again? Oh yes, a prayer warrior. I think that's it."

Conviction settled in right away. Okay. *Maybe her eyes really are blue.* "Thank you, honey." I reached to give her a hug. "I'll be praying for Amber."

I gave Nikki a wink as I headed across the bank lobby to the desk where my husband sat. Along the way, I gave a little wave to "Loan Officer Extraordinaire" — as Warren liked to call him — Richard Blevins.

"Hey, Richard."

"Oh, hi, Annie." He scarcely looked up from his work as I passed by. In fact, my finely tuned observation skills let me know that his gaze never actually locked on my own. *Avoiding me, eh? What's up with that?*

Odd. Richard was always so friendly and outgoing. Hadn't we voted him Sunday School Teacher of the Year last December? Why the unusual shift in behavior? Of course, he was going through a lot at home. Ever since his wife, Judy, was diagnosed with cancer several months ago.

"Hey, honey. What are you doing here?"

I nearly jumped out of my skin as Warren approached from behind. "I — I . . ."

"Something wrong with one of the kids?" His brow wrinkled in concern.

"No, I, uh —" I pulled the checks from

33

my bag. "Just need to make a deposit."

He took the checks from my hand. "I could've done that for you. There's never any reason for you to have to come down here, Annie."

Never any reason to come down here? Is that some sort of warning?

"I don't mind." I offered up a smile in an attempt at bravery. "I love coming to see you." I gave him a light kiss on the lips and a couple of the tellers let out a whistle. Warren turned all shades of red and gave me a "good grief" stare. In response, I grinned like a Cheshire cat and leaned over to give his jacket a sniff. "Mmm. You smell yummy." Must be that new cologne the girls had given him for his birthday.

"Annie, you're killing me."

"Yeah," I whispered. "But what a way to go." I gave him another light peck on the cheek and he shook his head in defeat.

As we headed to the counter together, I allowed my eyes to roam the lobby. From here, I could see quite a bit: a new painting on the far wall, dust on the paperweights, the balding spot on the top of Richard Blevins's head, even the bit of food between my husband's two front teeth. I gave him a little take-care-of-that-please gesture, and he quickly fingernailed it away. His cheeks turned a rosy pink, quite a dashing contrast against his wavy salt-and-pepper hair. *That's twice I've made him blush.*

The teller's voice brought me back to reality. "Good morning, Mrs. Peterson."

"Morning, Carl." I gave a polite nod.

Carl chattered on about the change in weather, but my mind remained otherwise engaged. Who had time to think about autumn with so much at stake?

We finished the transaction, and Warren ushered me to the door. A little too fast, to my way of thinking. *Is he trying to get rid of me?*

I summoned up the courage to ask him one more thing before leaving, something I should have asked days ago. I whispered the words, so as not to draw attention. "Warren —" I couldn't help but wring my hands. "I need to know — about the cash — you know — for the weddings —"

He pushed open the front door of the bank and ushered me outside. "I told you not to worry about that, honey. And I meant it. I've done a good job of handling our finances, haven't I? And you've always trusted me to do the right thing, right?"

As I offered up a lame nod, I couldn't help but notice the change in his expression — the etched brow, the tightening of the lips, the crease between the eyes. They all pointed to one thing.

I groped for coherent words, but all I managed was an "um" and an "ah." My soul mate of so many years must have heard my unspoken suspicions.

"Believe me. You have nothing to worry about." He gave my hands a squeeze. "That's our money. Ours. Every penny. So let the girls have it. And let the spending begin." He gave me a wink, which should have consoled me, but, instead, sent a little shiver down my spine.

Of course he would say that. What else could he say if he didn't trust me with the truth? I had to find a way to coax a full explanation from him without demanding it. I stood in silence a moment, then finally opted to change gears.

"Don't forget, we're eating out tonight," I reminded him. "That new steakhouse near the freeway. Seven o'clock."

"Ah. I'd forgotten."

Truth be told, I was a little nervous about tonight's dinner. The idea of meeting Brandi's future in-laws for the first time left me with a bit of a knot in my stomach, and I didn't have time for knots right now.

I had to get moving. I gave Warren one last peck on the cheek and then waved as if heading for home. And, indeed, I took a few steps toward home, just to throw everyone off a bit. However, once safely out of view, I slipped down the walkway on the north side of the savings and loan to do a bit of investigative work. I had to clamp eyes on the night deposit box, had to see for myself the location of the crime, to scope out the scene, as it were.

I inched my way along the wall, doing all I could to avoid the glances from folks sitting at the bank's drive-through just a few yards away. One lady stared in vague curiosity, and I shifted my gaze, avoiding her penetrating gaze at all costs. Where in the world was the night deposit box again?

Man. Turned out the metal contraption was smack-dab in the middle of the wall at the drive-through. *Mental note: Come back at night when there aren't so many people around. Be sure to bring a flashlight.*

With frustration threatening to eek its way into my pores, I turned to begin the walk home. This morning's verse ran through my head, taunting me. " *'You will know the truth, and the truth will set you free.'* "

In all honesty, I felt like a failure. Sure didn't have much to write in my notebook. I tried to cheer myself with happy thoughts, but the ever-present image of Warren in prison garb reminded me of my dilemma.

So, I had to get cracking. Had to at least speculate. If the truth refused to present itself, I'd continue on in my quest to find it. I would get to the bottom of this, if it was the last thing I did.

If I had to solve this riddle right here, right now, I'd still lean toward Nikki. I'd watched enough episodes of whodunit television to know you couldn't trust the innocent-looking ones as far as you could throw them. And what was all that stuff about being unnerved? What did she have to be nervous about, if not the obvious?

I allowed my thoughts to ramble that direction as I continued the journey toward home. By the time I turned onto our street, excitement had risen to an all-time high. I couldn't wait to settle down with my notebook to make sense of the facts now swirling through my head. Yes, Nikki had surely done this thing, and I would watch the cards as they stacked against her.

No sooner had I walked in the front door than the phone rang out. I answered it with a hint of frustration, wishing I could just stick to my work and avoid interruptions. I was startled to hear Warren's anxious voice. "Um, honey?"

"Yes?"

"Did you forget something?"

Forget something? I looked in my bag to figure out what I might have left. Got the deposit receipt. Got my notebook and pen.

"I'm clueless," I spoke into the phone.

His "Obviously" did little to set things straight in my mind.

Until I heard the barking in the background.

CHAPTER 03

Hardly a secret goes untold in our tiny town of Clarksborough, P-A. Whether it's the high school football coach's clandestine crush on the new postal carrier or Mayor Hennessey's eyebrow and chin lift — we hear it all. And "all" can be a lot to swallow, especially when you're not sure it's "all" the truth.

Now me, I avoid gossip like the plague. Always have. I mean, I'll occasionally chat with Sheila about this little thing or that — but most of our conversations revolve around prayer requests for the needs of others — like Mary Lou Conner's failed marriage or Betty Sue Anderson's good-for-nothing son who can't seem to stay out of the local jail.

But this thing about my husband stealing twenty-five thousand dollars I've managed to keep to myself. There are some stories you just don't need to have spread around.

People might get the wrong idea. And besides, I have my reputation to uphold. I've been a fine, upstanding member of the Clarksborough Community Church for over twenty years. And as president of the Clark County Ladies Political Action League, many depend on me for social guidance.

That's why when I opened my e-mail box after fetching Sasha from the bank, I knew I'd struck gold. The title of lesson two jumped off the page: *"A Good Investigator Develops Social Graces."* I could scarcely control my enthusiasm.

The more I read, the more intrigued I became. Turns out a skilled investigator needed more than just a keen intuition. She needed to be trained in the art of proper etiquette. Dinner parties, political gatherings, public events — a socially adept investigator should find herself at home in them all. I rubbed my hands together in anticipation. Now this, I could sink my teeth into.

With my back perfectly straight and my right ankle delicately crossed over the left, I scanned the lesson to review the basics of etiquette. I doubted there would be much to learn, all things considered. I might live in the North now, but my genteel Southern upbringing would surely give me an added advantage. If anyone understood the importance of the unspoken rules of society, a proper lady from Mississippi would.

Hmm. Turned out there was a bit more to this than met the eye. Some of the questions threw me a little.

"How do you receive a compliment?" *Graciously, of course, offering one in return.*

"Do you take a gift to the hostess of a party?" *Hmm. Looks like I owe Sheila a gift for that little soiree she held last Saturday night.*

"Does the twenty-first-century man still open the door for a woman?" *If he knows what's good for him.*

"If a wedding is called off, should the bride return the engagement ring?" *Whoa, Nellie. Stop right there. Return a diamond? Are you kidding?*

On and on it went. After awhile, I had to rest my eyes. I pondered the things I'd read. For the life of me, I couldn't figure out how "seating party guests in appropriate places" at my next big event could help me solve the Clark County Savings and Loan mystery, but I would give this "social awareness" thing my best shot. Yes, I would be a social butterfly before day's end.

Before day's end? A gasp erupted as I

glanced at the clock. Five twenty-five? After my escapade at the bank, the afternoon had pretty much slipped away from me. Warren would arrive home in less than an hour, prepared to leave for the steakhouse. And me . . .

Man, oh man. I flew into action, nearly tripping over poor Sasha in the process. "I'm sorry, little one." I gave her a scratch behind the ears, but she didn't respond with her usual burst of joy. *She's probably still mad at me for leaving her at the bank.* I crouched down to make a proper apology, one befitting a lady of honor. "I'm truly sorry for tying you to the flagpole, Sasha." Her tail gave a hint of a wag. "And I promise not to do it again." This time she leaped into my arms, as always, tongue lapping at my face in shameless glee. "Attagirl." One more pat on the back for my canine crime-solving partner, and I sprinted off to the bathroom.

It never ceases to amaze me, the ability of a woman to get ready for an "event" in a hurry. Truly, this has become almost an art form for me. I managed to shower, dress, curl my hair, and apply makeup — all within a matter of forty-five minutes. Granted, my shoes didn't match, my eyeliner came out a bit heavier on the right eye than the left, and my blue silk blouse required rebuttoning, but all in all, I think I made remarkable time.

As I headed to the closet to fetch the proper shoes — a lovely pair of fall pumps — I heard Sasha let out a joyful "yip" from the living room. *Ah. Warren's home.* I gave myself another once-over in the full-length mirror. *Not bad, not bad.* The face staring back at me conveyed genteel confidence. *Etiquette, schmetiquette. I've got this thing covered.*

Less than an hour later, we met up with Brandi and her fiancé, Scott, at Clarksborough's first-ever "fancy" steakhouse. CC's Steaks-n-More practically buzzed with excitement, and some of it rubbed off on me. I couldn't still my nerves, and the chaos of the place didn't help much. I glanced down one more time, just to make sure I'd remembered to put on my skirt. I've had that dream one too many times, I guess. You know the one — where you show up in public dressed in little more than your smile?

Brandi and Scott must've picked up on my nervousness. He nodded and smiled as she whispered, "You look great, Mom. They're going to love you."

God bless that precious daughter of mine.

She knows me, inside and out. She hit the nail right on the head this time around. For whatever reason, I was a little nervous about meeting Scott's parents. Sure, they were supposed to be wonderful people, but what if they didn't like us? What if we didn't get along or had nothing in common? Would Brandi's new mother-in-law sweep in and take my place, turning my daughter's head — and heart — away from the family? Would she talk Brandi and Scott into moving to Georgia? Would she raise my grandchildren in my stead?

Where in the world is all of this coming from?

I'd almost calmed myself when a syrupy voice near the door rang out: "How *wun-duh-ful* you look, *dah-lin'!*"

I pivoted on my heel and swallowed my fear. There she stood, in all her glory. Scott's mother. Nadine Cunningham. With her arms around my daughter, proclaiming Brandi's beauty to the masses.

Yep. She was definitely going to end up with the grandchildren. I could feel it.

On the other hand, she did have a pleasant-enough smile, and as she approached, I saw the laugh lines around her eyes. A very good sign. I reached out to take her hand, and we bonded the moment we touched. Tears rose to cover my lashes. The words must have come from the Lord. I certainly hadn't planned them. "We're going to be the best of friends," I found myself saying.

"Oh, *dah-lin'*, we are. I can feel it!" Nadine wrapped me in a warm embrace, and all the rules of proper etiquette flew right out the steakhouse window as two Southern women reveled in each other's presence. For a moment we giggled like schoolgirls, then began to ramble. "How lovely you look." "What an *a-dahr-able* shade of blue. Looks *mah-vuh-lus* with your eyes." I found myself caught up in the wonder of it all — and in the wonder of Nadine. It had nothing to do with her undeniable physical beauty; this was something different altogether. We were truly kindred spirits. I could sense it right away.

I also sensed Warren's humor as he watched me slip back into "Southern" gear. A playful smile crept across his lips. I smiled, too — until, of course, I remembered how he had acquired the money to pay for the wedding we'd gathered together to discuss.

"Are you cold, *dah-lin'?*" Nadine gave my fingers a little squeeze. "Your hands are trembling."

"No, no." I clasped them behind my back

and tried to imagine how my new friend would take to the idea that her daughter-in-law's father had stolen the funds to cover the cost of the wedding.

Thankfully, Brandi and Scott chose that moment for a "get-acquainted" session. The tall, silver-haired man to Nadine's left was introduced as Scott's stepfather, Brad. With his soft, round face, slightly protruding belly, and warm, laughing eyes, I couldn't help but think of the fellow as a premature Santa Claus. Warren reached to take his hand for a friendly shake, and I noticed the look of relief in Brandi's and Scott's eyes. Only then did I realize they had probably stressed over this meeting more than I had. Somehow, that put everything in perspective for me.

We spent the better part of the evening focused on the wedding. Brandi and Scott beamed as they shared their ideas. We all joined in with excitement, like schoolchildren released to the playground. Within an hour, most of the particulars had been penciled into my notebook, which I'd stashed in my oversized purse.

Date: Saturday, February 14 — Valentine's Day.
Time: 7:00 p.m.

Locale: The new Be Our Guest wedding facility about halfway between Clarksborough and Philly.

Colors: Wine-colored dresses for the ladies, black tuxedos for the gentlemen.

Wedding Party: Four bridesmaids (Candy and three of Brandi's best friends from church and school); four groomsmen (mostly college buddies); one flower girl (Nadine's "dah-lin' " granddaughter, Madeline); and one ring bearer (my great-nephew, Shawn).

Invitations: Personally designed and printed by the bride and groom, to be mailed early January.

Showers: Two. One for wedding gifts, another for lingerie. Mental note: Don't ask if you're invited to the second. Assume it's for the girls.

Food: Clarksborough Catering — Italian cuisine.

I bit my lip as I wrote that last one. I couldn't help but wonder how the fine folks at Clarksborough Catering would feel if they knew we were paying them with money my husband had stolen from them in the first place.

Thankfully, the wedding talk turned to other things, and Brandi and Scott lost themselves in each other's eyes. Warren and Brad took to discussing the ins and outs of investment banking, and Nadine and I . . . well, we talked about everything from our joy at becoming mothers-in-law to the Bible study she led on Monday mornings at her church in Savannah. Apparently there was more to this woman than met the eye. As she talked about caring for the homeless and feeding the poor, my heart twisted every which way. The love of the Lord literally beamed from her eyes, and I found myself captivated.

Throughout the meal, my mind wandered back to the lesson of the day. I couldn't help but be taken with Nadine's social graces as the evening continued on. Nothing contrived or fake. Simple. Genuine. Real. God-given.

If Nadine Cunningham didn't have her hands so full caring for the poor, leading a Bible study, and ministering to the sick, I daresay she would make an excellent crime fighter.

CHAPTER 04

Ah, Saturday. My favorite day of the week.

On the morning after our steak dinner, about halfway into a lovely dream about hauntingly beautiful willow trees in Savannah, Georgia, the piercing ring of the telephone roused me from my slumber. I groped for it and knocked my alarm clock off the bedside table in the process. It, too, rang out several times before I finally managed to shut it down. Amazingly, Warren slept through the whole thing.

That settled, I answered the phone, doing all I could to hide the grogginess, as morning phone-answerers often do. "H–Hello?"

"Mom?"

"Brandi, is that you?"

"Yep." She dove headlong into a lengthy, animated conversation about a wedding dress she'd seen in a bridal magazine, one she'd "have to have or die." I leaned back against my pillows and listened in rapt silence as I attempted to come awake. Hearing her happy-go-lucky voice reminded me of the plans I'd made for my own wedding, over twenty-seven years ago. Had I been this ecstatic, this . . . high-pitched?

"Sounds great, honey." I'm not sure how many times I spoke those words. At least a dozen. After Brandi finally wound down, she informed me that Candy wanted to chat. I couldn't help but grin. Even living on their own, these girls still needed their mama — nearly as much as I needed them.

True to form, Candy approached our conversation from a quieter, less emotional stance. And why not? Two very different girls; two very different ways to handle a wedding. Not that I minded. Thankfully, this daughter would give my pocketbook a bit of a rest. She and her fiancé, Garrett, had settled on a date in June, giving us a little breathing room between ceremonies. The two really seemed to suit one another. Warren and I had secretly confided in one another that Garrett would probably prove to be lower maintenance than Scott. And, of course, the fact that he worked as a computer tech didn't hurt. Might even come in handy one day.

I found myself relaxing as Candy spoke. She told me about the music she'd chosen for their first dance. My mind soared back to my own wedding. Warren and I had danced to "At Last" — one of my personal favorites and from that day on labeled "our song." Ah, love. The melody floated through my head and temporarily carried me off to a blissful state.

Until my husband let out a snore from his spot in the bed next to me.

I glanced his way and found him twisted up in the covers with Sasha sleeping soundly at his side. Nudging him with my elbow did the trick. He rolled over, and the room once again fell silent. The puppy whimpered then settled back down again, this time lopped across his feet. Warren never suspected a thing.

Warren. Suspect.

No, I wouldn't let my mind go there. Not this morning. I tried to focus on happier things — like wedding plans.

Candy continued on with her well-thought-out discussion, laying out an organized plan for the day, an hour-by-hour approach. I could hear Brandi arguing in the background, taking issue with this point or that, and found myself smiling. What interesting roomies these two made.

At some point, Candy's words sent my antennae shooting straight up into the air.

"We've set up a two o'clock appointment at Clarksborough Catering."

"Clarksborough Catering? Today?" I whispered the words again, so as not to awaken Suspect #1. "Clarksborough Catering?"

"Yes."

"Would you like me to go with you?" I offered.

When Candy answered in the affirmative, I knew the Lord must surely have special plans for me on this lovely fall day.

With my social graces firmly in place, I met the girls for lunch at the local diner. We giggled our way through soup and sandwiches as they showed me wedding-dress photos. How many squeals of sheer delight could they possibly manage?

After the meal, we drove to the tiny converted house that was Clarksborough Catering. The owner, Janetta Mullins, met us at the door. Even after years of doing business amongst us, the woman remained something of an oddity in Clarksborough — certainly not typical small-town material and not the sort to join our organizations — but what was it about her that intrigued me now? Perhaps her spiked hair with tips of blue? Or maybe the tattoo of a weight lifter on her upper arm, which she showed off by strategically rolling up the sleeve of her "Don't Mess with Mama" t-shirt?

She might look gruff on the outside, but Janetta had catered nearly every big social event in Clark County over the past ten years — and we knew better than to call on anyone else for our big to-dos.

I smiled as I reflected on my current www.investigativeskills.com lesson. Standing before me was a woman of social awareness, if I ever saw one.

Sheer curiosity settled in as she seated us at a table to discuss our options. Janetta got us off on the right foot. "Girls, take a look at this book while I go track down that daughter of mine to help out."

As she sprinted from the room, I couldn't help but wonder which daughter she meant. I understood her to have four or five. And a couple of sons, to boot. Of course, most had grown up and moved on, like my own children.

Nearly everyone in town knew Janetta had never married, and certainly more than one fella had been seen coming and going from this place through the years. Most of us never could quite put together which child went with which father, but I guess we figured that was none of our business. The family had managed not only to survive but to thrive. Their business was known for miles around. Catering business, not personal business.

A lovely young woman with sand-colored hair and sparkling green eyes entered the room.

"Hi, Kristina." Brandi gave her a warm smile. "How've you been?"

Kristina responded with "It's so good to see you!" and joined my daughters at the table, where they caught up on all they'd missed since graduating from Clark County High years prior. That done, Kristina handed out catering brochures, and the work began.

"Oooh! This looks great!" Brandi pointed to a photo of an elaborate serving table loaded with Italian goodies. "And look at that chocolate fountain!"

Candy's nose wrinkled in disagreement. "I was thinking of something much simpler than that. Hors d'oeuvres. Finger sandwiches. That kind of thing."

The three began a lengthy discussion as they flipped through the pages of the brochure, and I turned my attention to the caterer herself. Perhaps, in getting to know Janetta better, I could learn some things about the burglary.

"If you don't mind my asking . . ." I

shifted my gaze, so as not to make her uncomfortable. "How are you faring since the —"

"The unfortunate event at the bank, you mean?" Janetta let out a lingering sigh, and I couldn't help but feel sorry for her. But would she open up and share her heart with someone she scarcely knew? I hoped so, and not just because the "need to know" stirred the opening question. I wanted her to know that she had been on my mind and in my prayers.

"I've thought about you so many times," I started. "And so many of us have been praying, of course."

Her eyes locked on mine, and much to my surprise, I realized I'd stumbled upon another kindred spirit.

"Thank you for that. It's been tough, I'll tell you." She sighed, and a certain sadness set in. "We worked our tails off for that money — catered a three-day conference just outside of Lancaster with two hundred fifty attendees — in a little town called Paradise."

"Oh? Do you cater a lot of big events like that?"

"Quite a few," she explained. "But none like this. See, a lot of the Pennsylvania Dutch merchants from the area come together every fall to talk about new ways to promote their products. They called it the All Things Dutch Conference. Very interesting. I met a lot of new people, too."

I tried to picture Janetta in the Amish country, but my mind just wouldn't take me there.

She continued, oblivious to my thoughts. "I knew it was risky to make such a large cash deposit at night, but what choice did I have?"

Mental note: Why would a group of professionals, Amish or not, pay a caterer in cash? Something about all of this just felt fishy.

"If I had it all to do over again, I'd change everything." Janetta buried her head in her hands. "I feel like such a fool. But, to have it just disappear like that —"

My heart thumped madly as guilt settled in. *Don't worry, honey. You'll get some of it back as soon as we pay you.*

She lifted her head then brushed away what appeared to be a tear. "There's nothing I can do about it now. It's in the hands of the police. I feel confident we'll get it back."

"The bank won't cover the loss?" I asked.

"Well," she said, shaking her head as she explained, "since I made the deposit in cash, it's really a matter of our word against theirs. In other words, they didn't even view it as a missing deposit until I contacted them. They simply didn't know I'd made a deposit at all. And with the power being out, well, that just complicated things even further."

"Wow." I felt my cheeks heat up as I asked the dreaded question. "A–Any word about a suspect?"

For a moment, I thought the conversation had ended. She used the back of her hand to brush away another lingering tear as she opened up and shared more personal information. Her words surprised me. "They arrested my son a few days ago."

"Y–Your son?" This certainly raised my antennae. The infamous drifter was her son? This information felt a little too personal and almost gave me cause to think I had no right probing any further.

I was just in the process of shifting our conversation to the wedding when Kristina interjected her thoughts on the matter. I couldn't help but notice the sarcasm in her voice.

"These small-town cops don't have a clue what they're doing." She shook her head and frowned. "They caught my brother hanging around the bank at some odd hours, so I guess they put two and two together and came up with five."

"I'm not sure I understand." I fiddled with the catering brochure to busy my hands. Otherwise, the vibration might give me away.

Janetta cast a woeful glance my direction. "This is my youngest we're talking about here," she said, emphasis on *youngest.* "I guess you could say it's my fault. His daddy took off when he was little, and I was worn out from raising all the others, so I probably let him get away with too much."

"You did a fine job, Mama." Kristina gave a reassuring nod, and my heart warmed toward her right away. In many ways, she reminded me of my own girls.

"My son is —" Janetta's gaze shifted downward. "He's pretty messed up. I mean, he's mentally capable and all that, but he's had some serious drug-related problems. He's been away for years. In fact, I hardly recognized him when the police brought him in for questioning. He's so . . . changed. The drugs and alcohol really took a toll on him physically . . ." Her voice broke.

I joined her in her pain. *Oh Father, help her. Help them all.* My hand instinctively reached out to grab hers. "Oh, Janetta, I'm so sorry."

She closed her eyes for a moment, as if

trying to drive the whole thing from her memory. "It's water under the bridge. But apparently Jake — we call him Jakey — was hanging out at the bank late at night a couple of nights in a row, hoping Kristina would come by to make a deposit. He wanted to see if I'd take him back, since he'd sobered up and all. Least, that's what he says."

"It's the truth, Mama, and you know it." Kristina's eyes reflected her pain.

I didn't dare ask Janetta if she would have taken him back. None of my business, though the ache in my heart grew by the moment.

Her face tightened. "I just don't see how they can continue to hold him. There's no proof he took the money. In fact, they never found a penny on him."

"Doesn't make sense then." *Did I just say that out loud? Do I really want to narrow down the list of suspects this quickly, especially with my husband still at the top of the list?*

A look of frustration set in. "They're saying he probably rigged the night-deposit box somehow and then got to the money before the bank opened the next morning. But how could someone so . . . messed up . . . manage such a thing?"

"And where did the money go?" Kristina

threw in. "It's not like he's got a hotel room or some fancy car to hide it in. He's got nothing. No one."

"Have you asked them that?" As I shifted my gaze between both women, I could almost feel their pain.

I didn't think Janetta's face could tighten any more, but it did. "They're saying he did it to get even with me for kicking him out when he was seventeen." A hoarse laugh erupted from the back of her throat. "They didn't believe me when I told them I didn't kick him out. He ran off. On his own."

A lone tear rolled down Kristina's cheek. "We didn't know where he was for years. I prayed for him every night."

A lump the size of Mount Rushmore grew up in my throat.

Janetta rose from her chair and walked to Kristina. She leaned down and kissed her daughter on the forehead as she whispered, "We're just glad he's back. And we'll prove the police wrong if it's the last thing we do."

And I'll help you. I gave her hand a little squeeze. "I surely didn't mean to pry into your family business. I had no idea the man they'd been questioning was related to you."

She shrugged, and the strangest mixture of emotions ran through me. Complete relief — as I realize Jake's arrest probably let my husband off the hook, at least temporarily. And complete heartache — as I realized the universal pain of a mother agonizing over a wayward child.

I garnered up all the determination I could and turned my attention back to the weddings at hand.

CHAPTER 05

When you're the mother of twin girls, you don't have to join a gym or purchase fancy workout equipment from infomercials to stay in shape. Just following around after the little darlings — and their laundry — will do the trick. Add a young son to the mix, and you've got a *Why-do-I-need-to-do-sit-ups? I'll-just-chase-the-kids-around-the-park-to-get-my-exercise* kind of mama.

For years, this strategy appeared to be working. Thanks to good genes (*kudos, Mom!*), fairly healthy eating habits (*I'll have the salad, please, with low-fat dressing*), and an active lifestyle (*who would've guessed I'd learn to play football with my boys?*), I'd managed to stay in shape.

Until recently.

I could blame it on pre-menopause, but truth be told, it was just plain laziness on my part. The things I used to care so much about — counting calories, weighing food, fitting into that great new skirt — just didn't seem so important anymore, what with certain parts of my anatomy heading south. And now that I could purchase cute clothes in nearly every size, I'd decided to fill my closet with just that: nearly every size.

Warren didn't seem to mind. In fact, as we burrowed down on the sofa each evening with our oversized bowls of Moo-lenium Crunch ice cream, he seemed more content than ever. Sure, his size 32 waist had stretched to a 36, and yes, my jeans now came in one size larger, but who cared? We loved our lives and we loved each other — just as we were.

That's why, when I opened up lesson three on Monday morning, I couldn't help but groan. *"A Good Investigator Is in Tip-top Shape."* I slapped myself in the head. Were they kidding? What in the world did this have to do with anything?

I almost didn't read the crazy thing. What was the point, really? At forty-nine, I doubted I'd ever find myself chasing criminals down back alleys, even if I managed to shimmy the flab off of my thighs and upper arms with the latest advertised contraption.

Still, with two weddings coming up, it would be nice to take off a few pounds. A little shiver rippled down my spine as I thought about it. The mother of the bride was often put on display, much like the bride herself. *Mental note: Make sure all wedding photos are taken dead-on. Double chins don't show as much from the front as the side.*

Perhaps, in light of all that lay ahead, I should pay more attention to my diet. And a little exercise never killed anyone — at least not the kind that I might get involved in.

I started to sign off the Internet to contemplate my plan of action, but a whisper from the Lord reminded me I hadn't yet read my daily devotional. I scrolled to my favorite Word for the Day site. My heart rate doubled as I read the scripture verse: *"He must increase; I must decrease." John 3:30.* Another coincidence? I had to wonder.

Lord, are You trying to tell me something?

I reached over to grab a fistful of miniature chocolates from the bowl next to the computer as I pondered the possibilities. *I must become less.* Hmm. Yes, losing a few pounds and getting into shape appeared to be the message of the day.

I popped a couple of pieces of candy into my mouth and one apparently went down the wrong way. I didn't panic when the coughing fit started. But as I struggled to catch my breath, I found myself contemplating the inevitable stories people would share about me after my demise.

I could picture the headliner on the obituary in the *Clark County Gazette* now: LOCAL CRIME FIGHTER DIES WITH TELL-TALE SIGN OF CHOCOLATE ON HER BREATH. The dramatic piece would go on to reveal the particulars of my last moments on planet Earth — how I'd been found clutching pieces of candy-coated chocolates in my chubby fist. From there, it would discuss my inability to fit into the casket, due to the width of my hips.

The "melt-in-your-mouth" piece finally dissolved enough to slide down my throat, and after a few sips of water and an exorbitant amount of coughing, I managed to regain my composure. I prayed several heartfelt words of thanksgiving, drew in a few deep breaths, and shoved the candy dish aside. The Lord really was trying to tell me something — both through the lesson and the Bible verse. I must do something, and I must do it now.

Out of the corner of my eye I noticed Sasha jumping up and down. She let out a few frantic yips, capturing my full attention. I turned to face her, now able to speak. "Need to go out, little girl?" I stood and reached for her leash. As I did so, a thought occurred to me. *Taking the dog for a walk burns calories. Taking her for several walks will burn several calories.*

Only one problem with this idea. I glanced down at the slim, trim dachshund. She didn't look like she had many calories to burn.

As we made our way out to the sidewalk, I pondered my predicament. Whether I wanted to or not, I should probably join a gym. And it wasn't like I'd have to look far. I'd noticed the signs around town for the new Clark County Co-Ed Fitness Center on Main. I'd seen, through the large panes of glass out front, the sweaty bodies inside.

I just never dreamed I'd be one of them.

With Sasha leading the way, I headed into town. We sprinted along, enjoying the crisp autumn day. I couldn't help but focus on the leaves on my neighbor's stately oak as the afternoon sunshine rippled through them. For a moment, the sheer beauty of it all captivated me. God, in His goodness, gave me a glimpse of eternity as I gazed up through the trees and into the heavenlies.

I paused to reflect on the splendorous interruption. "How do You do it, God?" I questioned. "How is it that everything You create is so . . . perfect?"

For a moment, the wind seemed to offer a

response. "I created you, too."

Just the breeze, surely. Nothing more.

I picked up my pace once again, chugging along behind the puppy, who seemed to know just where I wanted to go. She led me to the end of the street and turned toward town.

We passed the Dairy Barn, where the lunch crowd swallowed down greasy fries and artery-clogging burgers. We continued on past the coffee shop, where customers nibbled at tasty baked goods, chased down by caramel mocha frappuccinos.

None of that for me. No sir. I swallowed hard and kept walking, stopping only when I landed in front of the new gym. Through the large panes of glass, I could see everything and everyone. The folks inside looked energized, mesmerized, slenderized.

Aw, who was I kidding? They looked just plain awful. And I would, too, if I dared to join them. I grew weary just pondering my dilemma. Even a really trendy sweat suit would do little to impress onlookers if the woman wearing it passed out cold after just two minutes on the elliptical machine.

I pressed my face against the window to have a closer look. What in the world? What was Richard Blevins doing here, in the middle of the day? I glanced at my watch.

Twelve fifteen. *Ah. He's on his lunch break. Interesting midday activity. Working off his guilt, perhaps?*

My finely tuned detective skills kicked in unannounced. It didn't take long to remind myself why this little episode with Richard felt strange. Just yesterday — with tears in his eyes, I might add — my husband read Richard's resignation letter aloud to a room full of stunned Sunday school class members. Turned out Richard and Judy weren't just stepping away from the class, they were leaving the church. Gone. Like a puff of smoke.

But why?

I peered a bit closer, eventually creating a haze on the glass with my breath. Even from here, I could see the frustration etched on Richard's face. He handled the Stairmaster like a man possessed.

Yes, he surely needed a sense of release from something. But what? The situation with his wife or something more?

I wanted to go inside, wanted to follow him from machine to machine, in search of clues. Wanted to ask him strategic questions. Wanted to find a way to pinpoint him as the perpetrator. Wanted to . . .

Help me, Lord.

With a sigh, I came to recognize the truth.

I wanted to exonerate my husband — to free him from the cloud of guilt that hovered over him like the branches of that old oak in my neighbor's yard. I didn't really want to incriminate anyone else, especially not a good friend and Bible scholar. Chasing Richard Blevins around the Co-Ed Fitness Center suddenly felt rather shameful. And a little silly.

Besides, I didn't really want to sweat. Not with so much work awaiting me at home.

I glanced down at Sasha, who had come to rest on the small grassy area to my right. "It's a pity I can't go inside," I told her. "But, alas, no pets allowed."

I secretly celebrated the fact. Honestly, I could hardly keep the grin from curling up the edges of my lips. Perhaps I had known all along I wouldn't carry through with this ridiculous notion.

On the other hand . . . I looked through the window again. It didn't look so bad. And I really could stand to tone a little. "Lord," I whispered to the skies, "if this is Your will —"

The honking of a horn interrupted me, and I turned as my son's voice rang out through the open window of our truck. "Whatcha doin', Mom?"

"What? Oh, I —"

"Are you joining the gym?" Devin pulled the truck to a stop, slammed it into PARK, and leaped from the door like a gazelle loping across the meadow.

"I'm not sure."

His face lit with more enthusiasm than I would have imagined possible for a seventeen-year-old male. "I think you should. And, in fact," he said, pointing to a sign, "you should sign up all of us. They've got a great family plan, and I've been thinking about working out more, anyway. I need to stay in shape, you know." He flexed a muscle in his upper arm and gave me a wink.

"Ah." I couldn't seem to force any more words to the surface. "Well, maybe someday."

What is it about sons? How do they melt the heart with a look? Devin flashed me that "Aw, Mom" face, and I dripped like butter through his fingers.

"The special ends this afternoon," he explained. "If we're going to do it, we have to do it now."

Sure enough. The sign on the door proudly bore today's date as the final day for the advertised price. But how could I go inside with Sasha in tow?

As if reading my mind, Devin scooped her

up into his arms. "Go on, Mom. And don't worry about Sasha. I'll take her home in the truck."

Without even asking my permission, he and my canine cohort took off and left me hanging in the lurch.

I pulled open the door and was met immediately by a young "fitness rep" as he called himself.

Fitness rep, my eye. "Joey. I remember you." He'd been in Devin's Cub Scout troop, if memory served me correctly.

Within minutes, "Joey the Fitness Rep Extraordinaire" handed me a pen so that I could sign on the dotted line. After a little coaching, I'd settled not for the "regular" family membership, but the "Twenty-Four-Hour Premium Membership." Man, he was good.

Or maybe I was just gullible.

Just before signing, I telephoned Warren to ask his opinion. He seemed a little surprised by my impulsive decision but heartily agreed, even going so far as to state, "We could all stand to lose a few pounds."

At that point, I passed my credit card off to Joey and the deed was done. Afterward, my new fitness rep ushered me into the small shop at the front of the center, where I selected a cute workout outfit. Navy blue with gray stripes. Not bad, not bad. Kind of reminded me of my junior high gym suit. Maybe someday I would actually put it on.

As if reading my thoughts, Joey pointed to the ladies' changing area and encouraged me to "dive right in."

Dive right in? Fifteen minutes ago, I'd been content to stare in the window. Now I was supposed to forget every concern and climb aboard the fitness express?

I scoped the room to see if I could locate Richard. Nope. Looked like he'd already headed back to the bank. No one would be any the wiser. I really could exercise without an audience. But, did I want to?

The title of today's lesson echoed loudly in my brain. *"A Good Investigator Is in Tip-top Shape."*

And so I did it. I donned the outfit. And with Joey's expert assistance, I made the rounds from machine to machine. Though I started off tentatively, my concerns lifted in record time. In fact, my excitement grew with each new piece of equipment. I felt so energized by the time I left that I practically sprinted home, not even caring what the neighbors thought.

I arrived at the house in breathless excitement. Sasha met me at the door, equally as pleased. We celebrated my victory together.

Then we headed to the kitchen, where I cooked a low-fat dinner: grilled chicken breasts, broccoli, and a salad. I even mixed up a batch of sugar-free brownies, just for fun.

Warren arrived home at six thirty, as always. He commented on the healthy glow in my cheeks, and I kissed him squarely on the lips in gratitude. A glance in the mirror let me know I did look healthier. And I felt healthier, too.

Why, in no time I would be in tip-top shape. I would chase suspects down back alleys, if that was what the Lord had in mind. And I'd catch 'em, too.

CHAPTER 06

I like to call them "Sheila-ism's" — the funny, off-beat things that slip out of my friend Sheila's mouth when you least expect them.

Like the time I complained about the appearance of a few wrinkles and she came back with, "I prefer to think of my body as a dried-up raisin — age has just condensed its sweetness." Or the time I chided her for not offering adequate support when a dispute with a mutual friend turned ugly and she retorted, "What do I look like, an underwire bra?"

When in doubt, I reach for a Sheila-ism. And I awoke on Tuesday morning in dire need of one. For one thing, my eyelids appeared to be the only thing working on my anatomy. For whatever reason, my back felt cemented to the mattress. And when I finally managed to sit up — truly one of the most painful feats ever accomplished by mankind — it took at least a minute or two to ease my legs over the edge of the bed.

With little else to do but sit there, I forced my mind to race backward through time in an attempt to figure out why my body had chosen to fail me. It took awhile to figure out what had happened.

Ah, yes. The gym. Ten minutes on the elliptical machine. Ten on the treadmill. Ten on the bike. Five on the Stairmaster. (How anyone in the world could handle more than that was beyond me.) From there, with Fitness Rep Joey's help, of course, I'd hit the weight-bearing machines, making the rounds to every single one.

Was it any wonder I could barely move this morning? I might never move again.

I crawled from the bed to the tub. Just leaning over to turn on the hot water proved excruciating. Surely after a long soak, all would be well.

I let out a cry as I eased my body down into the water. Sasha put her front paws on the edge of the tub and gazed over in sorrow, as if sensing my pain.

On the other hand, she might be experiencing a little pain of her own. Horror set in as I realized I had forgotten to let her out to do her morning business.

"Hold it as long as you can, little girl," I

encouraged. "I'll try to hurry."

Yeah, right. I leaned back against the bath pillow and closed my eyes. I tried to use the opportunity to pray, to seek the Almighty for His will concerning all of this. I found it difficult to focus, though I gave it a valiant effort.

Yesterday's scripture verse played back through my memory a thousand times over: *"He must increase; I must decrease."*

The Lord, who usually spoke to me in gentle whispers, appeared to be shouting in my ears this morning. Okay, so I had to admit, the verse had little to do with my weight. It had everything to do with my ego. I needed to let go, give the Lord full control of every area of my life. I had become entirely too self-sufficient, and that needed to change. Immediately, if not sooner.

My throat tightened — a warning sign that tears would soon follow. Why fight it? While the Lord "had" me, I might as well let Him deal with me.

And obviously He had a lot to deal with. As He began to point out problem areas, the lump in my throat grew until I could barely swallow. Whether I wanted to admit it or not, ambition had become my friend. Somewhere along the way, the insatiable desire to prove something to myself and others had taken precedence.

Had I really been chasing around after some sort of illusive dream, all in the hopes of freeing my husband from guilt? Why couldn't I just take Warren at his word? Had he ever given me reason to doubt him in the past?

A lone tear trickled down my cheek. I would've brushed it away, if my arms and fingers had cooperated. Instead, it plopped down into the soapy water, making itself at home. I lingered for a while against the edge of the tub and took the time to truly repent for my silliness over the past few days. I thought of Warren and the great sacrifice on his part to make sure we had the funds for the weddings. Common sense told me he must've cashed in an IRA to come up with that money. Doing so must have broken his "We-won't-touch-this-until-our-retirement" vow. And all for the love of family.

My heart swelled with overwhelming devotion for the man. Yes, he had surely proven himself trustworthy, and I'd been childish to doubt his actions or his intent. From now on, I would return to being his helper, his lover, his friend. I would cease to be his judge and jury.

Even if it meant I never found the actual perpetrator. Even if the crime went unsolved forever. I would follow the Lord's leading and only go where He wanted me to go. The words rushed out in a heartfelt prayer: "Lord, You've got my full attention this morning. I am sorry for taking the reins away from You. Again. I ask You to forgive me for running out ahead of You. Help me, Father. I want to do the right thing. If You want to use me in this, then I want to be useable. If it's not of You, then take the desire away. And Father, if You want to use me in some other way entirely, show me. I'm Yours, Lord. . . ."

The presence of the Lord suddenly shook me to my core. I somehow knew that He wanted me to do something, something specific. With fresh tears running down my cheeks, I responded. "Yes, Lord. I'll do that."

As soon as I can get out of the tub. I had apparently been sitting so long the water had turned cold. And if I thought getting in had been tough, I had made no psychological preparations for getting out. The process took a good ten minutes, if you counted the toweling off part. And all the while, Sasha whimpered in agony.

Finally dry — and nearly standing aright — I slipped on my robe and inched my way down the stairs and toward the back door. I had no sooner opened it than the frustrated puppy bounded out and located a spot to relieve herself. I filled her dog dish with a can of Macho Mutt — her favorite — and went about the task of preparing breakfast. With Warren and Devin already gone, after tending to their own breakfasts, I settled on a piece of toast and a cup of hot tea. Earl Grey, of course.

My knees didn't seem to want to bend, so I opted to stand while I ate. The pain in my back eventually forced me to lean against the countertop. I somehow managed to nibble the toast and sip the tea. Out of the corner of my eye, something grabbed my attention. There. Up on the bar. The newspaper.

I reached for the *Clark County Gazette* and nearly dropped my teeth as I read the headline: BURGLARY SUSPECT FREED.

The story focused on Jake Mullins, describing in some detail his release from jail after several rounds of questioning. Though the police still felt they "had their man" they simply couldn't provide adequate evidence to support their suspicions.

I whispered a "Thank You, Lord!" for Janetta's sake, though my heart twisted a little. With Jakey temporarily out of the picture, I couldn't help but wonder. . . .

No. Don't do this today. You've got your marching orders. Use 'em.

I pressed the paper aside and headed to the bedroom to begin the very tedious process of dressing. Though usually quite selective about my attire, I decided this wasn't the day to fret over the trimmings. Forget the jewelry. Limit the makeup. Wear the comfortable gray slacks and black turtleneck.

In short, stop worrying about what people will think. Just be yourself.

With a song of praise on my lips, I eased my way out to the car. After a brief stop at the new gift store on Wabash, I pulled the car out onto the highway and pointed it toward Philadelphia.

Yes, the Lord would surely guide my every step today.

By the time I reached the parking lot of Mercy Hospital, my nerves were once again an issue. I quickly settled them with a bit of prayer: *Lord, I know You've sent me here. Show me how best to honor You and to reflect Your love. May I truly decrease, Father, so that Your heart can shine through.*

Now, I'm not one for hospitals. Never have been. The creepy feeling that runs over me every time I visit a patient probably dates back to an episode as a youngster where I fainted at the foot of my grandmother's hospital bed. Something about the smell, perhaps. Still, the Lord had given me a sense of direction for today's visit. Surely He would see me through this.

I paused at the front desk to ask for the room number in question. East Wing 146. Then, with a "Lord, help me" on my lips — and the tiny gift in my hand — I wound through the halls, following the signs, the backs of my calves aching every inch of the way.

When I rapped on the door of room 146, a gentle voice from inside beckoned me to enter.

I found Judy Blevins in far worse shape than I had imagined. If I'd taken the time to visit her even once over the past few weeks, I would have been better prepared. She sat, completely alone in the stillness of this barren room, to face the ongoing treatments for pancreatic cancer.

"Annie." Her eyes filled with tears as she spoke my name, and her extended hand reached for mine.

I placed the tiny gift box on the table, then sat at her bedside and gripped her willing fingers. "Judy, how are you feeling?"

She drew in a deep breath before answering. "I'm blessed, Annie. Blessed by The Best."

The same answer you've given for years. But how are you, really? "You've been in my prayers, and the Lord specifically laid you on my heart today." I mustered up a smile.

"Did He?" Her eyes filled once more, and I found mine brimming, as well. "Well, maybe there's a reason for that." She went on to explain the results of her latest round of tests. None of them good. As she shared the news, I couldn't help but notice the confidence in her voice, the calm. She closed with simple words, but they shook me to the core. "You know, I'm ready to go, Annie. If the Lord chooses to take me, I can live with that."

I had to look twice into her twinkling eyes to catch the attempted pun. "Oh, honey —"

"I'm not afraid." She whispered the words, almost like a prayer.

Lord, what do I say? "I'm so proud of you, Judy. And I'm going to keep praying. We all are."

"I appreciate that. But please —" Her eyes lit up at this point. "Let's talk about something else. Something fun. Tell me all about the girls, the weddings."

Ah. Thank You for the diversion. I dove into some of the more humorous details concerning Brandi's plans. I told Judy about our meeting with the in-laws, and I laughed as I slipped into Southern gear once again. You can take a girl out of the South, but you can't take the South out of the girl.

Judy laughed, too. In fact, she laughed so hard, she set off her heart monitor and a nurse entered the room in a bit of a panic. Judy assured her all was well, and we were left alone to our own devices once again.

I would have forgotten to give her the tiny gift box altogether if I hadn't noticed it out of the corner of my eye. I offered it to her with great joy, hoping she liked what she found inside.

Sure enough, she oohed and aahed as her gaze fell on the tiny glass ballerina. She clutched the little figurine to her chest and whispered the words "I don't believe it!" several times over.

"What?"

Her eyes moistened as she spoke. "I'm sure it's going to sound so childish, but I always wanted to take dance lessons as a little girl, and my parents could never afford it." A dreamy look took over. "I used to do these silly moves all around the living room like little girls do, pretending I was on a big stage. I'd forgotten all about it until recently."

I fought to hold back the emotion as she continued on.

"See, about three weeks ago I started telling the Lord I wanted to dance. The desire just — returned. And —" Her voice broke. "He told me I could. Very soon."

I wanted to say something but couldn't. The presence of God washed over me afresh, and tears filled my eyes. The oddest conglomeration of joy and sorrow came in waves and kept me in utter silence for quite some time.

Judy didn't seem to notice. She continued to run her finger across the delicate ballerina, a look of sheer delight on her face. She eventually placed the tiny glass dancer on the bedside table, and we dove back into conversation. However, I couldn't help but notice she paused every few minutes to give it another happy glance. Funny, how such a little thing could mean so much. And funnier still that the Lord would have spoken so clearly to my heart to purchase that particular item.

We chatted at length about things at the church. She didn't mention anything about Richard's resignation from the Sunday school class, so I didn't bring it up. In fact, the tone of our conversation made me wonder if she knew at all. Before long, she shifted gears, and I realized she knew more than she'd previously expressed.

"I've been following the news — about the twenty-five thousand dollars." Her knuckles turned white as she gripped the bed railing.

"Oh?" My heart rate increased a bit.

She nodded and sighed. "Richard told me that Sergeant O'Henry had been around to question him. What about Warren?"

I nodded. "Yes. They talked with him, too. A couple of times."

"It's all so strange." Her brow wrinkled as she continued on. "But I've got to believe there's been some kind of mistake. How do we even know the deposit was made?"

"I don't know." Truthfully, that thought had entered my mind, too. Maybe Janetta's daughter had pocketed the money and . . .

Aw, who was I kidding? That scenario didn't make any sense.

On the other hand, none of the scenarios in my head made a lot of sense.

Judy and I shifted gears, diving into a chat about Sheila, and reminiscing about old times together when we'd worked on the "Get Out to Vote" rally. All of our stories were positive and upbeat. As we finished our time together, I reflected on three things.

First, Judy Blevins, weak as she was, was in "tip-top" shape spiritually. She might not be up to crime fighting, but she certainly understood what it meant to fight for the things that mattered. And, I daresay, she could chase the enemy of her soul down a back alley and snag him in a heartbeat.

Second, I wanted — and needed — a fresh reminder of the things that were important, truly important. And I wanted a heart that yearned to dance with my heavenly Father.

Third, my desire to mark Richard Blevins as the perpetrator of this particular crime flew right out the window the minute I looked headlong into his situation. No wonder he'd been so evasive. With so much going on, his desire to "slip away" was certainly understandable. Surely he just needed more time with his wife, while he had the opportunity. Yes, all the dear man needed from me was my prayers and a kind word in passing.

And perhaps all Judy needed . . . I glanced at the bed once again and observed — with my www.investigativeskills.com eyes — the peaceful expression on her face.

Maybe all she needed was a loving embrace.

I reached down to kiss her on both cheeks before leaving and whispered a quiet "thank you" in her ear.

She never asked why I thanked her. Somehow I think she just knew.

I drove home with the radio off and tears spilling every which way. Though I couldn't quite explain it — even to myself — I felt like a woman transformed. Yes, my body still ached. And yes, my upper arms still jiggled. But suddenly none of that mattered anymore. Right now, the important things — my relationship with my Daddy God, my marriage, and my children — flew like red flags before me. I made a conscious decision to address them all.

That night I cooked a delightful dinner for Warren. I cut back a little on the portions and opted to grill the meat instead of fry it. After the meal we settled onto the couch with our slightly-smaller-than-usual bowls of Moo-lenium Crunch ice cream. Once finished, I eased into Warren's arms and nuzzled against him as we watched a television show together.

Afterward, though still a bit stiff and sore, I slipped off into the bedroom and donned my favorite baby blue satin nightgown. Warren entered the room, took one look at me, and approached with the corners of his lips curled up.

"Annie, you look . . . amazing."

Apparently he didn't notice the cellulite on my thighs, the protruding tummy, or the patriotic waving of my upper arms. His eyes locked on mine, and I knew he only saw me as his beautiful bride once more. Warren swept me into his arms and kissed me as if we were newlyweds all over again. I couldn't help but lean my head against his and sigh.

For whatever reason, my thoughts gravitated to Judy and her desire to dance. The same sensation washed over me, even now.

"I've missed you these past few days," Warren whispered.

I knew what he meant. I hadn't been myself. Not even close. But I would remedy that right away. "I'm here now," I whispered.

He responded by wrapping me in his embrace. I rejoiced, not just in his presence, but in the overwhelming realization that the Lord had joined us in the room.

Immediately, my heart began to dance. And in that moment I understood what it meant to be in tip-top shape.

CHAPTER 07

My next days were filled with back and forth trips to the gym and a gradual lessening of pain from my now less-strenuous workouts. A tremendous excitement on the home front escalated as the girls came and went with wedding paraphernalia in their hands. Brandi arrived with swatches of deep red fabric and patterns to ask my opinion about bridesmaids' attire. Candy came with a magazine photo of a lovely three-tiered wedding cake adorned with fresh daisies. Nadine, still in town on an extended visit, joined us for lunch one day. Together, we listened to love songs and practiced making centerpieces. In short, we had the time of our lives.

In between their visits, I managed to squeeze in a few hours of work. My editing clients had been more than patient with me over the past week or so, and I owed it to them to get caught up on their various projects. With the zeal of a young warrior, I raced through their manuscripts, polishing and perfecting.

By Friday morning, I found myself back on track. A bathtub full of bubbles proved to be the perfect prayer closet. *Mental note: From this point on, purchase bath products with prayer time in mind. Some scents are far more heavenly than others.*

While soaking, I sought the Lord for His will concerning my day — and a swift resolution to the situation at the bank. After relinquishing my need to "fix" the situation, I rested much easier. In fact, His peace enveloped me as I leaned back and closed my eyes.

I almost dozed off, but Sasha's cold nose bumping up against my cheek roused me in record time. She peered over the edge of the tub with that woeful look I'd grown to love. I blew a little puff of the airy bubbles her way and she darted from the room. A giggle worked its way up from my belly, and I thanked God for life's simple favors.

After dressing and blow-drying my hair, I headed to the Internet to read my daily devotional. Still relaxed and happy from my bath, I whispered a prayer: "Lord, give me ears to hear Your voice today — and courage to obey." As I signed online, I prepared myself for whatever He had for me.

You know, a funny thing happens when you ask the Lord to speak to you.

He does.

I opened to a scripture verse, Proverbs 17:27–28. It was straight from God's mouth to my ears: *"A man of knowledge uses words with restraint, and a man of understanding is even-tempered. Even a fool is thought wise if he keeps silent, and discerning if he holds his tongue."*

Ouch.

Okay, I must admit, I had struggled a little in this area. Keeping silent wasn't a strong suit. My ability to listen was often pre-empted by my need to get a word in edge-wise. But I would work on that, with the Lord's help. After this gentle reminder, I would focus on keeping my ears open and my lips closed.

Before leaving the computer, I faced the ever-growing stack of e-mails head-on. Many were forwards from Sheila, those quirky things she liked to send to put a smile on my face. Still others were thank-you notes from clients, grateful for my help with their projects. And the rest, well . . .

For a couple of days, I had refused to open any of the lessons from www.investiga-tiveskills.com. I'd learned my own "lesson," to be sure. But by now, the irritable things were stacking up and curiosity got the better of me, so I opened the next one in line, lesson four, just for a quick glance. Interestingly enough, the title grabbed me right away: *"A Good Investigator Has Excellent Listening Skills."*

Yep. The Lord appeared to be driving home His point this morning. I took a closer look at the piece, chuckling as I read, "In order to better hone in on clues, an investigator has to focus on his or her listening skills."

A Sheila-ism popped into my head immediately. Just last week, in an attempt to conclude a story about an embarrassing moment she'd had at the grocery store, Sheila made me laugh with these words: "A closed mouth gathers no foot."

How beautifully that little phrase matched the message du jour.

I scoured the rest of the article, amazed at the biblical principles found within. Caught up in the excitement, I almost missed the gong of the hall clock. The final peal caught my attention. Noon? Already?

Warren's unexpected invitation to meet him for an impromptu lunch had provided a pleasant distraction, and I certainly didn't want to keep him waiting. Flying into gear,

I grabbed my sweater and my purse, then headed for the door. I arrived at the bank in record time but found him busy with a customer.

Nikki approached me with a broad smile and an apparent need for conversation. "I just wanted to thank you for praying," she whispered. "Amber is feeling much better now."

"Is she? That's wonderful."

With a glowing face, Nikki continued on. "So many good things have happened to me lately. It's obvious someone's been praying." She reached over to give my hand a squeeze.

I offered up a smile of support. "Fill me in. What's happening?"

"Well, to start with, I'm putting Amber in a private school." She hesitated a minute as her eyes misted over. "She was really struggling at the other school. It's hard being the new kid in a small town. And besides —" Nikki's expression changed. "Lots of the children were making fun of her because she didn't have a daddy, that sort of thing."

"That's awful."

"Yeah." She sighed. "But I've been there. I had a deadbeat dad, myself, and I know how mean kids can be." Nikki's eyes lit up as she continued. "But I heard about the

Clarksborough Christian School and went to check it out."

I knew the school well — also knew it cost a pretty penny to send a child there. How in the world could Nikki manage such a thing on a security guard's salary?

Slow down, Annie, and listen to what she's saying. Don't assume. After all, Nikki did put in extra hours at the diner in the evenings. She must really love her daughter to work so hard on her behalf.

I reached to give her a hug. "I'm so happy for you. And for Amber. I pray she does well."

"Thank you. I just want her to have a better life than I had."

"Oh?" My newly acquired listening skills kicked in as she forged ahead.

Nikki sighed. "I was so messed up as a teen. Hung out with the wrong crowd. Got into so much trouble. And I want so much more than that for Amber."

Trouble? What kind of trouble?

She continued on, her brow knotting a bit as she spoke. "For a while there, I really didn't think I'd make anything out of my life. I was, well, let's just say I was 'away' for a while. My mom could tell you all about it."

Away? As in, reform school? Jail?

I glanced across the room but found Warren still engaged in conversation with a client. Nikki didn't seem to notice my discomfort. She kept on talking, and I kept on listening.

And listening.

Turned out, today's Bible verse had arrived just in time, as evidenced by my recurring temptation to react to Nikki's woeful tale. Plenty of times along the way I longed to open my mouth, to interject a motherly thought or two. But I bit my tongue and just let her talk.

She went on quite awhile, covering details about her life as a single mom. The story ended on an upbeat note as she talked about being hired on at the security company Guards on Call.

"My uncle got me the job." She chuckled. "Not that I'm really security guard material, but he pulled a few strings."

I looked at the gun strapped to her side and swallowed hard. Yep. Something about all of this just sounded suspicious. Gun-toting security guards didn't just "get" jobs. They trained, prepared, acquired certification. I gave her another once-over as she kept talking. Sure, I heard what she said with her mouth, but now wondered if I should be reading between the lines. *Mental note: Check out Guards on Call on the Internet.*

Just then, Warren joined us. "I'm so sorry to keep you waiting, Annie," he whispered into my ear.

He slipped his arm around my waist and I cradled against him. "It's fine. Nikki and I were having a nice chat." *Actually, she chatted; I listened.*

As Warren and I left the building, I noticed a silver sports car in the parking lot. I'd seen a commercial advertising the expensive dream car some time ago and had drooled as I watched it. "Wow. That's beautiful."

"Sure is." Warren gave it a closer look. "Looks like it's a couple of years old, but it's top of the line, for sure. Look at that stereo system." He pointed in the window, and I peered a bit closer to absorb the luxury of it all.

"Man." I let out a little whistle of appreciation, and then my gaze shifted to the door of the bank. "Who do you think it belongs to?" I didn't recall seeing any unfamiliar customers inside.

Warren shrugged. "I don't have a clue. I know Richard was talking about getting a new car a few months ago, but I can't imagine it, with all he's going through —"

I shook my head in disbelief. "No way."

"Still, he has been worried about that old clunker of his making it back and forth to Philly every day." Warren rubbed at his chin, deep in thought. "But knowing how frugal he is, I can't imagine it."

"Me either."

We gave the car another admiring once-over, then, practicality setting in, Warren broke the silence with a question. "Where would you like to eat?"

I didn't have to think very long before responding. I'd seen the sign in the front of the Clarksborough Diner on Main. Their special of the day happened to be my favorite: grilled chicken Caesar salad. Yummy.

"The diner? Are you sure?" He chuckled. "I thought for sure you'd want something a little nicer than that."

"Nah. I'm a diner kind of girl."

With clear skies overhead, we made our way on foot to the familiar eatery. Once inside, we settled into the booth, and the waitress, an unfamiliar young woman with a pierced lip and eyebrow, handed us our menus.

"I don't need this, honey." I slid it back across the table. "I already know what I want."

Her eyebrows elevated a little at the word

honey, and I resisted the urge to explain my Southern upbringing. Most of the folks in Clarksborough had long since grown accustomed to my love terms. I snuck a peek at her nametag: Shawna. *Mental note: From this point forward, call her by her name only.*

As she took our order, I tried to guess her age. Midtwenties, most likely. Perhaps she knew Nikki. Maybe they were friends. I broached the subject with a smile.

"Shawna, do you know Nikki? She works here in the evenings, right?"

"Nikki Rogers?" She rolled her eyes. "Yeah, I know her. But we're not exactly on speaking terms right now."

"Oh?"

A look of aggravation took over as she explained. "She was supposed to cover my shift one night last week, and she never showed up. In fact, she hasn't been back since."

I felt that little "catch" in my chest that usually signifies one of those *Am-I-having-a-panic-attack?* episodes. "What?"

"She quit. Just took off on us. Really put Noah in a jam." Shawna pointed to the cash register where the owner, Noah Linder, took care of a customer.

"Wow." *Then how in the world can Nikki afford the private school? What's going on here?*

Warren gave me one of those *Annie-think-before-you-speak* looks, and I turned my attentions back to the menu. "I'll have a bowl of chicken soup to go with that salad."

After Shawna left to wait on another customer, Warren dove into a conversation about a new security policy at the bank. I should've been listening. I really should have — especially in light of my desire to see this bank riddle solved. But for some reason, my ability to focus skipped right out the window. The only things I heard were the scattered thoughts bouncing around in my head. And they were tough to keep up with.

We finished up our lunch, and Warren returned to his work at the bank. I went back to my work, too. I felt driven to look up Guards on Call on the Internet. Something about this whole thing just felt . . . off.

Sure enough, after a bit of tedious scrolling, I came upon a site that caused a tightening grip on my chest.

Hmm. Looked like Guards on Call was under a little investigation for lax hiring practices. I read the article with my jaw hanging in suspended disbelief. Apparently several of the guards hadn't passed the mandatory background check, and more than a few had failed the state-mandated drug test.

My thoughts sailed back to Nikki's exposé. What was it she had said about not being security guard material? Perhaps, if I'd really been listening, I would have discerned the true meaning of her words: *"He pulled a few strings."*

On the other hand . . .

Could be my listening skills had linked arms with my over-active imagination. Perhaps Nikki simply needed help getting her foot in the door and her uncle had served as a catalyst.

On the other hand . . .

Hmm. I rubbed at my neck to ease the sudden tension that rose up. What was it Sheila always said at times like these? Ah, yes.

"On the other hand . . . you have different fingers."

Before frustration could set in, I shut down the Internet and sprang from my chair. Sasha and I would go for a walk, and I'd tune my ears to something more peaceful . . . like the sound of the autumn wind whispering through the leaves on my neighbor's old oak tree.

Chapter 08

"Mom, are you listening?"

"Hmm?" I looked up from the china pattern I'd been staring at for the last several minutes into Brandi's face. Her wrinkled brow let me know she had some concerns about my apparent lack of interest in her bridal registration process. Probably wouldn't be long before she would voice them. At least, standing here in the fine china department of Philadelphia's largest department store, she wouldn't make too much of a scene. I hoped.

"Mom, you haven't heard a word I've said." She tapped her foot, and for a moment, I wondered if, perhaps, she had morphed into the role of mother, and I, the child.

"Sure I did," I offered up in retort. "You love the white china with the silver trim. Round, not squared." *How's that for not paying attention?*

She cleared her throat as she lifted a beautiful square plate in front of me. The wide black trim offset its deep ivory color.

"Wow. That's pretty."

I didn't think it was possible for the wrinkles between her eyes to deepen, but lo and behold if they didn't.

"I'm getting worried about you, Mom." At this point her voice dropped to a concerned whisper. "We all are."

All? Who's all? "Oh?" I tried to act natural, in the hopes that she would change the direction of the conversation. In the way of a diversion, I reached for an elegant crystal goblet and lifted it for her approval. "What do you think of this one?"

She shook her head and her lips tightened. *Uh-oh.*

"The same thing I thought the last time you asked me. I think it's awful. Gaudy. And Scott would never go for it. He likes the modern look. We both do."

"Right. I knew that." I placed the goblet down and flashed a smile that would've dazzled Hollywood paparazzi.

The words from yesterday's lesson came back to me in a flash: In order to better hone in on clues, an investigator has to focus on his or her listening skills. I stared into my daughter's troubled eyes and had to conclude . . . she was giving me plenty of clues with the wide-eyed stares. And they weren't pleasant ones.

With new resolve, I turned my attention to listening to her needs. This was her day. I shifted my mind — away from suspects, clues, and other such distractions — and toward the beautiful daughter standing in front of me. She needed me. And I needed to get with the program. Pronto.

Together, we picked out silverware — technically flatware, since she opted not to go with real silver. She chose a simple but elegant pattern that looked terrific with her new dishes.

From there we moved on to linens. I bit my tongue as she pored over the various patterns and textures and offered up a smile when she settled on "the perfect one." Should I tell her that satin sheets aren't really practical over the long haul? Tell her my own honeymoon story about wearing a satin nightgown in a bed with satin sheets — how the combination had nearly proven deadly? *Nah.*

After that, we headed to the bath department to select floor mats and towels. Purple? She's doing her bathroom in purple? I had to laugh. Internally, of course. As a new bride, I'd chosen brown and gold. Very trendy — back in the day.

Of course, a lot of things had changed since then. When Warren and I married, we registered for china and crystal. That was about it. These new-fangled brides registered for everything imaginable. Want to buy the lovely couple a wall clock? Simple! You'll find one listed on page three of their registry. What about kitchen towels or pot holders? You'll find several options on page five. Thinking about picking up a toothbrush holder for the master bath? Why stop there when you can buy a matching tissue-paper holder and soap dish? See page eleven of the registry for details.

Yep, you could register for just about everything these days. Heaven help the poor wedding guest who purchased the happy couple a set of bath towels without checking the list for the appropriate style and color. I shuddered just thinking about it.

Ah, well. Brandi and I did have fun making the selections. In fact, by the time all was said and done, I'd joined right in as if the presents would eventually be floating my way instead of my daughter's.

We finished out our "Saturday Shopping Spree" with a trip to a nearby pizza parlor, where we nibbled on Alfredo pizza, a favorite for both of us. I let her ramble on and on about the wedding, and enjoyed sitting in silence . . . just listening. Perhaps that's all she really needed from me right now — just an ear to fill.

My mind wandered a bit — and I grew a bit uneasy with the direction it took. Just an ear to fill . . .

Maybe that's all Nikki had needed from me, too. Maybe she didn't need my suspicions or my internal ponderings. Maybe she just needed my support. After all, the poor girl had her hands full with a daughter and a full-time job. Could be, a new friend — in a new place — could walk alongside her as she figured out how to do this "mothering" thing. Hadn't I leaned on older women when I was her age? Hadn't I made mistakes along the way? And hadn't the "mothers" of my day lent me their ears — and their shoulders?

Yes, I had to conclude, listening had its benefits. It drew me back to those who needed me — and those I needed.

"Mom, are you still with me?"

I couldn't help but laugh as I looked into Brandi's eyes. "Honey, I'm here. I promise."

I dove into a funny story about my wedding day, and before long, she was all smiles. We relaxed and enjoyed the rest of our time together.

After arriving home, I searched for Warren to tell him about our adventures. I knew he would get a kick out of hearing about the "Purple People Eater" bathroom. And he was sure to chuckle over the square plates.

If only I could find him. I searched the house but couldn't seem to locate him. Next I headed to the yard. Yep, the hedges had been trimmed, but "said trimmer" was nowhere to be found. Back inside, I decided to check the office. Perhaps some last-minute business had reared its head.

To my surprise, I found the office door closed. Weird. He never closed it. I leaned in to the door for a listen and was fairly sure I heard his voice. Sounded like he was on the phone. Ah, well. I could certainly talk to him later.

I'd just turned away when something caught my ear. *What was that he said?* I strained to better hear his end of the conversation.

"I can't believe I got away with it. And Annie doesn't suspect a thing."

That panic-attack feeling returned, and for a moment I felt as if I might faint. *"Annie doesn't suspect a thing?"* What in the world?

Everything began to spin, and I leaned against the wall to keep from going down.

Tears started at once, followed shortly thereafter by a fit of coughing, which I couldn't seem to suppress. I moved away from the door, hoping I hadn't aroused suspicions. No sooner had I caught my wind than Warren joined me in the hallway, his face oddly pale.

"Hey, Annie."

"Hey." *Felon.*

"I didn't know you were home."

Obviously.

He reached to pull the office door closed behind him, as if trying to shut the door on whatever had just happened in there.

"I'm here."

He slipped his arms around me and gave a squeeze. I tried to squeeze back, I really did. But something about hugging a criminal just felt . . . wrong.

He pulled back and gazed into my eyes. "Are you okay?"

Um, no . . . But thanks for asking.

"You seem kind of . . . quiet."

"Even a fool, when he is silent, people will think wise."

I could've slapped myself silly. *Why in the world did I say that out loud?* A Sheila-ism floated through my head, confirming my inability to turn back. "Once the toothpaste is out of the tube, it's hard to get it back in."

Warren looked at me as if I'd gone mad. "Annie, I'm getting worried about you."

"You are?" I backed away from him and tried to look normal. "Why?"

The perplexed look on his face did little to console me. "This whole wedding thing has you . . . out of sorts. Are you feeling overwhelmed?"

To say the least.

"Because I'm thinking you need to take a little time for yourself for a change."

"Oh?"

"How would you like a little getaway, Annie?"

Getaway? Sounded like something a bank robber would say. "What did you have in mind?"

I eased my way into the living room, and he tagged along behind me, still talking. I kept on listening, determined to stick to my lesson plan.

"What would you think about a little trip to that bed-and-breakfast you've always wanted to go to? Sound good?"

"W–What?" Forgiveness washed over me at once. A criminal would never offer to take his wife to a B&B in the Amish country. "Really?" I could see it all now — the rolling farmlands, the quaint shops, the ever-present buggies. Sounded dreamy, even if it meant spending time away with someone I wasn't sure I trusted at the moment.

He pulled me into his arms and rested his chin atop my head as he explained, "Yes. The girls and I were thinking you'd like a few days alone."

"Alone?" I pulled away as understanding set in. "You want to send me away?"

He gave me one of those *Is-this-your-hormones-speaking-or-is-this-really-you?* looks. "Of course not. We just thought you would like the peace and quiet. We were thinking Sheila could go with you." I could see the hurt in his eyes as he concluded: "I had a doozie of a time getting a reservation, but our travel agent owed me a favor." He pulled a brochure from his shirt pocket and placed it in my hand.

His words to the person on the other end of the phone now raced through my brain once again: *"I can't believe I got away with it. And Annie doesn't suspect a thing."*

Made perfect sense to me now. He'd been talking to our travel agent, Joan Edwards. Warren had been planning a surprise . . . for me! Suddenly I felt absolutely ridiculous. In an attempt to make up for everything, I planted approximately a dozen kisses on his pouting lips and then apologized for my off-beat behavior. "I love you, and I'm very grateful. Thank you so much."

He nodded and offered a mumbled response, then headed off to the yard to rake the leaves. With my emotions now firmly in check, I settled onto the sofa and looked through the colorful brochure. What a tremendous blessing, especially in light of all I'd been through. Surely the Lord had dropped this little weekend getaway in my lap. Out amongst the simplistic backdrop of the Amish country, I could clear my head, think more logically, spend time listening to His voice, get His perspective on things.

Then again, if Sheila came along, things might not be so simple. She always had a way of seeing deep inside me — to the places others rarely took the time to see. And she knew how to needle the truth out of folks, one painful sliver at a time.

Hmm. I contemplated the inevitable a bit longer. Yes, if Sheila came with me, I'd probably end up baring my soul — telling her what I'd been up to over the past couple of weeks. Before all was said and done, she'd know about my suspicions.

Would that be so bad? What would it hurt, really, for someone else to know? Maybe, between the two of us, we could get this crime solved, set my husband free from the cloud of guilt hanging over his head. Maybe we would become known as Clark County's "Crime Fighters Extraordinaire" — an example for all young would-be sleuths.

Or maybe we'd just spend the weekend eating chocolate and talking about pedicures.

Either way, we'd have a whopper of a time.

CHAPTER 09

I couldn't help but laugh as Sheila backed her SUV into my driveway. Her new HONK IF YOU LOVE PEACE AND QUIET bumper sticker seemed just right for our spontaneous getaway to Amish country. Surely she had purchased it with this occasion in mind.

In my heart, I did long for peace and quiet. Ached for it, in fact. That's why, as I watched Sheila's arrival through the living room window, I had to wonder if having her along on this little jaunt to "God's country" had really been His idea — or my husband's. Only time would tell.

She bounded from the front seat in her usual quirky fashion. I chuckled as I noticed the leopard-print scarf she wore around her neck. Very fashionable. The autumn wind snagged ahold of it and whipped it across her face, nearly knocking off her jeweled sunglasses. Sheila caught them with her index finger and pressed them back in place.

What a diva.

As she headed my way, I took in the rest of her outfit: The bright teal sweater and black jogging pants seemed to suit her, and the hot pink trim on the new tennis shoes finished off the colorful ensemble. *Girl, you are something else.* Everything about this woman just screamed menopausal.

And I totally got it. Which is why inviting her along suddenly felt just right.

Sasha and I met her at the door, tail wagging — Sasha's, not mine.

"Hey, girl!"

Sheila and I both spoke in unison, then the chuckling began. If I didn't know any better, I'd have to say we weren't just kindred spirits, we were "sisters from another mister" as Sheila liked to call us.

Within minutes I'd loaded my bags and we were on our way. In true Sheila form, the chattering began right off. She caught me up on all the action I'd missed at the political league, and I offered up a sigh, along with an apology for my latest absence.

She shushed my concerns with the wave of a hand. "You've got daughters to marry off. We all know that. Besides, if you stay away long enough, they might elect me president. So, take your time."

After the laughter died down, we dove into

114

a lengthy dialogue about Brandi's registry items and Candy's cake selection. Unlike Warren, Sheila really seemed to appreciate the self-made humor behind my Don't-forget-to-register-for-your-toilet-paper joke.

She got me. And that felt mighty good. So good, in fact, that I nearly forgot about the twenty-five thousand dollars. Nearly forgot about the mental image of Warren in a Pennsylvania State Penitentiary jumpsuit.

Nearly.

We arrived in Lancaster in record time and then turned off on a country road toward the smaller Amish communities I'd grown to love. Apparently Sheila didn't make it out to the Pennsylvania Dutch country very often, as was evidenced by her fascination with every shop and restaurant along the way. The childlike "oohs" and "aahs" warmed my heart.

Her fascination ended, however, as we encountered our umpteenth Amish buggy. She didn't seem to handle them with the same degree of kindness I would have displayed, had I been the one behind the wheel. Let's just say, the words, "Hey, mister, could you speed that thing up a little?" were a bit overused that day.

As we rounded the corner to the Heritage House Bed-and-Breakfast, my heart soared.

The surrounding property took my breath away, and the farmhouse, quaint and lovely, drew me with its simple charm. Colorful leaves had fallen in abundance, offering up a dizzying scene of reds, golds, and browns. I drank it all in and whispered, "Oh, God! You have surely kissed this place with Your beauty."

Sheila let out a whistle as we pulled to a stop. "You should've warned me," she said with a look of awe. "I would've brought my tissues. And some theme music."

"I knew you would love it. I just knew it."

For a moment we sat in blissful silence. Words would have spoiled everything, so I listened, instead, with every one of my senses.

Finally, a stirring on the driver's side roused us from our trancelike state. A portly woman in traditional Amish dress rapped on the driver's side window. Sheila pushed the button to lower the glass.

"*Wilkum!* Are you the Peterson party?" the woman asked. She ran her fingers along the edges of her white *kapp,* and I couldn't help but wonder if she ever tired of wearing it.

We nodded in unison, as kindred spirits would.

The jolly woman let out a laugh. "Well, get on inside, you's two! We're about to serve lunch and you don't want to miss it. I've prepared a lovely ham and a huge crock of the best corn chowder you ever tasted. And I just pulled a loaf of fresh bread from the oven."

"Mmm-mmm." Sheila and I spoke in unison again and my stomach rumbled in anticipation.

The proprietor, who introduced herself as Mrs. Lapp, continued on as we exited the car: "There's Shoo-Fly Pie for dessert — best to be had, if I do say so myself. I hate to brag, but folks from around these parts say I'm the best cook in the Dutch countryside." The zealous woman continued on talking a mile a minute as we snatched our luggage and headed inside. So much for peace and quiet.

After one of the most amazing lunches I'd ever eaten, Sheila and I rested in our room. She took the brass daybed with the colorful quilt and let me have the larger, double bed with the rich blue and white quilt. I'd almost dozed off when her voice roused me.

"I'd say it's about time you told me what's really been going with you these past few weeks."

I sat up and gave her a quizzical look. "What do you mean?" The thump-thumping of my heart nearly gave away my feigned innocence.

She gave me that *I'm-older-than-you-so-treat-me-with-some-respect* look and, in true Sasha style, I tucked my tail between my legs. Perhaps the time had come to spill my guts.

Sheila's penetrating gaze wouldn't let me off the hook. Yes, I needed to tell her what I'd been up to. She would run it all through her "Sheila-filter" and let me know her thoughts on the matter.

And so I began — tentatively at first, then with ever-increasing fervor. She listened to my tale with her lips clamped — a rarity. I tried to gauge from her expression what she might be thinking about my involvement in crime fighting. I told her, with a few tears, actually, about Warren and the twenty-five thousand dollars. I filled her in on Nikki Rogers, single mom and security guard. Sheila's brow knotted as I got to the story of Janetta Mullins and her wayward son. And her eyes misted over as I shared the specifics regarding Richard and Judy Blevins.

As I concluded, I expressed my concern about not being able to narrow down the suspect list. Sheila nodded and popped out a rather atypical remark: "Well, Annie, if all you have is a hammer, everything looks like a nail."

"What?"

"I mean —" She explained, giving me a pensive look. "You're swinging at anything and everything. You haven't narrowed down your list because you're all over the place with this. Truth is, you're just following whatever feels right at any given moment. You're not looking at the whole picture. You're not listening to the clues. Not really."

"Ah." *How do I do that?*

"You're the most trusting person I know," she added. "And that means you're easily swayed."

"Hey, I —" I really couldn't say more, all things considered.

Sheila grew quite serious. Kind of threw me. "Truthfully, we don't know if any of those people took the money. We don't even know for sure that Janetta's daughter made the night deposit drop like she said. The power was out, right?"

"Right." To be honest, that had worried me all along.

"So, really, you could be chasing around after absolutely nothing. And all in an attempt to exonerate a man you know in your heart couldn't have done this. Am I right?"

I swallowed hard and nodded.

119

"Maybe that's why we're here this weekend." She yawned and leaned back against the pillow. "Maybe you need to go back to square one and see where all of this started. If the Lord is asking you to be involved — and that's a big *if* — then you'll probably need to go back through all of the clues one by one and ask Him to help you sort things out."

"If the Lord is asking you to be involved . . ."

Her words caught me off guard a little. And kind of hurt my feelings. Didn't she know me well enough to know I wouldn't dive headfirst into something unless the Lord had prompted me to do so?

On the other hand, Sheila had witnessed my impulsive side on more than one occasion. And she clearly had my best interest at heart. Maybe that's why her opinion mattered so much to me. I wanted to ask what she thought about all of my suspicions — wanted to know if my ramblings had opened her eyes to any possibilities. *Come on, girl. Tell me what you think. Who did this?*

She never said a word. Instead, with all of the love of a true friend, she continued to encourage me to get alone with God this weekend — to seek Him on the matter. And not to let the "outside noises" sway me.

Outside noises, eh?

As Sheila settled down for an afternoon nap, I dismissed myself to spend a little time out-of-doors with the Lord. My heart swelled as I strolled across the countryside toward the little creek behind the bed-and-breakfast. In one hand I clutched my Bible, worn from years of reading. In the other, my notebook and pen.

I settled down on the embankment of the rippling creek and pulled my jacket tighter to ward off the chill, ready to hear from the Lord. Within minutes, the lyrical sound of the water as it rushed across the rocks lulled me into a blissful state. There, in that place, I found myself tuned in as never before to His voice. He seemed to speak through the water, the wind, even the colors of the leaves as they fell upon the water.

And His words rang out loud and clear as I stumbled across one of my favorite verses in the old Bible: "But blessed is the man who trusts in the Lord, whose confidence is in him. He will be like a tree planted by the water that sends out its roots by the stream."

I leaned up against the huge maple tree and spent some time in quiet reflection. I wanted to be like that tree — sturdy and strong. I didn't want to be blown about by every wind that came along. Not a hammer, swinging at every nail. I didn't want to bounce around from one "suspect" to the other, making mountains out of molehills. But how could I separate them in my mind? How could I see the bigger picture, as Sheila had suggested?

There was only one way, really. I had to approach this logically, thoughtfully. I had to listen to the clues, my heart, and the Lord's voice.

One by one, I went through the list, asking God to give me His perspective on each. Then I began to put together a comprehensive list, just to set things straight in my mind:

Warren Peterson.

Outward appearances: Godly husband, father, and man of my dreams.

Motive: Needed money to pay for two weddings ASAP. Fear of disappointing his two daughters.

Suspicious behavior: Appearance of envelope with twenty-five thousand dollars in cash. Closemouthed over the funds; won't talk to me about it. Secretive and somewhat sullen in behavior for the past few weeks.

Alibi: None available. As a banker, occasionally handles night deposits and was seen at the bank on the morning the money disappeared.

Possible mode of operation: Could have taken advantage of the power outage/disabled cameras to snag the Clarksborough Catering cash deposit.

My plan regarding this suspect: Check on our existing IRAs to determine if Warren cashed one in to pay for the weddings. Pray for discernment. Do not assume. Remember the innocent-until-proven-guilty rule.

Richard Blevins.

Outward appearances: Brilliant Sunday school teacher, devoted husband, and dedicated banker with thirty years at Clark County Savings and Loan.

Motive: Insurance company issues. Needed funds to help with his wife's ongoing cancer treatments.

Suspicious behavior: Usually handles night deposits. Has avoided friends and coworkers for an extended period of time.

Alibi: None available. His car was seen at the bank approximately fifteen minutes earlier than usual on the morning in question.

Possible mode of operation: Carries a key to the building and has access to all security codes. Probably knew about the expected night deposit. Could have taken advantage of the power outage to pocket the cash.

My plan regarding this suspect: Observe him carefully over the next few days to see if his behavior changes further. Spend some time at the gym with his friends and coworkers. Pray for discernment and pray for Judy.

Nikki Rogers.

Outward appearances: Loving, single mom, in need of a listening ear.

Motive: Tired of working two jobs to keep up with her life as a single mother; bitter over ex-husband/deadbeat dad.

Suspicious behavior: In the past week or so her financial state appears to be improving, in spite of quitting second job. Just enrolled daughter in an expensive private school. Possible suspicious hiring practices at Guards on Call make status as a "real" security guard questionable.

Alibi: None available. Works security at the bank and would have been there on the Tuesday in question (or at any point the night before). Maintains key/codes to the facility and can come and go 24/7.

Possible mode of operation: Could have easily entered the building in the middle of the night, taking the deposit just after it was made. Fellow Guards on Call could have aided her in cutting off the power ahead of time. Perhaps this is how the organization operates.

My plan regarding this suspect: Stay in touch with people who know/knew her to glean their thoughts. Further investigate Guards on Call. Pray for discernment.

Jake Mullins.

Outward appearances: Rough-looking. What I'd expect a "criminal" to look like. From family description, sounds like a prodigal son, craving the love of a parent.

Motive: To get even with his mother, or to acquire funds to escape life on the streets.

Suspicious behavior: Was seen hanging around the bank on the night before the money disappeared.

Alibi: Claims to have been looking for his sister, to obtain permission to return home.

Possible mode of operation: Could have rigged the night deposit box and taken off with the cash before anyone inside the bank noticed. Or . . . could have convinced his sympathetic sister to pass the cash off to him instead of making the deposit.

My plan regarding this suspect: Find out who he hangs out with. Take the time to meet Jake and pray for discernment regarding his involvement.

Wow. I certainly saw the "bigger picture" now. Four situations. Four very different people. And God clearly loved every single one with a passion, as was evidenced by the warmth that now filled my heart as I caught "His" view on things.

I delved into prayer, spending about a half hour totally dedicated to the four individuals I'd held in suspicion for so long. As I wrapped things up, I asked the Lord the inevitable question: *Is that all You want from me, Father — just to pray?* I braced myself for His response.

The answer gave me reason to pause. For, while none of these folks really came across as the criminal sort, I couldn't shake the possibility that someone I knew and loved had actually committed this crime. And, try as I may, I couldn't deviate from the idea

126

that God wanted me to play a role in bringing the right person to justice.

CHAPTER 10

There's something about a bed-and-breakfast that's conducive to sleep. On the morning after my creek-side chat with the Lord, Sheila and I dozed through the breakfast hour. Almost, anyway. At about twenty minutes 'til nine, Mrs. Lapp's all-too-cheery voice roused us from our slumber.

"Wilkum to a new day, you's two!" she shouted through the door. "There's breakfast to be had in the dining room."

I groaned and rolled over in a tangled mess of quilts to find Sheila still sound asleep in the bed next to mine. The whole thing kind of reminded me of the morning after my fifth-grade slumber party. Same telltale smudges of chocolate, different sleepwear.

"Sheila?"

"Hmm?" She stirred under the colorful mound.

I slung my legs over the edge of my bed and stretched. "Our hostess isn't going to rest until we eat."

Sheila sat straight up, eyes wide open. "Food? Why didn't you say so?"

Ten minutes later, with faces washed and clothes on, we took our seats at the beautiful breakfast table. I stared in disbelief at the amazing assortment of homemade jams, jellies, and other colorful goodies and wondered how any woman on the planet had time to devote to such things. Then I turned to face our blessed innkeeper. Her round cheeks glowed pink and her silver hair peeked beneath the edges of her kapp. She appeared nearly angelic.

Nearly.

"Good morning, you's two!" Mrs. Lapp's ample bosom met me head-on as she threw open her arms for a morning hug.

She then turned her motherly attention to Sheila, who handled the embrace with a little more finesse.

"Morning, Mrs. L." Sheila's cheeks broadened in joy. "I don't know when I've ever slept better."

The older woman clapped her hands together in glee. "Wonderful, wonderful."

"My husband, Orin, snores like a freight train," Sheila added. "But Annie here —"

she said, gesturing my way "— she's quiet as a mouse."

Wish I could say the same about you. I flashed a wide smile and stifled the giggle that threatened to slip out.

"My other guests finished breakfast nearly an hour ago," Mrs. Lapp explained. "But never you mind that. All the better to visit with just the three of us."

Visit?

She fixed our plates then plopped down in the seat at the head of the table. At that point, she dove into a detailed description of our breakfast foods. Dippy eggs, as she called them, turned out to be eggs over easy. Butter bread appeared to be her way of describing our toast with fresh creamed butter. Home fries were sliced potatoes and onions fried in a cast-iron skillet, seasoned with basil and oregano. But the pecan sticky buns, according to Mrs. L., were her specialty. A host of other goodies proved to be the icing on the top of our veritable breakfast cake. I didn't know when I'd ever felt more pampered. Or more stuffed.

I chuckled as I looked at the sign above the table. KISSIN' WEARS OUT; COOKING DON'T. Clearly, Mrs. Lapp's motto. And since there didn't appear to be a Mr. Lapp about, I had to imagine she didn't get much of the first. Judging from the size of her midsection, there appeared to be an abundance of the second.

As we finished up our breakfast, Sheila and I stood and rubbed our expanding bellies.

Sheila shifted her hands around to her hips. "Who needs buns of steel when we can have sticky buns?" She broke into raucous laughter and I joined in, feeling rather fat and sassy myself. For a moment, I almost let my mind gravitate back to the Clark County gym and my fitness rep, Joey. *Nah. Don't go there. Not today.*

Instead, I opted to do a little shopping. We had a look around the small storefront in the lobby, oohing and aahing over the various trinkets and treasures. I picked up a lovely handmade apron, mesmerized by its intricacies.

"Did you make this?" I asked our hostess.

Mrs. Lapp beamed. "No, I haven't the time, what with my guests, the cooking and all. My sister is the seamstress in the family. She has been making those since we were both young girls."

"It's amazing. I'd like to buy this one." I reached for my checkbook. "And please tell your sister just how much I loved it."

"I've sold them for her for years now." Her

chest puffed out a bit more — in pride. "My sister is pleased, to be sure. I just sold several dozen to the vendors at our local merchants' conference last month. You'll be seeing these aprons in shops all over the Amish country now."

Something she'd said piqued my interest. "Conference?"

"In Lancaster," she explained. "A couple hundred of us Dutch merchants meet every year to talk about marketing and promotional ideas. And we're always interested in new products to promote the Amish and Mennonite way of life, that sort of thing. It's great fun."

Sounded like it. It also sounded vaguely familiar.

"Are we going to spend all day gabbing, or are we going into town to shop?" Sheila interrupted our chat with her thoughts on the matter. " 'Cause all this talk about marketing has me in the mood to spend some money."

I chuckled. "We're shopping."

Mrs. Lapp took my check and folded it, then tucked it into her blouse. She followed us all the way out to our car, looking up at the skies before we parted ways. "Spritzing should begin any time now."

Spritzing?

"Best to take your umbrellas," she admonished.

Ah.

I had to poke Sheila in the ribs with my elbow to keep her from laughing aloud. We had too much to do to stand around gabbing about colloquialisms, cute as they might be. There were small towns to visit, shops to be explored, and more delicious foods to be eaten.

As we attempted to climb into the car, Mrs. L. went on to sing the praises of several of her favorite stores and restaurants — all within driving distance. "See as many as you can," she encouraged.

We nodded our thanks and headed out on our way, at once grateful for a bit of silence. I half expected Sheila to comment on the infamous Mrs. L., but she seemed to be lost in her thoughts this morning.

We drove along the winding country roads, pausing at every little town and store that drew our attention, some recommended by Mrs. L., others incidental. Within an hour or so of beginning our shopping, quilt envy had taken root in both of us. I wanted every single one. Above all, their detailed beauty amazed me.

Who in the world has the time to sit and sew like that? I could hardly sit still at the computer long enough to edit a client's manuscript. How did women sit for hours on end, visiting with one another, hand stitching one row upon another?

I snuck a glance at my best friend, her eyes glazed over in pure joy. Truly, she looked as though she'd died and gone to heaven. Perhaps, if we truly had the time to spend with one another, if we lived simpler, quieter lives, we would sit in silence and work on craft projects.

At this point, Sheila erupted in a warbling rendition of "Do a Deer," punctuating the "sew, a needle pulling thread" part.

Hmm. Then again . . .

We shifted our attention to the Amish furniture, taking note of everything from sturdy quilt racks to handcrafted hickory rockers to bent oak dining tables. I couldn't imagine owning such lovely things, though my heart connected with the beauty of it all.

While I couldn't justify the expense of a larger purchase, I did manage to find several other Amish delights to tickle my fancy. I bought a variety of things: several hand-dipped beeswax candles for Brandi and Scott's wedding ceremony, a lovely hand-painted box to give to Nadine as a gift, and the prettiest pewter plate I'd ever seen. The latter I expected to keep for myself.

Sheila couldn't seem to get enough of the pottery, hooked rugs, and handmade dolls. She purchased so many items I finally had to put a moratorium on the shopping. All along the way, she kept me entertained with funny stories and witty sayings, as always.

At some point in our journey, I stumbled across an outdated flier on the back wall of one of the shops, advertising the now-past All Things Dutch conference. Ah. That's what Mrs. L. was talking about. My mind reeled as another memory set in. Janetta Mullins. That's the conference she catered. No wonder it sounded so familiar.

My thoughts ran away with me until Sheila brought me back to reality — her version of it, anyway.

"Where can a girl get some food 'round these here parts?"

I chuckled and shifted our thoughts at once to food. We chose a nearby Amish-run restaurant. Once settled, we enjoyed the most lavish buffet I'd ever had the privilege of lingering over. Some of the foods were familiar, like the beef-and-noodle Amish stew. Others I'd never heard of. Scrapple and sauerkraut surprise custard pie, for example. And Amish ham salad, also made with sauerkraut.

Interesting. Sheila, ever the adventurer, tried a small helping of everything. Yep, everything. I erred on the more cautious side. Ironically, most everything I sampled proved to be quite tasty.

After lunch, we drove the back roads for a while, drinking in the beauty of the place and admiring some of the prettiest farmland on planet Earth. We found a couple more shops to explore but grew weary with the process as late afternoon sleepiness set in. Finally, just as the sun dipped off into the western sky, we landed back on Mrs. Lapp's doorstep once again.

"Well, there you are!" She clapped her hands together, obviously satisfied to see us at last. "I'd begun to wonder if you'd changed your minds about coming back."

I stifled a yawn and assured her we were thrilled to be "home."

Though still stuffed from lunch, Mrs. L. insisted we sit for yet another meal. Bean soup and friendship bread. As we settled down for supper, I took the opportunity to ask our hostess a couple of questions that had been niggling at my brain all day.

"I wonder if you would mind telling me a little more about the merchants' conference you were talking about this morning," I started.

She sliced huge chunks of the bread as she spoke. "What would you like to know?"

I garnered up the courage to ask the question on my mind. Why beat around the bush? "Well, specifically, I'd be interested in hearing your take on the food."

"The food?" She gave a bit of a shrug as she set the bread down. "I don't remember hearing any complaints. Now, mind you, it wasn't as good as my cooking, if I do say so myself."

I pressed back the smile that threatened to sneak up on me as she continued.

"But the caterer did a fine job with both quantity and quality, all things considered. We're a picky lot, what with so many of us being cooks ourselves."

"How did you meet her?" I asked.

Mrs. L. shrugged. "From what I remember, we hired the woman based on references and personal recommendation. I found her to be kind of an odd bird, physically speaking; certainly not what I would have expected, but her work was impressive."

I couldn't help but smile at her description of Janetta. And at this point, I felt safe sharing my information.

"I'm only asking because the woman who catered your event — Janetta Mullins — is an acquaintance," I explained. "We've just hired her to cater my daughter's wedding this coming February."

"Ah." I couldn't help but notice the hesitation in her voice or the way her gaze shifted ever so slightly.

"What?"

"Well, she's a good cook, as I said, but her business practices are a bit . . . unusual."

"Oh?"

As Mrs. Lapp took a seat at the table, her demeanor changed. "I've been on the conference planning committee for years," she explained, "and we're accustomed to dealing with all sorts, but this one really took the cake."

My www.investigativeskills.com antennae rose right away.

"We couldn't figure out why she insisted upon being paid in cash, especially since we were talking about such a large amount of money." Mrs. L.'s brow wrinkled. "Something about it just felt . . . odd."

Felt odd to me, even now. And I could tell from the look on Sheila's face what she must be thinking.

"Mrs. Mullins didn't seem happy when we explained we didn't work that way. Took some time to convince her we had no other choice. She took our check, but I could tell she wasn't happy about it."

"Can't say as I blame her much," Sheila piped up. "I always say the quickest way to double your money is to fold it over in your pocket. Just doesn't work the same with a check."

"Still," I argued, "it's no way to run a business, insisting on cash."

"Funny thing is," Mrs. Lapp threw in, "she stayed on after the conference ended Sunday night. On Monday morning, first thing, she went down to our local bank to try to cash that check. My brother-in-law was in there making a deposit at the same time. He said she pitched a fit. Told 'em she wanted her cash and wanted it now. They usually put a hold on such large amounts, you know." Mrs. L. leaned back in her chair, satisfied that I would understand.

"What happened?"

"She somehow talked them into making an exception and headed out of town with twenty-seven thousand dollars cash in her pocket that same afternoon."

Twenty-seven thousand, not twenty-five? And why in the world didn't Janetta wait to deposit the check into her account back in Clarksborough? Why the rush?

On the other hand, it was really none of my business, was it?

Mrs. Lapp continued on, oblivious to my thoughts. "And then, just a day or so later, when we heard the news about the arrest of that young man in Clarksborough, well —"

Well, what?

"The whole thing was just too suspicious. We put two and two together and realized the missing cash deposit was probably the money we'd paid her." She sighed. "I can't explain why this hit me as strange, but it did. And I'll tell you this: If you're using that woman's company for your daughter's wedding, just be sure to get everything on paper. And don't be surprised if she won't take your check."

I suddenly felt sick inside. I'd passed off two thousand dollars cash to Janetta Mullins as a down payment for Brandi's reception. Cash. What if she'd skipped town, taken off with my money? What if . . .

A thousand what-ifs floated through my head before reality hit.

Looks like I needed to update my crime notebook.

Whether I wanted to admit it or not, I had just acquired one more suspect to add to my ever-growing list.

CHAPTER 11

"I take it Sasha missed me while I was gone?"

I stared down at the mounds of shredded toilet paper on the master bath floor, then back up into Warren's eyes. He looked like a whipped man. Puppy-whipped, to be precise.

"I guess." He let out a woeful sigh. "She was a handful. And if you think this is bad, you should've seen what she did with the trash can in the kitchen. I don't think she was happy with your leaving."

"Clearly." I shook my head in disbelief. If the little monster could do this much damage in a forty-eight-hour period, I hated to think of what she might accomplish in a week without me. Looked like I'd be spending a lot of time at home from now on.

Warren raked his fingers through his hair, lifting the salt-and-pepper waves into a mess almost as big as the one on the floor. "Seriously, Annie," he said. "She's a pain in the neck. And she's not getting better with time."

"Time for a little doggy obedience training?" I gave her my toughest stare, and she responded by shifting to a "begging" position. How cute was that?

Warren groaned. "They'd kick her out of class. Wouldn't be worth the money."

Still . . .

I looked down at my little crime-fighting cohort as she settled to all fours. Her tail wagged a mile a minute and she leaped up, hoping I'd catch her for a little "cuddle time."

Aw. How could I resist?

Once safely in my arms, she settled down, as always. I scratched her behind the ears as I explained my addiction: "I know she's awful, and I don't know why I love her so much. Maybe —" Tears rose to my eyes right away, and I had to confess, I did know. "Maybe it's because the kids are growing up and leaving —" The tears tipped over the edge of my lashes, and Warren stared at me as if I'd gone mad.

"So, you're saying that keeping the dog around is therapeutic?"

Sasha nuzzled her face against my cheek and I whispered, "Uh-huh."

Warren made a face and headed into the bedroom, muttering all the way. Seemed like he'd been doing a lot of that lately. I set the dog down and started scooping up heaps of toilet paper. All the while, Sasha stood at my side, tail beating against the toilet seat. She might be a little on the disobedient side, but I loved her.

Within minutes, Warren reappeared at the bathroom doorway dressed in his boxers and a t-shirt. "I'm worn out. Are you nearly ready for bed?"

I nodded and he came into the bathroom to help me finish up. In typical Warren style, he reached down to rub Sasha behind the ears. I'm pretty sure I even heard him whisper, "Are you helping Mommy?"

The man was smitten, whether he wanted to admit it or not.

That night, I slept like a stone. My weekend in the country, amazing as it was, still couldn't compare to the beauty of sleeping in my own bed with my husband at my side and my puppy at my feet. I dreamed the strangest dream — something about Janetta Mullins dressed in Amish garb, serving food in a small-town restaurant. Dollar bills tumbled from her pockets in every conceivable direction.

Crazy, the things we dream when we're troubled.

I awoke to a brilliant fall morning. I threw back the covers and sprang from the bed, ready to start the day. But first things first. I nudged Warren, who groaned, then eventually crawled from under the sheets in slow motion. I couldn't blame him. He had tossed and turned all night. *Mental note: Why is he suddenly having trouble sleeping? Is he hiding something?*

He showered, dressed for work, gave me a gentle kiss on the lips, and reached down to pet Sasha before leaving. *Yep. He's puppy-whipped.*

With my son at school and my husband on his way to work, the heavenly sound of morning silence fell over the house. I loved this time of day. After a quick shower I headed off to the computer to check my daily Internet devotional. Sasha hopped into my lap as I sat down. You know, I've discovered that typing with a dachshund in your arms is possible, though somewhat debilitating.

This morning's scripture from the second chapter of Proverbs answered some of my weekend ponderings. The very things I'd asked for all along now seemed possible after reading these verses: *"If you call out for insight and cry aloud for understanding, and if you look for it as for silver and search for it as for hidden treasure, then you will understand the fear of the LORD and find the knowledge of God."*

True, true.

I needed — and wanted — His knowledge, not my own. And according to this verse, I could have what I asked for.

So I asked. With Sasha now dozing, I took advantage of the stillness to ask God to give me something I'd neglected to request in weeks prior: understanding. Knowledge. If the Lord truly desired my participation in this investigation, then I had to be willing to accept wisdom from on high. This wasn't the kind of knowledge acquired in school; I needed something that far superseded that.

I could almost hear Sheila's voice now: *"It's what you learn after you know it all that counts."*

Perhaps I'd come at this thing from a know-it-all approach, but that ought to change. Today, in fact.

In this new, dedicated frame of mind, I opened lesson five, which had been waiting in my e-mail box for days. I read the title with great anticipation. *"A Good Investigator Is 'Street-Smart.'"*

Wow. Looked like this was the day to

smarten up. I couldn't help but grin at God's apparent sense of humor in coordinating all of this. *Perhaps I'd better take a closer look. . . .*

Street-smart, eh?

In our little town of Clarksborough, we occasionally saw a little street action. There was the Fourth of July parade hosted by the political league and the Children's Festival, held on the corner lot of Main and Wabash each May Day. And, of course, we had the annual Get Out to Vote barbecue and the ever-famous lighting of the Christmas tree on the day after Thanksgiving.

Then again, that probably wasn't the kind of "street-smart" they had in mind, now that I thought about it. To be street-smart meant . . .

To be honest, I didn't have a clue what it meant. Perhaps I'd have to do a little investigating to figure this one out, particularly if I wanted to understand the mentality of a young man like Jake Mullins, who had apparently lived much of his life out on the streets.

Street-smart, street-smart . . .

I did a search on the Internet to find out about life on the streets. Several Web pages later, I realized I had plenty to learn. And I recognized right away that folks on the street were apparently quite savvy, in their own right. Most had probably already learned far more than I ever would about things like . . . basic survival skills, for example. How else could they cope with drastic weather conditions, constant hunger pangs, and the ever-present threat of violence from so-called friends?

I shuddered as I thought about that. How awful, to live alongside people who had no hope. And how much more awful still, to lose hope yourself.

Over the next hour or so, I scoured Web sites, looking at specific stories of those on the fringes of society: the homeless man, the downtrodden veteran, the prostitute, the drifter. . . .

My mind stopped right there as I contemplated Jake Mullins. He'd spent a lot of time on the streets, no doubt. Probably in nearby Philadelphia. Any one of these stories could have been written about him. And surely, during his time "out there," he had acquired plenty of "street smarts." Perhaps he knew what it was like to beg for a bite to eat or to fight over a bridge to sleep under. Perhaps he knew what it meant to celebrate over a hot shower at a local shelter or cry over a holiday spent alone next to an open fire in the parking lot of an abandoned tenement building.

Jake Mullins.

I pushed the emotions back. As a mother, I simply couldn't imagine my child on such a frightening learning curve.

Sasha wriggled a bit, coming awake.

"Need to go out, sweet girl?"

As she stood in my lap and gave a little shake, the tags on her collar jingled. She leaped to the floor, her tail wagging in anticipation. I simultaneously reached for her leash and grabbed my jacket, sensing this walk would take a bit longer than the norm. For whatever reason, I needed to get out of the house for a while.

Out onto the streets.

I tagged along behind the little darling, past the morning paper at the end of the driveway and beyond the piles of leaves spread across my neighbor's yard.

All along the way, I looked over my street with new eyes. Lovely middle-class homes lined each side, and cars, bright and shiny, sat in each driveway. Landscaped yards spoke of people who cared about their environment, and fall decorations displayed a feeling of warmth for the season. Someone must be burning leaves nearby. Smoke lifted in a spiral, of sorts, and the heavenly scent of blazing embers filled my senses.

I loved that smell.

In fact, I loved everything about small-town life.

How much had I taken for granted, dwelling in such safe, comfortable surroundings? A little shiver needled its way down my spine as I contemplated the truth. I lived a good life. A safe life. A life with ice cream socials and Sunday school parties, Fourth of July picnics and weekends at the lake. I didn't have to deal with the kinds of things I'd read about on those Web pages, and I was grateful for it. So, how in the world could I go about acquiring street smarts? Where would this knowledge come from?

This morning's verse raced back through my head again. *"Look for it as for silver and search for it as for hidden treasure. . . ."* I had the strangest sense the Lord wanted to teach me a few things today. Specific things. But I'd have to dig deep to find them.

Sasha and I walked a good, long ways — into town and beyond. I let her lead the way, up to a point. When we got to Clark County School Road, I turned off to the left. The sound of children's voices drew me, and I made the journey, as much from memory as anything.

I came upon the familiar schoolyard at the elementary building. As the boys and girls played kickball, their squeals rang out against the quiet of the late morning. One of the little girls from the church gave a jubilant wave.

"Hi, Mrs. Peterson!"

This started a round of shouts and waves from children who knew me. Before long, their teacher, a young woman named Jodie, who had graduated with my girls, ushered them back into order again. "Come on, boys and girls! Back to the game."

I offered a shrug in the way of an apology and called out, "Sorry!"

She gave me a thumbs-up then shifted her attention back to her young charges.

I watched for a moment as they returned to their game. How many times had I stood at this fence, watching my own children play ball? And how many times had my heart swelled, as it did now?

Reminiscence eventually took over and emotions kicked in. Instinctively, I reached down to grab Sasha and cradled her into my arms. I pondered the passing of time. I ran my fingers across the puppy's floppy ear, and she responded to my attention by nuzzling up against my cheek.

Yes, Warren, she is therapeutic.

I needed her more than I'd acknowledged. And perhaps I needed to grieve a little, too.

I hadn't really done that yet, to be quite honest. Sure, I'd helped my girls settle into their own place, and yes, I'd felt an unusual heart-twisting on the night they announced their respective engagements. But . . . grieving? Was this to be part of the learning process for me?

I stood, deep in thought, until the ache passed. At some point along the way, Sasha got antsy, and I put her down. So much for therapy.

At that point, I made a conscious choice to step away from my sadness. With so much to be grateful for, I should probably be looking toward the future, not the past. And standing here, in front of these jubilant children, provided me an opportunity to do just that.

I looked at their smiling faces once again and reflected on my gratitude — and my hopes for the future and safety of our little town. My own daughters had grown into wonderful, knowledgeable adults, and my son soon would, as well. These children would grow into intelligent young men and women, too. Most would probably attend college. Some would even acquire degrees — and spend the rest of their lives passing on the things they knew to future Clarksborough generations, just as Jodie did now.

My mind drifted back to Jake Mullins, and troubling thoughts set in. How did he slip through the cracks? What went wrong? Hadn't he attended this same school? What had happened to send him off on a journey of destruction? Why had he opted to leave home at seventeen, to pursue life on the streets?

I thought about Nadine and her work with the homeless in Savannah. My admiration for her soared through the roof. What was it she had said about the Lord calling us to reach out to the poor and needy? Something from Isaiah, I think. Oh yes, *"The Spirit of the Sovereign Lord is upon me, because the Lord has anointed me to preach good news to the poor."* And there was more, too. Something about ministering to the downtrodden.

Was Jake Mullins downtrodden? If so, was the Lord asking me, in some way, to minister to him?

Only one way to know for sure. I would arrange to spend a little time with him, get to know him better. Figure out who he liked to hang out with, and why. Perhaps doing so would solve two problems for me: First, it would help me discern his role, if any, in the disappearance of the money. Second, it would give me a glimpse into the life of a young man who'd struggled like so many others I'd just read about on the Internet.

Sasha tugged on the leash and I turned toward home. As I walked along, I felt led to pray for Jake. I'm not sure why. Perhaps this thing about being a prodigal hit me so hard because of my own son. I couldn't imagine what it must feel like to have a family member living in such hopelessness.

In my mind's eye, I could see Devin in his football uniform, chasing a ball past the fifty-yard line. I could not — prayed I would not — see him on the run from his family, his friends, his relationship with God. I would do everything in my power to prevent such a thing.

Then again, perhaps Janetta Mullins had done everything within her power, too. Maybe she'd spent the last few years praying for her wayward son, as she'd said. If so, we had every reason to hope — to believe — he had returned for the right reasons. To enter back into relationship with his family.

I pondered that awhile. If, after all he'd learned on the streets, Jake Mullins had turned his heart toward home, then I wanted to help free him from the cloud of guilt that now hovered over him. Perhaps, if the two of us linked arms, we could convince the police . . .

I stopped right there. Sheila's comment at the bed-and-breakfast roused me from my ponderings. *"If all you have is a hammer, everything looks like a nail."*

Funny thing was, Jake Mullins didn't look much like a nail right now. In fact, he looked every bit like a young man in need of a hand.

And I just happened to have a hand. Two, in fact.

CHAPTER 12

I guess you could say I caught a break. On Wednesday afternoon, at approximately 2:15 p.m., I happened to notice Jake Mullins through the window of the diner, seated in a booth. Alone.

Could I help it if the sudden urge for a piece of homemade apple pie pushed me through the front door of my favorite eatery and into the booth next to his? And could I help it that my former Don't-call-me-honey waitress happened to be serving both of us simultaneously?

I slipped off my jacket and looked up into Shawna's eyes from atop the plastic-coated menu. For the first time, I observed their color. Green. Quite pretty. In fact, she was a pretty girl, all the way around.

Take note, Annie. If you look beyond the tattoos and piercings, you might just find a beautiful person underneath.

"Can I help you, honey?" I took note of

the sarcasm as she pulled the pencil from behind her ear to take my order. My gaze shifted to the assortment of earrings lining her right ear. All the way up — and in some of the oddest places I'd ever imagined anyone poking a hole. *Wow. That looks painful.*

"Mmm, yes." I glanced at the menu — for effect. "I'll have the apple pie, à la mode. And a cup of coffee."

She reached to take the menu, and I commented on her fingernails — black with a various musical notes painted in white on each one. "Very cool. Where did you get them done?"

Now, me — I always had mine done at Clarksborough's salon, The Liberty Belle. But I knew for a fact my nail tech, Maureen, didn't customize quite like that.

Shawna held her hands out for my approval. "My sister in Philly does nails. So every time I go back home for a visit she experiments on me. Do you like them?"

"Very much. I take it you're a music lover."

Her face lit in a smile, the first I'd seen. "I'm in a band," she explained. "I play the keyboard and sing."

"Very appropriate, then. What kind of music do you play?"

"I write most of our songs," she added, a flush now covering her cheeks. "We do mostly alternative stuff."

"Ah." *Mental note: Look up alternative music.*

She went to fetch my pie, and I focused on the young man I'd come to connect with. Jake never seemed to notice me. Instead, his gaze appeared to be focused on one thing: Shawna.

As she returned to plop a dish-sized wedge of apple pie in front of me, he piped up from the next booth. "Did I hear you say you're from Philly?"

"I lived in Northeast Philly 'til I was seventeen." Shawna took a step his direction, and I couldn't help but notice that the color in her cheeks deepened as she drew closer to Jake. And why not? Despite his rough life, he was a good-looking young man.

"How in the world did you end up in Clarksborough?" He reached to put his coffee cup down. "I mean, I can see moving from here to there, but to do it the other way around —"

My keen observation skills kicked in. I took note of Shawna's tightening grip on the menu as he asked the question. *Is she nervous? What's up with that?*

"My cousin lives here," she explained. "My parents . . . well, let's just say they thought it was time I got out of the city for a while. They wanted to get me away from my, um, friends."

Jake gave her an inquisitive look. "Ah. I lived in Philly, too. 'Til just a few weeks ago."

Shawna set the menu aside as she carried on. "I miss my old neighborhood." She dove into a lengthy explanation about the street she'd grown up on, and I tried to turn my attention to the cars driving by on the other side of the window but couldn't seem to. Something about this pair intrigued me.

Before long, the three of us found ourselves in an enlightening conversation that would've made my Internet teachers proud. I learned more in those few moments than I had in years.

With no other customers to wait on, Shawna took a seat at Jake's table and eventually encouraged me to join them. I slipped in with the comfort of a cat easing onto a sunlit windowsill. Of course, this cat had to take her pie with her. Waste not, want not, and all that.

For whatever reason, Jake felt comfortable enough around the two of us to open up and share about his life in the big city. Over the next hour, I heard all about his yearlong residence in the underground world of Philadelphia's subway station, where commuters would occasionally toss a bit of change his way, or shift their eyes, pretending to look the other way. He talked about bitter cold nights spent in shelters, where he listened to street preachers "do their thing," in exchange for a hot shower and a much-needed rest in a real bed.

"Never really paid much attention to what they were saying," he admitted at one point. "Guess I didn't feel like I needed what they were peddling. I just wanted a clean bathroom and a shave. Or a new shirt."

My heart nearly broke as he told his story. For several reasons. I wanted to ask him how he could've heard their words of hope and not responded, but he answered that for me.

"I was too messed up to hear what they had to say, anyway. My mind was —" His hand flew up, as if in a sign of surrender. "Shot. I was completely messed up by the drugs and alcohol."

He went on to talk about the countless bottles of cheap whiskey he'd purchased over the years, which he'd swallowed down between drug hits. I squirmed in my seat and tried to settle the ache in my "mama

159

heart" by tracing circles in my now-empty pie plate with my fork.

I thought, once again, about Nadine, and her work with the homeless. How wonderful, to give yourself so freely to those in need. But how difficult it must be to watch so many return to their habits, in spite of your encouragement and help.

As Jake spoke, I wished a thousand times over I could bolt from this place and not look back. But something held me firmly in place. *Lord, is this what You meant by street-smart?* To be honest, this isn't quite what I had in mind. I could have lived the rest of my life without hearing all of this.

On the other hand, I had asked the Lord for His help with the investigation. Perhaps something Jake said would stir up an answer to the questions rolling around in my head.

"If you look for it as for silver and search for it as for hidden treasure, then you will understand the fear of the Lord and find the knowledge of God."

Hmm. There it was again. That verse.

Well, no point in beating around the bush. I might as well come out and ask the question that had been on my mind all along. "I just need to know one thing." I could feel the frustrating sting of tears as I interrupted him.

His brow wrinkled as he looked my way. "What?"

"If you had family here, what were you doing there? Why didn't you just come home?"

Jake and Shawna both gave me that *you-wouldn't-get-it* look, but I refused to let the question go unanswered.

"I want to understand." I offered up an imploring look, in the hopes that both would trust me enough to bare their souls. "I'm a mom. And all moms want to know what they could have done —" dare I say it? "— differently."

Shawna's musical fingernails tapped on the tabletop. "It's not always that easy to explain." I took note of the strain in her voice. "I mean, I got along with my mom okay, but my dad —"

"At least you had a dad," Jake interjected. "With me, there was no one to talk to but my mom, and she just didn't get me. At least not during the bad years."

I thought back to my conversation with Janetta Mullins. She had acknowledged making a few mistakes, not offering her youngest child the same discipline as the older ones. But was that really enough to send him running to a life in the streets?

"So leaving was the best choice?" I asked.

161

Jake's gaze shifted to the table. "I'm not saying that. There are a lot of things I wish I'd done different. My mom —" His eyes clouded over here.

Was he going to cry?

"My mom did everything she could. I know that. She wanted me to just snap out of it. Like it was that easy. She even sent me to a counselor."

"Been there, done that," Shawna whispered. "My parents sent me to a shrink. Paid a fortune."

I couldn't help but notice the admiring gaze Jake cast Shawna's way as he forged ahead. "After my dad left, I just kind of folded up — like a deck of cards. Shut down. It wasn't long before a couple of my friends offered me something that took away the pain."

Drugs.

"I knew I'd end up as messed up as they were." He shrugged. "But to be honest, I didn't care. I didn't care about anyone back then, especially not myself."

Whoa. Brutal honesty. I guess that's what I got for asking God to show me His heart in all of this.

Jake's lips pursed and silence took over. He finally spoke, though a tremor now laced his words. "My dad obviously never cared anything about me. I didn't figure I mattered to him — at least not enough to send a lousy birthday card or Christmas present. So I guess it made some kind of sense that I didn't care about myself either. Like father, like son, you know?"

How do I get rid of this knot in my throat without creating a scene?

Jake's face tightened as he finished. "I just wanted a way to kill the pain. And the drugs took care of that."

I noticed Shawna's eyes brimming over. Apparently her heart was softer than it appeared. "How did you end up in Philly?" she asked.

Is that tenderness in her voice?

Jake took another swig from his coffee cup before answering. "The money. I figured I could deal drugs, like my buddies. They made it sound pretty appealing. But I've already told you how all of that ended up." He cleared his throat and shifted his attention out the window.

My heart felt as if it would break. I wanted to wrap this young man in my arms, to tell him everything would be fine, that he could start all over again.

Shawna interrupted my thoughts with a few thoughtful words. "Sometimes I wish I could go back and do things over."

"Me, too." Jake looked up, and their eyes seemed to lock.

For a moment I said nothing. When I did interject my thoughts, they came bathed in silent prayer. "Everyone feels that way at some point. We've all got stuff behind us we wish we could change. But it's what's in front of us that matters."

Jake gave a slight nod. "Looking back is hard. I don't even like to remember what I was like in Philly." Again, his gaze shifted to the table.

I reached to squeeze his hand. "Jake, you're no different from any of the rest of us."

His eyebrows arched in surprise. "You're kidding, right?"

"No. And I think you know it, too. I think you probably heard just enough from those street preachers to get you thinking. You're not interested in going back. You want to move forward. That's evident."

He leaned back in the booth and put his hands behind his head. "Maybe. But the police sure don't seem to think I have any kind of a future — except maybe one behind bars. They took one look at me and assumed the worst. Didn't even give me a chance."

My heart rate increased immediately. *Oh, here we go. . . .*

"What's up with that?" Shawna asked.

I leaned in as Jake responded, my need-to-know kicking in.

"They said they found my fingerprints on the night deposit box. Big deal. So I'm not a customer at the bank. What does that have to do with anything?"

What, indeed? Probably hundreds of people have touched that box.

"I told them I'd touched it. Even tried to open it. I was just messing around, waiting for my sister to show up. I'd been watching her for days and kind of figured she'd eventually turn up to make a deposit for my mom's business."

"Did she?" Shawna leaned in, elbows on the table, in rapt attention.

He shrugged. "From what my sister told me later, she made the deposit around one in the morning, but I never even saw her. I fell asleep around midnight on the backside of the building, just beyond the trees."

Ah. So that answered one question. "I fell asleep" probably hadn't been the strongest alibi, to a law enforcement officer's way of thinking.

"The police must think I'm a lot smarter than I am. There was some sort of power outage, and I guess they figured I rigged it somehow." He shook his head, clearly frustrated. "I can think of a thousand things I'd rather do than mess with anything electrical, I'll tell you that."

Amen, brother. I hear ya.

"And how in the world they think I rigged the night deposit box is beyond me. Supposedly they found some scrape marks on the edges, but they're really grasping if they think that incriminates me in any way." He finished up the story with a smirk on his face. "I guess these local cops took one look at my record from Philly and made an assumption I stole the money to buy drugs. But I've been clean and sober for nine months. Nine months."

"Wow." Shawna and I spoke in unison.

I could see the anger in his eyes now. "The thing that really made me mad was the part where they said I did this to get even with my mom. They have no idea —" His chin quivered, and Shawna reached to squeeze his hand. "They have no idea I came back to Clarksborough to make peace with my mom. I was coming home . . . for good."

The silence at the table grew a bit eerie, and I finally snapped to as I looked at my watch. *Four thirty? No way.* I glanced out the window just in time to see Devin drive by on his way home from football practice. Even from here, I could see the smudges on his face.

Oh, my son. My wonderful, innocent son.

I thanked Jake and Shawn for their vulnerability and told them I wanted to stay in touch. Then I dismissed myself to return home. I spent the brief drive in a somewhat frantic, choppy prayer, pleading with God to reach down and touch Jake — to give him a new perspective of himself and his future.

Lord, please help him see that You're for him, not against him. Help him, Father. And if You want to use me in any way to bring him to You —

I could see myself, now — reaching out to Jake, giving him motherly advice, offering counsel and encouragement. Perhaps I'd even go to the police and explain his situation, try to help them see beyond the circumstantial evidence to the truth.

When the Lord interrupted my zealous ponderings to share His thoughts on the matter, I very nearly missed Him altogether. His words, familiar and poignant, took me aback.

God grant me the serenity to accept the people I cannot change, the courage to change the one I can —

— And the wisdom to know it's me.

Funny, the Almighty sounded for all the world like Sheila.

CHAPTER 13

On the morning after my encounter with Jake Mullins, I decided to stop by the Clark County Sheriff's Office for a little chat with his arresting officer. Mind you, I knew little about law enforcement and even less about criminal investigations — other than what I'd learned through the terrific courses at www.investigativeskills.com, of course. Still, I couldn't shake the idea that meeting with "the big guys" would serve me well.

Sergeant Michael O'Henry, a former Sunday school student of mine, met with me, albeit unwillingly. He didn't seem keen on swapping stories about Clark County's key suspect, but I tried not to take that personally. My gut told me the police didn't have their man this time around.

O'Henry, a rather rotund and red-faced fellow, led me into his cold and uninviting office. He took a seat behind the desk, and I sat in the stark metal chair on the opposite side. *Mental note: If anyone in the family ever decides to go into law enforcement, offer to decorate their office.*

The sergeant took a seat in the squeaky leather swivel chair, leaned back to put his hands behind his head, and the conversation began.

"Well, Mrs. Peterson —"

"Call me Annie." I had to admit, it felt kind of weird calling him "Sergeant." Weirder still to see him with a receding hairline instead of those cute blond curls he'd always pushed out of his eyes while coloring pictures of Jesus and the disciples.

"Fine. Annie, I'm not sure what else I can tell you that you haven't already read in the papers or heard through the grapevine."

Grapevine? What does he think Clarksborough is, anyway? A rumor mill? Hmm. Then again . . .

"Is Jake Mullins still a suspect?" I pulled out my notebook to begin writing.

O'Henry pursed his lips. "I can't really talk to you about that."

Oh, sure you can. "Why not?" I scribbled a couple of circles onto the page to make sure my pen was working. Just in case this fine law enforcement officer decided to spill his guts. "Obviously you've released him. Does that mean you don't have a case against him, or are you just working to obtain more evidence?"

The man didn't even bother to blink.

"We're dealing with an ongoing investigation here," he explained. "And I can't really divulge anything more than that."

I gazed through the glass into the outer office, distracted as the various officers came and went. The radios strapped to their sides blared out bits and pieces of messages, but I couldn't make out any of them. Couldn't figure out how they did, either. The whole thing was pretty dizzying.

I regained my focus and slipped into Sunday-school-teacher mode. "Michael, you must know in your gut that Jake Mullins is innocent. All of the evidence is circumstantial. I've heard his story. I can't imagine he's guilty. Talk to his family. They'll fill you in on why he was hanging around the bank."

Michael picked up an ink pen and twisted it around in his fingers. My keen observation skills clued me in on the fact that my words had made him nervous. Or possibly irritated. Still, his response surprised me.

"Every snowflake in an avalanche pleads not guilty, Mrs. Peterson."

Good grief. Is everyone on the planet going to end up sounding like Sheila?

With my most motherly voice in place, I

went on to ask him how he knew so much about Jake Mullins. After all, poor Jake was just a kid in need of a mother's love. Couldn't O'Henry see that?

His answer threw me for a loop.

"I've been tracking that kid for nine years. Nine years. You wouldn't believe all the stuff he got into as a teen."

My mind soared back to the conversation in the diner. Plenty of Jake's stories had wowed me. Plenty.

I noticed O'Henry's brow creasing. "This is one messed-up young man we're talking about here," he said. "And I owe it to the taxpayers to finally bring him to justice. He's gotten away with too much over the years. Too much. And he's made me look like a fool on more than one occasion."

Whoa. Do I smell a vendetta here, or what?

"I know he says he's changed." O'Henry reached up with his palm to swipe it through his thinning hair. "But that's hard to believe. And a little too convenient, to my way of thinking. Once a troublemaker, always a troublemaker."

"Interesting words, coming from the kid who set off a round of fireworks in the baptistery during the Christmas play. You were fourteen at the time, if memory serves me correctly." Now I was the one leaning

172

back in my chair, smug look on my face.

Michael turned all shades of red. "I, um —"

"A rough past doesn't dictate a person's future," I prompted.

"Listen, Mrs. Peterson, it's like this —" The fine sergeant went on to tell me about Jake's arrest history. He listed countless drug charges while Jake was in his late teens and a case of breaking and entering at seventeen.

"He's been in and out of this jail more than I have," O'Henry said with a smirk, "and I've worked in this building fifteen years."

Clearly an exaggeration, but I did have to wonder about Jake at this point. His "record" seemed to be heftier than I'd imagined. Of course, he had never minced any words about his past. He'd simply left out the parts where he had "done time" in the Clark County Jail.

O'Henry continued on. "Mind you," he said, "I'm only free to mention all of this because it's a matter of public record. If you go back through the local papers from a few years ago, you'll find most of this same information. It's all there."

Ouch. So much for playing the role of "Super-Sleuth Extraordinaire." I'd never thought of looking through old newspapers for evidence.

Sergeant O'Henry stood, and I followed his lead by standing as well. All the while, a strange mixture of thoughts tumbled around in my head. Maybe Jake hadn't completely bared his soul in our diner discussion. But people could change, couldn't they? All of these things really were just a reflection of his past, not his present. Hadn't we talked about that? What difference did a shady past make, after all?

I tried to shift the conversation a little by explaining my reason for coming — at least one of my reasons, anyway. "I'm trying to understand the mentality of a young man who would turn to life on the streets."

"Why?"

There must be a course at the police academy on how to give a piercing gaze, because his left me feeling more than a little cold.

"I, um —"

"Annie." The officer extended his hand and I took it for a good-bye shake. "I think you're better off leaving this to the sheriff's office. That's why you pay your tax dollars. And we're here to serve you."

"I don't doubt that. I just want to —"

"I know what you're trying to do." He

ushered me to the door as he carried on. "You're softhearted and all that. Nobody ever wants to believe the worst, especially of a guy as young and innocent-looking as Jake Mullins. But someone stole that twenty-five thousand dollars."

"Indeed." My heart rate doubled immediately. "But this troubles me, too. I've not heard you mention any other suspects." *None. Nada. Zip.*

"That's right, you haven't." He gave me yet another cold, hard look. "And if we had other suspects, you still wouldn't — at least not until an arrest had been made. As I said, this is an ongoing investigation."

I can't explain the cold shockwave that rode down my spine as he looked into my eyes. It was almost as if Sergeant O'Henry could read all of my troubling thoughts at once. *Mental note: Figure out how to give that stare. Very effective.*

Perhaps the Clark County Sheriff's Office had shifted their sites to another suspect and I knew nothing of it. Maybe, even now, they were tailing my husband's every move, in the hopes that he would slip up, make a mistake.

Maybe they knew I carried a large amount of cash in my purse at this very moment to pay the Clarksborough Catering Company toward the balance on Brandi's wedding reception.

I opted to change gears. "Has it occurred to you that the Mullins family might not have actually made the deposit? Perhaps Jake's sister pocketed the money. Or maybe —" I was going to bring up Janetta's obsession with being paid in cash, but something stopped me.

"Mrs. Peterson, we're more than aware of all the angles." O'Henry looked more than a little perturbed. "That's why we're here. We'll look under every bush, I can assure you. And we'll catch our man. Or woman. The right person will be brought to justice."

He shifted the conversation to the weather as we approached the parking lot. I tried to do the same, tried to think happier thoughts. But they would not come. Out of habit, perhaps, I reached to give him a hug before leaving. The bulletproof vest served as a reminder of the weight of his job.

He is an expert. And I am . . .

Hmm. Not sure what I am. Mother of the brides? Editor? Housewife? Responsible pet owner?

I made the drive home in a mixed-up state of mind. Even after all of my conversations with Jake and the police, I didn't feel any smarter. True confession: Sergeant O'Henry had made me feel, well, a little dumb. Kind of like Jake's conversation yesterday had done.

Nope. I surely didn't know much about crime fighting. Or life on the streets. Or drug busts. Or missing cash. Or anything, outside the realm of my own safe little world. And perhaps that's how it was supposed to be.

"If you call out for insight and cry aloud for understanding, and if you look for it as for silver and search for it as for hidden treasure, then you will understand the fear of the Lord and find the knowledge of God."

The niggling voice of the Holy Spirit whispered in my ear again. Maybe I'd been going about this "street smarts" thing all wrong. I'd been digging, all right, but didn't find myself much closer to the truth. Honestly, it felt like I'd been digging myself deeper and deeper into a hole.

I opened the door to the house, and Sasha met me, tail wagging. I didn't notice anything amiss — at first. It wasn't until I entered the living room that reality hit. The room was covered in white fuzz. It kind of looked like someone had peeled back the roof and invited in a snowstorm.

What in the world?

The throw pillows had been shredded to

smithereens. The white, fluffy stuff was now spread about in wisps. Sasha jumped up onto the sofa, her tail wagging a hundred miles a minute. I stared down at her in disbelief. "Bad girl, Sasha. Bad girl." After that, I vaguely remember muttering, "Daddy's going to kill me."

I went to work, cleaning up her mess, all the while trying to figure out why she would have done something like this. Boredom? Rebellion? Frustration?

Had I somehow played a role in all that? Perhaps I had been so busy "out there" that I'd forgotten to take care of things "in here"? *Perhaps.*

After racing through the living room with the speed of Mr. Clean, I headed off to the kitchen to load the dishwasher. Sure, I'd meant to do it last night before bed, but the time had gotten away from me. *Mental note: Remember that speech you used to give the kids — "Dishes do not wash themselves."*

After thoroughly cleaning the kitchen, I shifted my attention to the bedroom. Piles of laundry greeted me. I even noticed a pair of panties sticking out from under the bed. *What in the world? Note to self: Be careful where you leave your laundry basket, particularly when there are unmentionables involved. Sasha enjoys hiding things.*

After loading the washer, I settled down at the computer. I found a note from Devin taped to the monitor. *"Don't forget the food for the homecoming party."* Oops. I *had* almost forgotten about the party he'd planned for this coming Friday night after the homecoming game.

Hmm. I'd have to deal with that later. Right now, a monstrous stack of e-mails from clients awaited me. I couldn't help but groan. Had my investigation really taken me away from my work this long? I read through them all, surprised to find a couple of my favorite clients weren't terribly happy with me right now. Good rule of thumb: Never make a promise to a client and then walk away and forget about it.

After responding to the e-mails, I decided to listen to my phone messages. Whoa. Eleven. Had it really been that long since I'd checked them? I zipped through the messages, startled to hear one from my mother and another from our pastor, asking for my help with the church's booth at the annual Get Out to Vote rally later in the month.

I leaned back in my chair and drew in a deep breath. I'd let life pile up on me. And now I had to pay the piper.

I thought back to my last lesson. Street

smarts, eh? Looked like the only kind of "smarts" I needed were the kind that would teach me how to stay on top of the day-to-day things. I very nearly picked up the phone to call Sheila, to ask her advice. But, why bother? I could pretty much imagine what she'd have to say: *"Annie, you used to have a handle on life . . . but it broke."*

And she'd be right.

To further torment myself, I decided to open up the next lesson from www.investi-gativeskills.com. I'm pretty sure it was accompanied by a heavenly choir this time around, that's how powerfully the words hit me when I read the title to lesson six: *"A Good Investigator Is Able to Multitask."*

Yikes.

I stared at the screen in disbelief. Why even read the lesson? Hadn't I already struggled enough in this area? Hadn't I proven that I couldn't handle one thing piled upon another? Why in the world would I want to rub salt into an open wound?

Still . . . I could use a few suggestions for how to bring balance to my life, as the opening paragraph suggested. I needed to know how to be all things to all people.

Didn't I?

CHAPTER 14

Sometimes I wish life had subtitles.

Seriously. There have been certain instances in my life that would have been greatly enhanced by a few carefully thought-out words written beneath them. Take, for example, the time I tried to rewire the thermostat in the downstairs hallway and short-circuited the fan in the air-conditioning unit outside. *Subtitle: If you don't have a sense of humor, you probably don't have any sense at all.* Or the time I insisted I could change the oil in the car and ended up in the emergency room with eight stitches in my right hand. *Subtitle: Should have gone to Jiffy Lube.*

Yep, there were just some things a twenty-first-century woman shouldn't attempt without subtitles. In fact, there were some things a woman like me shouldn't be allowed to attempt . . . at all.

So why, then, did I agree to make all of

the foods for Devin's post-homecoming-game party next weekend? Thirty high school boys and their dates? Was I crazy?

I sifted through the bags of groceries with a sigh and attempted to put together a plan of action. Where should I start? Animal, vegetable, or mineral? I took a look at the hodgepodge of high-carb, high-calorie goodies and slapped myself in the head. What a way to spend my Saturday afternoon. I could think of approximately ten thousand other things I'd rather do.

The bag of frozen meatballs looked up at me, teasing, taunting. "Get to work!" they screamed. I supposed I could drop them into the Crock-Pot before next week's game and pour some barbecue sauce over them. I glanced through my cookbook for a recipe for sausage-and-cheese puffs, which Devin had specifically requested. *Hmm. They'll have to be made earlier in the day, but it doesn't look too complicated.*

I stared and the monstrous bag of frozen hot wings. What in the world was I supposed to do with those? I'd never cooked a hot wing in my life. I flipped over the bag and drew in a relieved breath as I read the instructions. Looked like they could be popped into the oven on a cookie sheet to be warmed just before serving. No problem.

Now for the complicated one — the salsa dip. I read Sheila's hand-scribbled instructions one more time before starting: Take a jar of salsa and mix it with creamy cream cheese. Spread it in a dish and chill. Then spread chopped onions, tomatoes, and peppers all over the top. Cover with shredded taco cheese mix and serve with chips.

Goodness. Why didn't I just buy a container of dip at the store?

I finally turned my attention to the things that troubled me most — the sweets. Devin had shown up with the oddest assortment of goodies to be pieced together, everything from chocolate chip pizza cookies to homemade caramel corn. Add to that about a zillion bags of chips and enough dip for a small army, and I knew my hands were more than full.

I paused a moment from my ponderings to think about Janetta Mullins. The woman was terrific at pulling together food for parties like this. A real pro. Should I give her a call?

Thinking about Janetta got me thinking about the missing money. Thinking about the missing money got me thinking about Jake. Thinking about Jake got me thinking about the plight of the homeless. And thinking about the homeless made me feel kind of bad about complaining about food preparation at all.

The telephone rang, interrupting my reverie. Thank goodness.

"Mom?"

Brandi. She sounded anxious. Nothing new there.

"What's up, honey?"

"I need you."

Ah, the bliss of those words. They were enough to make any mom throw her son's snacks overboard and focus on the things that really mattered in life.

The bride-to-be needs me.

I quickly put the groceries away, content in the fact that next week's game night would be a smashing success. Within minutes, Brandi arrived at the house with a large bag in her hand and a suspicious gleam in her eye. I knew that look all too well, which explained the sudden splattering of fear that trickled through me.

My beautiful eldest daughter gabbed all the way from the front door to the kitchen. When we arrived at the table, she pulled from the bag the loveliest red rose I'd ever seen. It was large, full, breathtaking, and . . . fake. I had to look twice just to make sure my eyes hadn't fooled me.

"What made you decide on silks?" I asked

as I fingered it.

Brandi shrugged. "We're spending so much on the facility and the food, I needed to cut back. So I thought silk flowers would be a nice way to do that. They're so real-looking, no one will ever know. Aren't they pretty?"

Indeed, they were. In fact, they were eerily true-to-life. I had to give it to her. The girl really knew her roses. Then again, with nearly a dozen boyfriends coming and going over the past several years, she should.

"So, here's the thing," she said with a crooked grin. "I know you're really crafty and all —"

"I'm really what?" My mind gravitated at once to the women in the Amish country, seated with their quilting projects in their laps.

"Crafty. You're so good at putting things together. Remember those centerpieces you and Nadine worked on? They turned out great."

"Well, yes, but she did most of the work," I argued. "To be honest, I'm not —"

Brandi continued on, undaunted. "I've had the most fabulous idea, and it will save us so much money. I want you to put together the bridesmaids' bouquets for the wedding."

"S–Say what?"

She emptied the bag of voluptuous roses out all over the clean end of the table.

I took one look at the whole mound of red silk goodies and clutched my head in my hands. *Subtitle: When life gives you lemons, make . . . bridal bouquets?*

My mind reeled. *What do these kids think I am — a decorating diva? Sure, I watch a little home-improvement TV, but that's purely recreational.*

Brandi rambled on and on. Something about boutonnieres for the guys and corsages for the mothers and grandmothers. I'm not sure I heard a word of it. I mean, I saw her lips moving, but it was almost like I'd instantaneously lost all of my hearing the minute those roses hit the table.

Funny thing was, it returned when she began to sing my praises once again. "You're the best, Mom!" She finished her zealous speech, planted a kiss on my cheek, and beamed with joy. "I just can't wait to see what you come up with."

Um, me either.

My expression must've spiraled downward, because Brandi reached out to give me what felt like a sympathetic hug. "I need you, Mom," she whispered.

Ah, those words. Those magical, lyrical

words. They sprinkled pixie dust on a mother's weary soul. They roused her from her slumber and caused her to believe she could attempt the impossible. Even when she knew in her gut she shouldn't.

I thought about my lesson plan once more. *A good investigator is able to multitask.*

Accomplishing several things at once might appear difficult to the average human being, but I'd never claimed to be average. No, in my daughter's eyes, I was Supermom — able to leap tall buildings in a single bound — and certainly capable of piecing together red silk roses in a fashionable display. I could do this. I could.

My courage elevated as I chewed on that idea. Hadn't I already proven myself as an editor, investigator, wife, friend, neighbor and civic leader, and overall terrific person? Surely I could make my mark as a floral designer, as well.

Brandi's eyes lit with pleasure as she looked over the flowers. "Oh!" She clutched her hand to her chest. "I nearly forgot. Nadine asked me to call when I got here. She wants to talk to you." Brandi pulled her cell phone from her purse, and within seconds, I found myself chatting by phone with my sweet Southern sister. The words just flowed.

"Yes, *dah-lin'*, the roses are *luv-lee!*" and "Bless your heart, Nadine, I do hope I can do them justice."

She went on to encourage me in my task, even giving me pointers. *Question: Why does it not surprise me that Nadine has conquered the art of floral arranging? Is there anything the woman can't do?* Truly, I wanted to be Nadine when I grew up.

Um, if I ever grow up.

By the time I hung up the phone, I felt strong, invincible. It's amazing what ten minutes of an "Encourager Extraordinaire" will do for you.

Brandi left with a smile on her face and an "I love you" on her lips. Then, with scissors in one hand and floral tape in the other, I turned my attention to transforming my kitchen table into an artist's pallet.

The red roses toyed with my imagination. I picked up a few and rehearsed my strategy by pressing them together in a bundle and winding a bit of ribbon around the stems. Yep. I could do this.

Subtitle: Woman of God discovers amazing new talents and abilities. Story at eleven.

I put the bouquet to my chest and practiced walking the aisle, just to see how it might look. With no mirror in sight, I tried to follow my reflection in the kitchen window. No such luck.

I hummed the wedding march and reflected back on my own big day. Somehow, prancing around the kitchen with a bundle of flowers in my hand got me tickled. The giggles began quite innocently but quickly escalated into full-blown laughter.

Sasha sprang up and down, up and down, trying to get in on my glee. I snatched her up in my arms and danced around in circles, flowers now forming a halo around her head. Round and round we went, spinning like maniacs.

"Annie?"

"W—Warren." *Subtitle: Oops!* "Sorry, I thought you were replacing the windshield wipers on the truck."

"I'm done." He gave me the strangest look. "Are — are you okay?" He reached to take Sasha from my arms, as if sensing the need to protect her from me.

"Who, me?" I snatched a lone red rose from the bundle and stuck it in my teeth, tossed the rest on the table, then took the pose of a Spanish dancer. "I'm just terrific!" I mouthed the words through clamped teeth and very nearly dropped the flower. For effect, I clapped my hands in a cha-cha off to one side.

"Annie, I —" Warren shook his head then

stared in silence.

I pulled the rose from my teeth. "What?"

"Nothing." He put Sasha on the floor, and she rubbed up against my leg, ready to play once more.

"Come on, honey." I stuck the rose behind his ear, then slipped my right arm around his waist and my left into his unsuspecting palm. I leaned in to whisper, "Doesn't all this talk of love and weddings make you feel like dancing? Doesn't it make you feel — invincible?"

"Um, I —"

Subtitle: Confused husband contemplates psychiatric help for deranged wife.

But I didn't need psychiatric help. On the contrary. I simply needed to know that the man of my dreams would still ask me to our high school homecoming game all over again, if he had the chance.

I managed to get him to take a couple of turns around the kitchen with me. He even added an impromptu spin at the end of our choreography, a sure sign I'd gotten to him. Warren tipped up my chin with his finger and gazed into my eyes. A feeling of warmth flooded over me as he leaned down to plant a gentle kiss on my lips. *Yep. He'd still ask me to the homecoming game.*

After a moment, he snapped to attention.

"I almost forgot why I came in here."

"Ah. I have that effect on you, do I?"

He laughed as he pulled the rose from behind his ear and placed it back on the table with the others. "Yes, you do. I came in to tell you that Richard Blevins just called on my cell phone. Something about the Get Out to Vote rally. He wants to pass off the brochures and placards to you. He's not going to be able to participate this year."

Something about hearing Richard's name sent a ripple of guilt through me. I'd been so busy, I hadn't gone back to visit Judy. And from what I'd heard through the prayer chain, she had taken a turn for the worse.

"When is he coming?"

Warren shrugged. "Sometime tomorrow afternoon. Is that okay?"

"Sure. The kids are all coming over for dinner after church. I'm making pot roast."

"Mmm."

"We'd planned to play board games after," I explained. "But nothing out of the ordinary, so it's fine if he stops by."

Still, it did hurt my heart a little. In the old days, Richard would have passed the items off to me before or after Sunday school. I still couldn't get used to the idea that he wasn't teaching our class anymore. In fact, I couldn't get used to the idea that he seemed to have distanced himself from the rest of the world. Something about that just felt . . . wrong.

"Maybe I can talk him into staying awhile." Warren tag-teamed my thoughts. "I want him to know how much we all miss him."

"Great idea."

My hubby left to work in the yard, and I turned my attention, once again, to the table. I put together one of the bouquets, for real. Just as I finished, the telephone rang out, and I reached to pick it up with the bouquet still in hand. "Hello?"

Sheila's cheery voice greeted me. "Annie, is that you?"

"It's me." I clutched the bouquet to my chest, trying one last time to catch my reflection in the window. "How in the world are you?"

We dove into a lengthy conversation about weddings, homecoming dates, floral arranging, and my new knack for Spanish dancing. She chuckled her way through most of it, even adding a bit of advice on how to put together the bouquets. Finally, our chat took a bit of a turn.

"How are things going with the investigation?" she asked.

"I paid a little visit to O'Henry," I said

with a sigh.

"Oh?"

"Yeah, but he wasn't as helpful as I'd hoped. In fact, I feel a little foolish after talking to him," I confessed. "Most of my suspicions have turned out to be false alarms." I let out a sigh of resignation. "Maybe I'm not supposed to solve anything. Maybe I'm just supposed to pray that the right person will be brought to justice. You know how I am. I dive in with both feet before thinking twice."

"We all do that," Sheila said. "But don't feel too bad, Annie. After all, we can't all be heroes. Somebody has to sit on the sidelines and clap as they go by." She let out a giggle, and I couldn't help but join her.

"Yeah, I know," I agreed. "And it's not like I don't have other things to occupy my time. Seems like everyone needs me right now." I paused for a moment before adding, "Still, I can't shake the nagging feeling that the Lord wants more from me. It's kind of like He wants me to stay tuned in to hear His thoughts on the matter. Like . . . there's something more to hear."

Sheila must've noted the seriousness in my voice, because her response reflected genuine concern.

"Then keep praying, Annie," she encouraged. "You just never know what He might do. And you know as well as I do, following Him is a great adventure. That much is for sure."

Subtitle: Friendship with Sheila is a great adventure, too. One I wouldn't trade for anything in the world.

We wrapped up our little chat, and I returned to my role as mother of the brides. For now, that suited me just fine.

CHAPTER 15

It would be wrong to accuse Sheila of being prideful where her singing voice was concerned, but . . .

Well, she didn't give me much choice.

Now, mind you, Sheila had had a lovely voice as a younger woman. Note the word *had.* But the last three or four times she'd sung a solo at church, I'd noticed folks squirming in their seats, clearly uncomfortable. No one said a word. Ever. Wouldn't dare. But I had to wonder how long her illustrious singing career would go on. Seemed to me, she had already passed her expiration date in this area of ministry.

And of course, to add insult to injury, she always came to me after each performance, asking my opinion. "Did you like it? Do you think it ministered to the congregation?"

There were only so many ways you could say, "Honey, God has truly gifted you in a unique way," before she became suspicious.

That's why, when I arrived at church on Sunday morning to discover Sheila would be singing the special music, I got that familiar sinking feeling in my heart.

Maybe I should volunteer to work in the nursery this morning. No, only a chicken would use such devious means of escape. I needed to do the right thing, needed to stay put in the sanctuary and offer my support and encouragement. With that in mind, I braced myself for the inevitable.

The service started off quite well. Our praise and worship leader, Bob Lemuel, came forward and led us in a mix of several choruses and hymns. After that, we welcomed our visitors. I almost dropped my teeth as I turned to discover Janetta Mullins and her family seated in the pew directly behind mine. The strangest emotions overtook me, particularly as my gaze traveled to Jake, who offered up a polite smile. Were the police still following him? Were they tailing him, even now?

Forcing those thoughts aside, I reached to give Janetta a hug and took note of the fact that she responded with a broad smile. I returned to my seat, puzzled, yet intrigued.

Lord, surely You've brought her here for some reason. Am I supposed to get to know her better, try to figure out if she is somehow to blame for the missing cash?

My heart resonated with a loud *no!* Either this wasn't the place to worry about it, or I shouldn't focus on Janetta at all. I wasn't quite sure which.

The announcements followed and then, finally, the moment arrived. Sheila stood and approached the pulpit. Her deep purple cowl-necked sweater proved an interesting match for the long, flowing black skirt, but what made the ensemble even more conversational was the choice of jewelry. How the woman could stand aright with so many bauble-laden chains hanging around her neck was a miracle in itself. And the violet-colored flower clip in her red hair really set the whole thing off.

The music for "Softly and Tenderly" began, and she lit in headfirst. I sat still as a mouse, determined not to look around me. And I did pretty well — until she attempted to hit a high note about midway into the piece. She missed it by about a .5 on the Richter scale, which, for some reason, got Devin tickled. I heard the slightest bit of a snort to my left, followed by the vibration of the pew as he lost it in silent laughter.

I jabbed him with my left elbow, never looking his way. I didn't dare. I did notice Warren to my right. His eyes were closed. *Is he praying or in pain?*

On and on Sheila sang, "Come home, come ho–o–ome . . ." The notes wrapped themselves around the room in a tremulous vibrato. Pastor Miller's cheeks flamed red as Sheila set out to hit an impromptu high note at the end. *So close, and yet so far.* She held the note for a good thirty seconds, long enough to allow me to drive fingernail prints into Devin's right arm.

As she ended the song, I breathed a huge sigh of relief. A couple of ladies to my right fanned themselves as the pastor stood and approached the pulpit.

"Thank you so much, Sheila," he exclaimed. "Surely even the angels themselves can't sing like that."

Ya think?

He opened his Bible and began the sermon. In an interesting irony, he talked about the Prodigal Son, the words of his message not far off from the lyrics Sheila had just sung. I wondered if Jake, who sat behind me, "got it." Several times I wanted to turn around, wanted to see if I could catch his expression, but stopped myself.

Instead, I focused on the part of the message that was meant for me . . . the part about the older brother who held his sibling in judgment. Yep. I was more like the other brother, whether I wanted to admit it or not. *Mental note: From this point on, read between the lines of familiar Bible stories for hidden messages.*

The service ended on a high note, albeit more in tune than Sheila's song. One of the teenage girls, Claudia, came forward in response to the pastor's message, and one family, new to town, came to the front to join the church. We celebrated together then closed in prayer.

I lingered awhile after the service to talk to friends. And I wanted the opportunity to visit with Janetta — as soon as the welcoming committee around her dissipated a bit.

She looked at me with tears in her eyes. "Annie, it's so good to see you."

I gave her a big hug. "Good to see you, too. And Jake —" I flashed a smile. "My apple pie partner. How are you?"

Our family members gave us a few curious looks, but he forged ahead undeterred.

"I'm great, Mrs. Peterson. It's good to be back home." His emphasis on the word *home* let me know he'd understood the message.

After a little more conversation, my girls headed off in search of their friends, and Devin settled into a conversation with Jake about the upcoming homecoming game.

Well, if that doesn't beat all.

Janetta took me by the arm and whispered, "Can we talk a minute?"

"Of course." I tried to push Mrs. Lapp's story about Janetta out of my mind as we eased our way through the crowd to a quieter spot. No point in worrying about the missing twenty-five thousand dollars today, of all days.

Sheila chose that very moment to show up at my side. She didn't seem to notice that Janetta and I were engaged in conversation. Or, if she did, it didn't stop her from interrupting.

"Annie," she spoke breathlessly, "what did you think of my song? And be completely honest. Do you think it ministered to the congregation?"

I'd just opened my mouth to say something rehearsed and brilliant when Janetta caught me off guard. She took hold of Sheila's hands, tears erupting, and spoke with genuine passion. "I just want you to know," she said, "how much that song has touched me."

What?

She continued on, swiping at the tears with the back of her hand. "My mother used to sing 'Softly and Tenderly' when I was a little girl," she said. "And I've always loved it. But I haven't heard it since she died. The words —" She broke down and wept. I reached into my purse for a tissue. "The words reminded me of the faith I used to have as a young girl. The faith I need to return to."

Nope. One tissue wouldn't cut it. This was going to be a multi-tissue cry if I ever saw one.

Sheila began to softly sing the chorus, "Come home, come ho–o–ome, ye who are weary, come ho–o–ome." As she did, Janetta erupted once again, this time using the second and third tissues to mop up the moisture on her cheeks.

"Thank you," she whispered.

Sheila wrapped Janetta in her arms. "I'm so glad," she whispered. "I always pray before I choose the song and ask the Lord to show me what to sing."

"Well, He certainly did this time," Janetta responded. "And I'm so grateful. You'll never know how much that meant to me. Made me want to come home — to Him and to the church."

Lord, I am a worm — a terrible friend and a spiritual worm.

I gazed up at my friend with new eyes. Admiring eyes. Sheila asked Janetta if they could pray together — and lo and behold if

201

they didn't stop and pray, right then and there, in the foyer of the church. The little flower clip in Sheila's hair bobbed up and down as her enthusiastic prayer went on. I watched it all with my jaw hanging down, taking careful notes.

We stayed on and chatted a few minutes before we all finally parted ways. I promised both ladies we'd try to get together for lunch one day soon. And I promised the Lord I would never again doubt His ability to minister — in any way He pleased.

Devin made a rapid-fire decision to head over to a friend's house for lunch, which left Warren and me with some alone time as we made the journey home. *"Come home, come ho—o—ome."* For some reason, the words wouldn't leave me.

The last few weeks had been so busy, it felt nice to have my husband to myself again. And it would feel just as good to spend an afternoon with the girls.

Warren clicked the radio off, and we sat in delirious silence for a moment before either of us spoke.

"That was a great service," he said at last.

"Mmm-hmm."

"Hearing the story of the Prodigal Son again reminds me of how blessed I am," he continued.

This certainly caught my attention. "Oh?"

Warren nodded and I noticed tears glistening in his eyes. "I've got such a great family." He spoke softly, seriously. "And I'm so thankful to the Lord for all of you. When I see the struggles that so many other fathers face, I'm so grateful — grateful that our kids have stayed close to the Lord — and — and close to us."

Yep. Those were definitely tears in his eyes. I leaned over to rest my head on his shoulder. "They have a great dad," I whispered. "So why would they turn their hearts in a different direction? They see a real picture of their heavenly Father every time they're with you."

Listen to what you're saying, Annie. This is a true man of God, incapable of the kinds of things you've suspected. He has clean hands and a pure heart.

I could see the quiver in Warren's chin and noted his obvious silence but didn't hold it against him. He couldn't talk right now. I understood.

We arrived home minutes later and I dove into action. I opened the Crock-Pot to check on the pot roast. Mmm. Looked and smelled yummy. With the *click* of a button, I turned on the oven to warm some rolls.

Just about that time, the girls and their guys arrived, and the conversations began to layer, one on top of another. I watched Warren's face as Brandi and Candy bounced wedding and honeymoon ideas off of him. Yep. Those were still tears in his eyes. I wondered if the kids noticed.

We shared a terrific meal together, laughing and joking our way throughout. Afterward, we turned our attention to a couple of board games. *Mental note: Future sons-in-law seem to excel at movie trivia. From this point on, choose literary games.*

I served up generous slices of the angel food cake with berry topping, and we opted to watch a movie together. Brandi argued that we should watch a romance. Scott felt strongly about an action flick. Candy opted for a musical and Garrett said he'd rather watch football. Warren was already snoring in the easy chair by this point, so his opinion didn't factor in.

In the end, we settled on *Father of the Bride* — a logical choice, all things considered. Just as everyone got settled down in front of the television, the doorbell rang. I excused myself to answer it.

I'd honestly forgotten Richard Blevins had planned to come by until I laid eyes on him. He reluctantly entered the house at my bidding. Took a bit of persuading on my part, but I didn't want to let this opportunity slip away from me. I'd looked for a chance to talk with him for weeks now.

I ushered him beyond the crowd in the den, and on into the living room. We settled onto the sofa, and a groggy-eyed Warren joined us, offering coffee as an incentive to stay awhile. To my surprise, Richard agreed.

Preliminary chatting aside, I garnered the necessary courage to broach the most important subject. "Tell us about Judy," I urged.

His gaze shifted to the floor at once, and I wondered if I'd crossed a line.

"We don't want to pry," Warren spoke softly.

Richard looked up at us with tears in his eyes. "No, it's okay. Might do me some good to talk."

Neither of us interrupted him.

"I know what everyone must be thinking," Richard continued. "It's got to seem strange that I just . . . disappeared."

Funny. When I'd placed him at the top of my suspect list, his disappearing act had seemed strange. But now that I empathized with him, I'd almost come to understand it.

I wanted to tell him so but didn't dare. The lump in my throat wouldn't allow it.

"I spend so many hours at work already," he explained. "And it's such a drive back and forth to Philadelphia to see her at the hospital. I just want to have every possible minute with her."

"That's understandable, Richard," Warren said. "And I don't think you need to worry about what other people are thinking or saying. It's irrelevant."

"I —" Richard's voice broke. "I don't know how much longer she has." At this point, a lone tear slipped down his cheek. He didn't even try to wipe it away.

Again, I wanted to speak, but no words would come. But Richard seemed to have more on his mind, so it was probably for the best.

"Judy and I have been married nearly forty years," he said. "None of the people at the church knew us when we were newlyweds. We didn't move to Clarksborough until after our son died."

I tried not to let my surprise show. In reality, I did not know Judy and Richard had lost a son.

"He was my namesake," he explained. "Richard Jr., the cutest thing you ever saw — born about a year and a half after we married. Richey was a happy, healthy boy for the first few years, but when he turned four —" Richard's voice broke again. "When he turned four, he was diagnosed with leukemia."

My hand went straight to my heart. "Oh, Richard, I'm so sorry."

He forged ahead, clearly on a mission. "See, I was a different man back then. Very driven. My job meant everything to me. I guess it was my way of hiding from the truth. Richey was in and out of the hospital, and Judy stayed by his side every minute."

Oh, you poor, poor man. You've already lost your son and now . . .

"I should've been there more." The tremor in his voice intensified. "But I couldn't face the pain of what was happening in that hospital room. I left it to Judy — wrong as that was. Her faith was so much stronger than mine back then. It still is."

"You're stronger than you think, Richard." I reached out to squeeze his hand. "You are. Everyone sees that."

He shook his head. "I know the Bible inside and out — studied it for years. But that doesn't mean my faith is strong. In fact, I don't know when I've ever felt weaker." He buckled, and the tears started. He dropped his head into his hands and wept aloud.

My heart twisted into knots. I wanted to

tell him everything would be okay but decided against it. *Oh, Lord, help him. Walk him through this.*

Warren's steady voice brought a sense of calm to the room. "Then let us be strong for you," he said. "That's what the body of Christ is for, to lift the arms of the ones who are struggling. We want to support you, Richard. Everyone does."

Richard looked up at us with bloodshot eyes. "I don't know the first thing about how to let you. I just know that I have to be there for Judy. This time around, I'm going to do right by her. I have to." His voice broke again. "I — I have to."

He cried again, this time huge, silent tears. But I heard them as loudly as any wailing I'd ever witnessed in my life. They were the cries of a broken man, a man afraid of losing the one human he cherished above all.

"We want to help," I added softly. "We care about you. Both of you. And we know this is a hard time for you."

"I don't want anyone to feel sorry for me," he interjected through the tears. "Being there for Judy is a blessing, not a curse. It's not that I *have* to care for her." He looked at us with imploring eyes. "I *get* to care for her. It's a privilege, and I don't want to miss a minute of it."

His impassioned words rocked me to the core.

"And when I'm not with her," he continued, "I spend nearly every waking moment on the Internet, searching for solutions the doctors might have missed. I've found out a lot about the holistic approach to cancer. If all else fails . . ." His voice trailed off, then picked back up again. "I'd have to get her to another state, and I know insurance wouldn't cover much of it. But I would do anything for her. Anything. Even if it meant depleting every account we've got. And I want her to know that." Again, the tears flowed.

We spent the next few minutes trying to assure him, and then Warren and I prayed with Richard before he left. The pain in my chest was unbearable, but I couldn't let loose and cry with either of the men around.

A short time after Richard left, I climbed into a bubble bath with tears streaming. The whole course of the weekend ran through my mind: the party foods, the silk flowers, and the dance with Warren — all of it. In one instance, I saw the devastating losses Richard Blevins had faced, starting with the death of his son. I thought again of the Prodigal Son's father — how he'd welcomed that young son back home into his arms once again. Richard would never know the joy of sweeping his son into his arms. And, on top of that, he might soon have to release his wife into the arms of her heavenly Father.

"Come home, come ho–o–ome . . ." Sheila's words played over and over in my mind as I sat in the now-cold water. They became a multi-layered mantra, driving me away from the events of the past few weeks and into a deeper place with my Lord.

I prayed for Richard Blevins as I'd never prayed before. *Oh, Father, how can one man bear so much?*

From outside the bathroom door, I heard the sound of Devin's laughter and realized he'd returned home, safe and sound. My heart twisted as I thought about all of those aggravating snack foods I'd grumbled over. I would gladly put together a hundred parties for my son, now that I saw it all in perspective.

I fought to keep my emotions in check, then closed my eyes and leaned back against the edge of the tub. In my mind's eye, I replayed my "rose in the teeth" dance with Warren. Tears tumbled once again. I wept for Richard, and for all of those who had no one to dance with. I cried myself completely dry. Then, just about the time I'd totally given myself over to emotion, the Lord reminded me once again of Judy's comment about dancing across the living room as a little girl and His promise that she would soon dance again — with Him.

In an instant, God gave me His perspective. This time around, I got it. I truly got it.

CHAPTER 16

I remember, years ago, reading a sign that said REALITY IS A NICE PLACE TO VISIT, BUT I WOULDN'T WANT TO LIVE THERE. I've thought about those words hundreds of times since, but never so much as in the week that followed Sheila's infamous solo.

The trouble really started on Friday morning — the morning of the homecoming game — when the man from the electric company came to shut off our power.

For one thing, Sasha's incessant barking set my nerves on edge right away. She carried on so loudly, in fact, that I could scarcely make out a word the poor guy was saying. I finally caught the gist of it.

"Sorry, ma'am," he shouted for the umpteenth time, "but I have no choice. You didn't pay your October bill."

I reached down to pick up my little guard dog as I responded. "What do you mean? Of course we paid it." Warren never forgot to pay bills. Ever.

He even went so far as to say they had mailed a DISCONNECT notice. No way. Warren would've seen that, for sure.

The trembling in my hands must've convinced Sasha we were dealing with a perpetrator, because she attempted to leap from my arms in the young man's direction, growling all the way.

"I'll just find your meter." He backed up and acted as if he might turn to leave, right there on the spot.

"No, please don't go yet. I can give you the confirmation number. Hang on."

"Mmm-hmm."

He stood at a safe distance, and Sasha and I scurried into the house to set things straight. I always got a confirmation number when I paid by phone with the credit card. I fished around the top of my desk but found nothing. Then I opened the drawer where Warren usually kept the bills and found the hard truth. Way down in the stack sat two unopened envelopes from the electric company. Horrified, I tore open the top one, the DISCONNECT notice the man had mentioned. My husband had indeed forgotten to pay the Clark County Lighting and Power Company, just as the serviceman had said.

I returned to the door and pleaded with the fellow to give me an hour or so, but he informed me that company policy must be strictly adhered to.

These guys from the electric company must take special courses in how to deal with hysterical, menopausal women. He handled me with grace, charm, and finesse. Almost an art form on his part. How he did it, I'll never know, but this tough guy managed to see past my tears and the check I quickly presented.

"Sorry, but you'll have to take that to one of our payment centers," he explained. "I'm not authorized to accept reconnect fees at the door." He handed me a notice with a list of local payment centers on it, our local grocery store making the top of the list. I looked over it as he disappeared around the side of the house.

And with that, our house went black.

Okay, a slight exaggeration, perhaps. Morning sunshine streamed in through the windows, but my world, as I knew it, ceased to exist the minute the hum of electricity faded.

No computer, which being interpreted, meant I could not work. *Mental note: Remember to keep laptop battery charged at all times, just in case.*

No lights. Only a problem in a couple of rooms, to be noted, but a serious challenge should this situation last very long.

Perhaps the worst of all: no power in the refrigerator. This could have devastating consequences if I didn't get the electricity turned on right away.

And so, off to the grocery store I went to pay my bill. I stood in a lengthy line at the customer service booth until I reached the counter. Bob Lemuel, our beloved praise and worship leader, greeted me from the other side. Yikes. It would have to be some-one I knew.

"Hi, Annie. Can I help you?"

"Um, yes —" I went on to explain our predicament, and he helped me through the process with a smile. "Happens all the time," he explained.

Not to me it doesn't.

"Yep, it could've happened to anyone." He dove into a story about his wife, Nita, and her inability to keep up with the family's bills, and I felt my cheeks warm. I hoped he didn't feel as free to share our story with others.

Bob handed me my receipt and I glanced at my watch. Ten fifteen. "How long will it take before the lights come back on?" I asked.

"You got this payment in before noon." He gave a little shrug. "I'd say they'll be on by midafternoon, early evening at the latest. But you'll have to call and give the fine folks at Clark County Lighting and Power the receipt number first."

"Terrific."

I pulled my cell phone from my purse to call the electric company but opted to call Warren first. No point in beating around the bush. He apologized profusely, blaming the oversight on his hectic work schedule. We somehow managed to make it through the conversation with good moods intact, though I secretly wondered at this mistake on his part. He'd never forgotten to pay a bill before. *Why now? Distracted, perhaps?*

I punched in the number to the power company and was greeted by a recording. While waiting for an operator, I decided to pick up a few grocery items. I also purchased a few more last-minute items for Devin's post-homecoming party tonight. *Mental note: As soon as the power comes on, start working on those sausage-and-cheese puffs.*

As I hit the checkout line, another call came through. I'd been on hold for over ten minutes at this point. The way things were going, I'd switch to the other line and the operator would choose that very moment to take my call. Regardless, the other phone line continued to beckon. I opted to take it. I couldn't help but notice the emotion in Candy's voice as she spoke. Candy, the unemotional one.

"M–Mom."

"What, honey?"

"Mom, you've got to stop Brandi. She's driving me crazy."

Candy went on to explain her latest dilemma as I inched my way up through the line. Once I reached the conveyer belt, I unloaded the milk and eggs. In the process, the phone slipped from my ear, nearly falling. I caught it on the way down. The clerk gave me a "down the nose" stare and shook her head. Apparently she'd seen one too many customers with a cell phone incident in her line. I gave her my best *I'm so sorry* look.

"Mom, are you there?"

"I'm here." I pressed the cell phone between my shoulder and my ear as I continued to unload the basket.

Candy forged ahead. "She's using silk flowers at her wedding. *Silk flowers.*"

"Yes, I know. I —"

"The problem is," she interrupted, "she's absolutely insistent I do the same thing. But

I don't want silk flowers. I want real flowers. Fresh daisies. I think silk flowers are tacky."

"Well then, use real flowers." I reached for my purse to pull out my debit card so the clerk could see I was paying attention to the task at hand.

"I wish it was that easy." On and on she went, telling me all of the details of why this silk versus real dilemma had grown to such proportions. I tried to take it all in, but the glare from the clerk made it difficult.

I swiped my debit card through the little machine and punched in my password. For whatever reason — distraction, probably — my card was rejected. Panic set in immediately. *No money in our account? Has Warren been wrestling with insufficient funds, on top of everything else?*

Thankfully, the clerk, whose name I duly noted as Jeanene, pinpointed the problem. "Wrong password."

"Ah." I tried again, this time taking great care to enter the right number.

This time everything went through properly, and Jeanene handed me the receipt with a brusque "Thank you." I nodded in her direction and kept talking on the phone as I pushed the basket from the store.

"I need to know what you think," Candy

implored. "It means so much to me. Tell me."

"Honey, it's your wedding." I stated my opinion on the matter. "You're the bride. You should do what you want."

At this point, my normally unemotional daughter erupted in tears. "I d–didn't know it was going to be this c–complicated. Sometimes I wish we could j–just elope."

Tell me about it.

Just as I reached the car, a beep on the phone let me know I had another call. "Honey, I have to go. I'm getting another call. Stay strong — and get your fresh flowers. Any kind and any color you like. This is your wedding."

"I love you, Mom." And with a sigh, the call ended.

I clicked to the other line and couldn't help but groan as I heard Brandi's voice. "Mom, we've got a problem."

We? What's up with this we *business?*

"Candy is driving me absolutely crazy. I don't think I can go on living with her."

"Oh?" I opened the backseat door to unload the groceries. "Tell Mama all about it."

She dove in, in typical Brandi fashion. "She's such a snob. She doesn't like any of my ideas, thinks everything I'm doing is tacky. Tacky, Mom. She actually said *tacky.*"

Lord, if we live through these next few months, it's going to be a miracle.

"I need your opinion, Mom," Brandi spoke with great passion. "It means so much to me. Tell me what you think."

I encouraged her with the same words I'd just used with her sister. "It's your wedding, honey. You should do what you want."

She eventually calmed down, and we had a few nonemotional words before ending the conversation. I climbed into the driver's seat and leaned my head back against the headrest. *Lord, I know You said You wouldn't give me more than I could bear. All I can say is, You must trust me a lot.*

I started the car and reached to put it into REVERSE. At that very moment, reality hit. *The electric company.* I still had to call them with the receipt number.

I punched in their number with great speed and breathed a sigh of relief when I actually reached a human. The woman on the other end of the phone assured me my lights would be back on by three o'clock. *Just enough time to put together the foods for tonight's party. Thank You, Lord.*

At this point, it took everything in me just to get the car from point A to point B — point A being the grocery store, point B being the house. All along the way, my mind flooded with a hundred things.

Janetta Mullins, seated in the pew behind me last Sunday morning. Judy Blevins, lying alone in a hospital room. Nikki Rogers, caring for her daughter alone. The tears in Warren's eyes as he talked with me on the way home from church.

Lord, help me. In spite of my heartfelt compassion, I couldn't get past the fact that someone had stolen the money from the bank. But who?

All of my ponderings now melded together with today's daughter encounters. For a minute or two, I could scarcely separate out one thing from another. How could I, with so much going on at once?

In that same moment, I remembered my prayer in the bathtub last Sunday night. I could hardly justify complaining about being overwhelmed with a houseful of healthy family members. And besides, most of these messes were of our own making.

I arrived home with groceries in hand and entered my still-near-dark house. I could hear Sasha barking in the backyard, where I'd left her nearly an hour ago. I set the grocery bags down on the kitchen table and then started the task of putting them away. Afterward, I swung wide the back door to greet my adorable pup.

For a second, I thought perhaps I'd landed in the wrong house, was looking at the wrong yard. Then, after a second glance, realized . . . *Nope. It's my yard, all right. At least it* was.

Off to my right, where the flowerbeds used to be, I found a chaotic scene. All of my marigolds had been ripped up and gathered into messy clumps. To my left, my evergreen bushes had been pulled up as well. And in the middle of the yard — holes. Probably five or six. Not itsy-bitsy tiny holes, but great big, halfway-to-China holes.

I stared in disbelief at Sasha, wondering how in the world one tiny dachshund could have accomplished such a feat. Had she cloned herself while I was away?

Nope. There she sat, tail wagging, completely alone.

Well, not really sat, exactly. She sprang up and down in an attempt to get my full attention, the mud and twigs flying everywhere. *Oh, you want to be held, do you?*

"No way," I said with a shudder. "I'm not holding you. And when Daddy sees this —"

A very real shiver went down my spine as I thought about what Warren would do when he saw the backyard. *What if he asks me to get rid of my beloved puppy? What will I do?*

Hmm.

I couldn't really accomplish much inside the darkened house, so I opted for the yard work. Over the next hour I replanted what was salvageable of the flowers, set the bushes back in place, and filled in the holes. Sasha stuck by my side all the way. Indeed, she almost looked repentant at one point. And, by the time all was said and done, the whole yard looked very nearly perfect. Well, unless you counted the missing sod part. But it would grow back.

Around one o'clock I entered the house, tidied up, and fixed myself a sandwich. I settled down at the kitchen table, thankful for the peace and quiet. The gentle ticking of the battery-operated clock on the wall distracted me for a moment, but only just that. After that, I lost myself in my thoughts.

As I sat in the silent stillness of that near-darkened house, I reflected on the missing deposit once again. The electricity had gone out at the bank on the night of the incident. I still didn't have an answer to the "why" question. A power surge, presumably, but what did that mean? Had someone deliber-ately shut it off, or was it simply a co-incidence someone had taken advantage of?

I needed to check into that, to be sure. I reached for my now-worn notebook and scribbled in a reminder to myself.

Then, as I looked around the room, I thought about all of the changes brought on by my lack of electricity. Whoever had stolen the money that infamous night had faced those same challenges. No power. No lights. No . . .

No cameras. No cameras in operation whatsoever. And cameras were, I knew, an integral part of the counting of the night deposit money. I remembered Warren telling me all about the process — how he stood at the counter with the camera angled down at his hands as he counted, counted, counted the money from the night deposit bags. With no cameras in operation, anything could have happened.

Clearly, my next challenge would be to find out who had counted the remaining money on the morning after the power returned. After all, no other deposits had turned up missing. According to the *Gazette,* three other merchants had made successful deposits in the night: Neva McMullen from the grocery store, Corey Stephens from the local dairy, and Ginny Tompkins from the courier service. No cash in the mix.

Once again, I thought of Mrs. Lapp's words, how Janetta had insisted upon being paid in cash. I couldn't make any sense of it, but surely, somewhere between the darkness and the light, that twenty-five thousand dollars had found a new home. And the lack of power had clearly played a major role.

I let my imagination run away with me for a while, racing down a variety of rabbit trails. Each one led me to exactly the same place: frustration.

I'm not sure when the electricity in my house came back on, exactly, but I remember hearing the hum of the refrigerator at some point and realized the light above the sink had returned.

Though the day felt half wasted, I had enough on my plate to keep me busy for the rest of it. Between now and tonight's game, I had to edit an article for a new client and prepare enough food for an army of teens.

First things first. I signed on to the Internet with great fervor, almost like an addict stumbling off the wagon. My stash of e-mails beckoned with the strongest intensity. Probably should've skipped them and gone on to my work. But somewhere in the mix of things, I came across lesson seven from www.investigativeskills.com: *"A Good*

Sure. Easy for them to say. Whoever wrote that particular lesson had apparently never had a day like I happened to be having today.

I shut the crazy thing, refusing to read it. Perhaps another day.

Following directly on its heels was an e-mail from Sheila. I expected it to be one of those goofy forwards she liked to send but was surprised to find a personal note instead.

Dear Annie,

In praying for you this morning, the Lord laid a particular verse on my heart and prompted me to share it with you. It comes from Psalm 18. "In my distress I called to the Lord; I cried to my God for help. From his temple he heard my voice; my cry came before him, into his ears." I'm not sure what you're facing today, but God knows and already has a plan to see you through it. Hope this helps.

Lots of love,
Sheila

Whoa.

For a minute, it felt like all the wind had

been knocked out of my sails. Had the God of heaven really just interrupted my up-to-now pitiful day to speak directly to me through my up-to-recently nutty friend? How in the world could she have known?

Funny. Twice this week I'd seen Sheila in action, touching people's lives with something directly from the Lord. *Lord, I want to be like that. I want to touch lives, make a difference.* Though I never thought I'd hear myself pray these words, I found myself asking, "Lord, make me more like Sheila." And I meant it. She apparently had a direct line to Him and I wanted that, too. From now on, I'd have to take everything my best friend said far more seriously.

I started to click the REPLY button, to let her know how much I appreciated her note, when something caught my eye. There, just below her name, I discovered a little tag line. It read: "If at first you don't succeed, skydiving is not for you."

I nearly fell out of my chair laughing. A prophet and a comedian. Sheila was truly the most well-rounded friend I'd ever had.

CHAPTER 17

If dogs could raise red flags, I'd have to say Sasha raised one. She needed to visit the vet anyway, what with her booster shots being due and all. But the bizarre "episodes," as I liked to call them, now had me wondering if she needed a bit of psychiatric help as well.

Yep. My dog was going through bona fide "spells" — hyperactivity, combined with strange withdrawal symptoms whenever one of us would leave the house, even for a few minutes. Over the past couple of weeks, on top of the pillow incident and garden fiasco, she'd chewed up the legs on the coffee table and left scratch marks on the inside of the front door. Something was definitely up. So, on the morning after the game, off to the vet I went. Saturday or no Saturday, my puppy needed help.

Dr. Andrews saw us right away. He swooped my baby into his arms, and she hid her face in his armpit.

"I don't have a clue," I said with a shrug. "She's been acting so weird."

"Tell me about it."

As he placed her on the table to begin the examination, I relayed her symptoms. Extreme mood swings. Temperamental. Whining. Bizarre behaviors.

"Mmm-hmm." He continued to examine her. "Any change in her eating habits?"

"Slight. I've noticed she's not eating quite as much."

"Has she been a little clingy?"

"Very."

"I see. And have you been gone from the house more than usual?"

"Well —" I stumbled a bit across the words, thinking about my latest escapades related to the investigation. "Maybe a little. But other people leave their dogs at home alone for more than an hour or two, and they don't destroy the house."

Sasha looked up at me with imploring eyes as he took her temperature. I had to turn my head the other way. This was as tough as taking my kids to the pediatrician, but I would never have admitted it.

"Have you tried crating her?"

My heart sank right away. I couldn't bear the thought of it, in all honesty. "She's never been a problem 'til recently," I explained. "Seriously. No accidents on the floor. No destructive behavior. Nothing. So we've never had a need to."

"So —" He continued on, checking her out. "She doesn't even sleep in a crate? What is her bedding situation?"

"Well, I —"

"I thought so." Dr. Andrews paused as he looked at me. "I think some changes might be in order. The sooner, the better."

"Changes? Why? What's wrong with her?"

He scribbled a few words into her chart before answering. "Sounds like your pup has a classic case of SAD — separation anxiety disorder."

"Say what?"

He went on to explain the diagnosis. "Dogs with this problem don't like to be alone. And dachshunds are particularly susceptible because they're prone to 'shadow' one person in the home. If that person goes away, even for a short period of time, the dog is liable to act up. Do you mind if I ask you a few questions?"

"Sure. I guess so." I swallowed hard.

"Does Sasha follow you around the house?" When I nodded, he continued, "And how does she react when you reach for the keys or head for the door?"

"She, um —" I scratched her behind the ears. "She cries, but I always reach down and play with her. Tell her I'll be home soon, that sort of thing."

He shook his head. "Nope. Just exactly what you shouldn't do. If your good-byes and hellos are exaggerated, she's more prone to act up while you're gone. Tell me how you greet her when you come in the door."

"Well —"

Should I tell him that I always scoop her up in my arms and love all over her, telling her how much I'd missed her while I was away?

"Uh-hum. Never mind." He scribbled something in her chart.

My heart raced. "What can we do?"

"Call in a specialist," he suggested. "Obedience schools usually have trained experts on staff who can come to your home to show you how to deal with this. Or —" He gave me an inquisitive look. "Get another dog. That way she wouldn't be alone, even if you had to leave." He smiled, as if that settled the whole thing.

"Heavens to Betsy." I tried to imagine the look on Warren's face. "Another dog?"

Dr. Andrews shrugged. "These are just suggestions, of course, but you'll go on seeing these behaviors until her situation changes."

He called in the technician, a perky girl named Angela. She entered the room, took one look at Sasha, and let out a couple of "oohs" and "aahs."

"She's so pretty." Angela reached to scratch Sasha behind the ears. "Have you thought about showing her?"

"Showing her? You mean, like, dog shows?" I let the idea mull around in my brain a minute before answering. "Nah. Never really thought about it."

"She's a purebred, right?"

"Well, yes."

Dr. Andrews threw in his two cents' worth. "Might be good for her. Get her out around people and give her a sense of purpose."

A sense of purpose? What is she, Miss Canine America? Next thing you know, she'll be campaigning for world peace.

"She looks like a winner to me." Angela's face erupted in a smile.

As I looked into Sasha's eyes, they appeared to morph into dollar signs. "Really?"

Angela led me out to the front office, where I reached for my debit card, praying it wouldn't be rejected again. I swallowed hard when she gave me the total: $185.00. *Yikes. Maybe I'd better put Sasha to work to pay the vet bills.* As I contemplated this possibility, the little monster lay curled up in my arms, completely content. *Puppy, you clingy little thing. What am I going to do with you?*

While waiting for the card to process, I glanced over at the corkboard on the wall. Nearly a dozen photos of puppies and kittens greeted me. My eye gravitated toward a photo of a male dachshund, a bit larger than Sasha. *What's up with this?* The note beneath it read, "Male dachshund, one year old, reduced price."

A thousand questions entered my mind at once. Why in the world would anyone reduce the price on a pedigreed dog? And why sell a one-year-old?

I looked over the rest of the ads on the board, finding a few to be completely unrelated to animals at all. In fact, I felt a familiar catch in my throat when my gaze landed on the photo of a familiar sports car. *That's the car from the bank parking lot.*

"Excuse me." Still juggling the dog in my arms, I took the photo to Angela and pointed at it. "Do you know who this car belongs to?"

Her cheeks pinked over as she reached to grab the piece of paper. "Oh, I'm sorry. I was supposed to take that down a couple of weeks back. That was Dr. Andrews's car. He sold it ages ago."

My heart rate increased immediately. "Do you have any idea who he sold it to?"

"Hmm." Her lips pursed as she thought it through. "Oh yes. I remember now. It was someone who works at the bank."

Bingo. "Yes, but do you know who?"

Now the spot between her eyebrows crinkled. "Oh, I do remember. It was a woman — that new security guard from out-of-town. Nikki something or another."

"Nikki Rogers?"

"Yes, that's right." Angela tore up the paper and tossed it in the trash. "She came into the office to pay him. In cash, no less. Now there's a girl with some money to spend."

My heart felt as if it would explode in my chest. "Do you . . . do you have any idea how much?"

Angela shrugged. "I know he was asking just under twenty thousand dollars for the car. Blue book value was a bit more, but the car had a lot of miles on it. I do seem to remember him saying he got his asking price. Why?"

"Oh, no reason." I excused myself and backed out of the office, suddenly feeling dizzy.

Nikki Rogers. In the crazy mix of things, I'd almost forgotten all about her. An ocean of possibilities swam through my mind. With twenty-five thousand dollars cash in hand, she would've had enough money to pay for both the car and the tuition for her daughter's school.

How ridiculous I now felt. How completely, utterly ridiculous. Nikki Rogers had access. She had motive. What else did I need to pinpoint her as the thief?

Sure, she'd played that *I'm-just-a-single-mom-caring-for-my-daughter* bit to the hilt. But her acting skills had raised my antennae from the beginning, hadn't they? And all of that business about Guards on Call — had I forgotten all of that?

I struggled with a host of thoughts and ideas as I drove home. Sasha made the drive a bit complicated, what with insisting on sitting on my lap and all. *Mental note: Perhaps a crate wouldn't be such a bad idea, particularly in the car.*

Then again, the little darling enjoyed sticking her head out of the window to catch the wind in her face. Wouldn't want to steal that from her. And, if Nikki Rogers turned out to be the Clark County Savings and Loan perpetrator, Sasha would be a local hero, after all. Had she not required a trip to the vet's office, I would never have pieced together this latest bit of information.

Still . . .

I couldn't get a settled feeling about Nikki's guilt. Every time I thought about her in a negative light, my sympathies kicked in and I saw her innocent face lit with joy as she talked about her daughter.

Oh well. Enough of this.

I deliberately switched my thinking to the dog, trying to figure out how to go about telling Warren about her "condition." How would he take that news that his wife wasn't the only one in the family with "issues"? Only one way to know for sure.

I found him in the kitchen, rooting around in the refrigerator.

"Hey, baby." I reached to give him a peck on the cheek and he responded with a grunt.

"Bad mood?"

"No." He continued his search through the fridge. "Just trying to figure out what to make for lunch."

And no doubt having trouble, what with all of the leftovers from Devin's celebration party last night. They swallowed up most of the eye-catching space in the refrigerator.

"Let me take care of that for you."

He stepped out of the way and I took over the process of pulling out the lunchmeats and cheeses to make our usual Saturday afternoon sandwiches. Moments later, we settled down at the table and I started to tell him about Sasha. Note *started to.* But something in Warren's eyes led me a completely different direction. He looked . . . lonely. A bit lost, even.

"Honey, are you okay?"

He shrugged. "I guess." Which being interpreted meant *no.*

"What's going on?"

He bit into his turkey sandwich and gave another little shrug. "Things just seem kind of weird lately. You're usually so . . . talkative."

"And I haven't been lately?"

Another shrug.

"I'm sorry, Warren. I'm trying to be there for the girls and be there for my clients. And this thing with the dog —" Nope, I wouldn't go there. I wouldn't usurp my husband's needs for that of a dachshund. "I'm just overwhelmed."

"I miss you, Annie."

Whoa. Huge red flag, waving right in my face.

"I — I know."

Man, is this ever weird. For years, I've been the one initiating these kinds of conversations. Feels kind of odd for the shoe to be on the other foot.

"We should plan a date night," I offered. "At least one night a week. No television. No computer. Just some one-on-one time — either here or in a restaurant or something."

He reached to take my hand. "Okay. I think you could use the distraction."

After that, he dove into a story about something that had happened at work the other day, which sent my thoughts soaring back to Nikki and the money. *No, no, no. Not going there. Focus on the man sitting in front of you. He needs you.*

In that very moment I came to realize the truth. My puppy wasn't the only one in the household with separation anxiety disorder.

Apparently my husband had a pretty severe case of it, too.

CHAPTER 18

You hear about those wives who dig through their husband's pockets in search of evidence of wrongdoing? Well, I'm not one of them. Never have been. The only thing of value I ever pulled from Warren's pockets was a stick of gum he'd left there weeks before. That's why, when I first saw the little folded note in his slacks pocket while doing the laundry that same Saturday afternoon, no alarm bells went off. Probably just a *don't-forget-to-pick-up-the-dry-cleaning* reminder to himself.

Wrong.

For whatever reason, I felt compelled to open the silly thing before throwing it out. Just in case it turned out to be something important, you understand. The words inside, written on bank stationary, completely floored me. "We pulled it off without a hitch. Easy money, my friend."

The tiny piece of paper slipped out of my

hand and floated down to the floor. *"Pulled it off?" "Easy money?" And what's up with this* we *business?*

A host of ideas raced through my imagination. Did Warren and Nikki work together to steal the money, then split the proceeds? *Nah.* How could she have paid for the car? Maybe Warren and Richard plotted this whole ugly thing. Maybe they . . . *Nah.* Nothing made any sense, especially the part where Warren played a role in the burglary — at all.

I picked up the paper and stared at the handwriting in an attempt to analyze it. Scribbles and scratches. A child could've written it, for all I knew. Didn't really look like Warren's, but how could I be sure?

Ask him.

Just two simple words, but they terrified me.

I mulled them over as I worked on Brandi's silk wedding bouquets. I dissected them as I cleaned up the mess in the kitchen Devin and his friends had left behind the night before. I pondered them as I started a second load of laundry.

And I agonized over the awful truth as it stared me down. My husband, innocent as he looked, could very well have pulled the wool over my eyes from the get-go. Maybe that's why he'd seemed so distant lately. Perhaps that's the real reason he looked so . . . lost. Maybe he was wracked with guilt, filled with remorse.

I'd promised the Lord I wouldn't entertain these thoughts. And I really tried to dismiss them and think of something positive, uplifting. But my brain simply wouldn't cooperate. I sent a plea for help heavenward.

A familiar case of nerves kicked in. I let myself get completely wound up inside, and my stomach turned to knots. Maybe I needed that Internet lesson on handling stress more than I thought.

While Warren clipped the hedges outside — safely out of sight — I slipped into the computer chair and signed online, determined to read the lesson through, even if it killed me.

It almost did. On and on it went, about not letting the ups and downs of the investigation steer you from dead-center. "Getting pulled to the right and left will cause undue stresses," it read. Well, no kidding. But what else could I do? According to the lesson, keeping my eyes on the goal would prove most valuable when it came to de-stressing. *Hmm. Sounded almost . . . biblical.*

I shut down the Internet and paced the office. Sheila's cryptic e-mail message flooded my mind once again. *"In my distress I called to the Lord; I cried to my God for help. From his temple he heard my voice; my cry came before him, into his ears."*

What was it she had said? *Ah yes.* The Lord already saw my situation and had an answer for me. He could handle all of this, surely. I lit into a heartfelt prayer, completely assured of the fact that God could handle it all. And I would remain focused. More so than ever. I would ask for the Lord's help every step of the way.

At that point, I went out into the living room and began to vacuum. *Mental note: Vacuuming can be a stress reliever when agitated.* After that, I dusted all of the furniture. *Goodness, I didn't know the coffee table could shine like that, even with the chewed-up leg.* And cleaned all of the windows. *Don't want the neighbors to think we're slobs.* And washed and waxed the car. Why not? *Looks like good weather, after all.*

As I moved from job to job that afternoon, I sorted through the mess in my mind, concluding the obvious. *Warren is a godly man. Period. There is a logical, sensible explanation for the note. Ask him.*

At this point, a sense of peace fell over me. I drew in a deep, relaxed breath and knew the moment had arrived. I could face Warren and just ask him — point blank — about the mysterious slip of paper. Surely he would offer up a logical explanation.

I'd just worked up the courage to enter his office for a friendly chat when I heard his voice ring out.

"Annie!"

Something about his tone worried me. He sounded almost . . . angry?

I eased my way down the hallway and into the door of his office. "What's up?"

Warren turned away from the computer with a dazed look on his face, one I didn't recall ever seeing before. "Annie, I went on-line to pay our credit card bill, and —"

Oh no, oh no, oh no.

"What in the world is this?" He pointed to the screen.

Yep. There it was, clear as day — my $150 charge to www.investigativeskills.com.

"Oh, I, um —"

I half expected the man to pull a Desi Arnaz and say, "Lucy, you've got some 'splaining to do," but he didn't. No, his silence spoke far more than words ever could.

I pressed my body against the doorjamb, in case I had to make a clean getaway. Warren stayed seated in the swivel chair, a puzzled expression on his face. He drummed his fingertips on its arm, finally speaking, "Annie, is there something you'd like to tell me?"

The sudden rush of blood to my face made me feel a little faint, but there was no time for drama now. I had to face the inevitable. I'd known this moment would come all along, of course. I must tell my husband the awful truth — about the investigation, about my personal suspicions, everything.

No time like the present. With a prayer on my lips, I dove in, headfirst.

You know, a funny thing happens when you finally open up after a long period of silence. A certain sense of relief floods your soul and gives you the courage to say the very things you've been terrified to say all along. And at great speed, to boot.

Warren must have sensed my need to get it all out, for he kept quiet. I poured out my heart, gave away every tiny detail. I started with my suspicion of him, using the note I'd found as my first piece of evidence. The look on Warren's face was, well, heartbreaking. At one point, I had to look away. Couldn't stand the pain in his eyes. Next, I moved on to Richard Blevins, stating my initial concerns there, as well. Warren just shook his head in silence. I shifted to Nikki

Rogers, my voice intensifying as I told him about the latest bit of news I'd garnered at the vet's office. And, over the lump in my throat, I told him the whole story about Janetta Mullins and her wayward son, including my questions about the cash deposit.

Warren heard it all in painful silence. I lost count of how many times I saw him shake his head in disbelief. And I think I heard him mutter a couple of things under his breath, though I didn't ask him to repeat them.

"So you're saying —" he finally offered "— that this note you've found is supposedly evidence linking me to the stolen money?"

"Well, I —"

"And you think I stole the money from the bank to pay for the weddings? Is that what you're saying?"

"I'm not saying I believe that," I argued. "I'm just saying the thought has crossed my mind. And you have to see that your phone conversation with the travel agent a couple of weeks back just added fuel to my fire."

"Conversation with the travel agent?" His face paled. "I don't know what you mean."

With frustration mounting, I forged ahead. "Sure you do. Couple of weeks back, on a Saturday? The day you told me about the bed-and-breakfast surprise."

"I — I —"

"See, I overheard part of your telephone conversation from outside the office door and drew my own conclusion," I threw in, "but I was wrong. I misjudged what I heard and turned it into something else. There was a logical explanation all along."

He shook his head once again. "I don't have a clue what you're talking about. I never called the travel agent from the house. Never."

"What?" He had to be mistaken. I'd heard his words, plain as day. *"Can't believe I got away with it. Annie doesn't suspect a thing."* If he wasn't talking to the travel agent, then who? And about what?

I suddenly felt a bit faint and excused myself to sit on the loveseat. Alone. Warren continued to stare at me from his spot in front of the computer desk, as if I'd just landed on planet Earth in a spaceship and had antennae sticking out of my head.

"Annie, there are a thousand things I don't understand about women," he said, "and I guess I'll just have to chalk this whole thing up as one of them. How in the world could you let your imagination run away with you like this? And if you suspected someone we knew of stealing the money, why didn't you come to me, ask for my help?"

"I — I don't know." And I truly didn't. Fear, maybe?

At this point, Warren got really specific, asking questions about the Internet courses I'd signed up for. I told him, with a smile actually, about all I'd learned. I didn't resort to bragging, but I did feel — at least to some extent — I'd gotten my money's worth. Er, his money's worth.

Warren's brow wrinkled as I tied the pieces of the puzzle together — all of my odd behaviors over the past few weeks. Joining the gym. Tying the dog to the flagpole. All of it.

Finally, I ran dry. Couldn't think of another thing to say. I wanted to distract him, wanted to ask about the note I'd found in his pocket. Wanted to clarify the issue of the phone conversation. Wanted, no needed, to know where he came up with the twenty-five thousand dollars cash he'd pressed into my palms weeks earlier.

But somehow I never made it that far. My bewildered husband stared at me in absolute silence for a good sixty seconds, then did something that completely stunned me. He turned back to the computer and, without saying a word, paid the credit card bill.

Paid it.

That simple. Never asked another question. Never offered up a response of any kind, even to my would-be accusations against him. Never so much as breathed a word to ease my mind. No, he apparently wanted to let me stew awhile. Wanted me to wallow in the mess I'd made.

I so desperately needed to turn this thing around, to find out the answers to the questions that continued to plague me, even now. But Warren didn't appear to be in a talking mood, as was evidenced by his unwillingness to carry the conversation one step further.

And so, with little else to do, I resorted to the unthinkable. Went into the kitchen, opened the freezer, and pulled out a brand-new, never-opened halfgallon of Moolenium Crunch ice cream. I didn't bother to grab a bowl. No point. Just a spoon would do. I dove in headfirst, my thoughts rolling almost as fast as the spoon as it ping-ponged from the carton to my lips.

Mental note: Ice cream eaters are far more susceptible to brain freeze when they consume large quantities at breakneck speed.

You know, there are some things you just have to learn the hard way. I rubbed my temples, begging the pain to ease. After a minute or two, it started to let up. I plopped down into a chair at the breakfast table, deep in thought.

I'm pretty sure I set a new world record that day, consuming nearly half of the carton in one sitting. Afterward, I reached for my notebook and crossed the room to my favorite easy chair. As I eased my way down, tummy now aching, Sasha leaped up into my lap. I scooted over to make room for her. After pulling the cap of the pen off with my teeth, I started writing. Or, rather, I tried to start writing.

For once, no words would come.

Nothing.

I stared at the blank page, unable to think of one sensible thing to say. I had made a mess of things, a complete and utter mess. I'd offended my husband, the very last person on the planet I'd ever wanted to hurt. Would he ever forgive me?

On the other hand, he had hidden something from me, too. The note. I couldn't get it out of my mind, no matter how hard I tried. And that phone call. *I know what I heard. I'm not going crazy. Am I?*

I snapped the notebook closed and leaned my head against the back of the chair. For whatever reason, I could just hear Sheila's voice now. In her usual, motherly way, she would lay it out straight for me: "Annie," she would say, "some days you're the bug. Other days you're the windshield."

Today just hadn't been a windshield kind of day.

CHAPTER 19

Did you ever stop to think and forget to start again? I guess you could say that's what happened to me on Saturday evening. I found myself completely distracted by the complexities of the day. So much so that I couldn't sleep that night. How could I, with all of the guilt and anxiety eating me alive?

That, and the incredible bellyache from the ice cream.

A couple of times I rose from the bed, which totally threw poor Sasha off. "No sweetie," I whispered. "It's not morning yet."

Both times she settled down and dozed off again. On my second trip, I eased my way into the bathroom, where I fished around inside the medicine chest for an antacid tablet, which I promptly popped into my mouth. Afterward, I paced the bedroom, praying, thinking, and clutching my tummy. *Mental note: Next time you're stressed, head to the gym, not the freezer.*

Thankfully, Warren never budged, though I almost willed him to, at times. I was terrified to stir up more trouble, yet I knew that one heartfelt conversation between the two of us could fix everything. If he'd wake up, we could get to the bottom of all of this. Afterward, we could kiss and make up, then spend the rest of the night wrapped in one another's arms.

I gazed over at him several times with a serious longing in my heart as I continued to trudge back and forth, wearing a path in the carpet. The lines of gray in his hair glistened against the glow of the tiny nightlight. Sure, his scalp was a bit more apparent than when we were younger, but he was every bit the handsome devil I'd fallen in love with. Paunchy middle or not. Raucous snore or not.

I reached to brush a curl from his forehead and he stirred a bit. Yes, I loved this man with every fiber of my being. Loved the way he laughed at my jokes even when they weren't funny. Loved the way he danced with me when I felt like dancing. Loved the way he cared for his family through thick and thin. I pulled back my hand and stared in silence, reality setting in.

But this wasn't about my love for him,

was it? I couldn't let my feelings run away with me here. This was about not getting to the truth of the matter before we fell asleep. What about that biblical principle of not letting the sun go down on your anger? He'd quoted that line to me a million times over the years. So why had he gone to bed upset, without talking to me? Sure, the Word of God said that love would cover a multitude of sins, but I had to wonder if we'd crossed some sort of line here by "dozing before dealing."

I finally crawled back under the covers and leaned back against the propped-up pillows, attempting to pray. To be honest, I wasn't sure where to start. My marriage? The upcoming weddings? The investigation? As I pondered these things, the knots in my stomach grew. Finally, in spite of my anxiety, my eyelids gave way to the sleepiness.

Things didn't get much better after the sun came up, though it wasn't for lack of effort on my part. In fact, I don't recall ever trying harder. I dressed for church, as always. Wore a dress I knew Warren loved. Put on the earrings he'd bought me for Christmas. Sprayed on the perfume he'd given me for my birthday. Fashioned my hair in a style I knew he liked.

In short, I did everything I could to get

him to look my way — and open up for a heart-to-heart chat. Preferably before we left for church.

For whatever reason, he refused to budge. He moved from bathroom to bedroom to closet in steady succession, readying himself for the day. All in stony silence.

Not a word during breakfast.

Not a word as he sat to read over the Sunday school lesson, which he'd agreed to teach in Richard's absence.

Not a word as Devin joined us to leave.

We climbed into the car for a very quiet, strained drive to church. Even Devin took note of our silence.

"What's up with you two?" he asked.

I hoped Warren would respond, but he kept his eyes focused on the road and his lips glued shut.

"Oh, it's just been a stressful weekend," I offered. "Nothing to worry about."

"Is that your final answer?"

Good grief. My son should really consider a career in law.

I nodded, but he refused to let it go. Devin, never one to worry until now, crossed his arms and cast a pensive gaze my way. "Right. Whatever."

I stared out the window as Warren made the familiar drive. The leaves had, for the most part, fallen now. We would be heading into winter before you knew it. Somehow, that thought depressed me, especially in light of the fact that my oldest daughter would be married in the late winter. *Lord, everything is changing. Everything.*

I shivered as we exited the car at the church. Sometime in the night, the temperature had dropped. Seemed to fit our mood, truth be told. I pulled my jacket tight, but it did little to relieve the shivering. *Am I really cold, or have my nerves become an issue?*

Devin ran on ahead of us to meet up with some friends, which left Warren and me alone. At last. I turned to him for one last attempt at breaking the ice before entering the church. "Warren, you have to talk to me. You have to."

"What would you like me to say?" His rock jaw was tighter than a snare drum.

"I don't know," I pleaded. "Something. Anything. Tell me I'm crazy. Tell me I haven't heard from the Lord. Tell me I've wasted your money. Tell me you know —" My courage rose. "Tell me you know who took the money, and I'll let this thing go. I promise."

"I can't tell you that." He kept walking, never looking my way.

"You can't or you won't?" I spoke in a

hoarse whisper.

He shook his head. "I *can't* tell you that."

We paused at the door of the church. Others walked around us to enter, but I refused to go inside until I said one last thing.

"Warren, I have to show you something."

"Later, Annie."

"No, now. This is important." I pulled the folded-up note from my purse and shoved it into his palm.

As he read it, the color drained from his cheeks. "Where did you get this?"

"From your pants pocket. I found it yesterday, just before you opened up the credit card bill. I was headed to the office to ask you about it."

He took the note and ripped it in half.

I knew it. There's more to that note than meets the eye. He's up to something and he doesn't want me to know what it is.

"Warren, I wish you would —"

At that moment, Candy and Garrett appeared at my side. "Hey, Mom. We're going out to eat after church today — that new buffet up on the highway. Would you and Dad like to come with us? Garrett's parents are coming."

Great. We'll have to air our dirty laundry in front of our children and our good friends, all at once.

"You'll have to ask your father." I shrugged. "It's up to him." I shot another glance Warren's way. He discreetly crumpled the paper in his balled-up fist, then pressed it into his pants pocket. *I guess this means our conversation is over.*

"Okay." Candy turned to face her dad. "What do you think, Dad? They've got the best carrot cake in town. I know you love that."

"Sounds great." Warren pulled open the front door of the church and we entered together. I tried to catch his eye, but he refused to look my way. I couldn't tell if he was angry or worried, but something was wrong . . . very wrong.

Once inside the vestibule, Brandi and Scott joined us.

"Hey, Mom. How are you coming on the bouquets?" My daughter's eyes sparkled as she asked the all-important question.

"Making progress. Nearly finished with them, in fact."

I managed a weak smile. She didn't seem to notice my discomfort, as was evidenced by her continued chattering.

We turned our attention to talking about floral arranging, and Warren slipped away to talk with a friend. The look of sadness in his eyes alarmed me. I'd never seen him hang on to a grudge this long. Or maybe it wasn't a grudge. Maybe he felt as confused as I did right now. *Lord, You're going to have to help us through this. I don't know what to do anymore. I really don't.*

Brandi continued to chatter away, and I tried to listen, I really did. But I couldn't stay focused. I could feel my hands shaking and knew that tears would soon come, so I dismissed myself to the ladies' room. She gave me the oddest look as I turned away, but I couldn't pause long enough to worry about it. I felt the sting of tears and knew I must make my escape as smoothly as possible.

Once inside the restroom, I fought the line of familiar women to get to a stall. Most everyone was so busy touching up lipstick, fussing with hair, or chatting to notice my misty eyes. Once inside the safety of the tiny stall, I pulled the lid down on the toilet and took a seat, fully dressed. At that point, I allowed the tears to tumble. In silence, naturally.

I stayed in there so long, a couple of the ladies must've felt the need to check on me.

"Annie, you okay in there?" Nita Lemuel called out.

This was followed by a chuckle and a quip from an elderly woman named Margie.

"You didn't fall in, did you?"

"I'm fine," I assured them, trying to make my voice sound normal. "Just need a few minutes to myself."

They went back to chatting, their voices eventually fading away as they disappeared out the door. With the restroom now emptied out, I could hear the music begin in the sanctuary on the opposite side of the wall. I continued my emotional breakdown on the toilet with my head in my hands, my chin quivering like a bowl of gelatin. I cried over the look I'd put on Warren's face yesterday afternoon. I cried over the look that must've been on my own face when I'd found the note in his pocket.

As I heard the door to the restroom open, I quickly dried my tears. The pointed toes of a pair of deep green pumps appeared just under my door.

"Annie, I know you're in there."

Sheila. Naturally.

"You can't stay locked up in that stall forever," she said. "Might as well come on out and let me know what's going on. Everyone is getting worried."

"Everyone?" I choked back the lump in my throat. "Did Warren send you in here?"

"No." She hesitated. "Your girls did. They think you're sick. You're not, are you?"

Leave it to Sheila to know the difference between physical sickness and sickness of the soul, even without laying eyes on me.

I sat in my confession booth a bit longer, unwilling to move. She could coax all she wanted. I wasn't coming out, and she couldn't make me.

"Annie, did you get that e-mail I sent?" Her voice softened in an un-Sheila-like way.

I nodded, then realized she couldn't see me. "I got it."

"I was right about the stressing thing, wasn't I? You're overtaxed. Too much going on at once?"

"Yes. You were right." At this point, I raced forward, telling her everything — right down to the note in my husband's pocket. Her exaggerated silence went on for so long, I suspected she'd left the building.

Finally, when I could take it no longer, I cracked the door and peeked out of the stall.

"Aren't you going to say anything?" I queried.

She shrugged. "I'm thinking. Sometimes I speak too fast. Didn't want to do that this time around. Besides," she said with a small smile, "I kind of figured you just needed to get all of that off your chest. Didn't really figure you needed anyone to tell you what to do."

Her face lit into a broad smile and I couldn't help but notice she'd styled her hair differently.

"You look great," I commented. Her dark brown and green sweater caught my eye right away. "Is that new?"

"Mmm-hmm." She turned in a circle, and the rich brown broomstick skirt made her look like a little girl spinning around the living room to impress her parents. "You like it?"

"Yeah."

"Bought it at the mall on clearance."

The woman had an uncanny way of lifting me from my woes, even through her wardrobe.

I let out an exaggerated sigh, then gazed in the mirror at the bags under my eyes.

"How do you do it, Sheila?" I queried. "How do you stay in such an upbeat mood all the time?" I knew she'd been through her own personal tragedies: an unexpected hysterectomy, her husband's bout with prostate cancer, and watching her grown children marry and move away to other states.

She shrugged. "I get down, just like everyone. I really do. And I find myself in predicaments that get me stressed out, just like you. If anyone knows how to get into hot water, it's me."

True, true.

"I guess I just have a theory about all of that."

"Okay." I paused to see if she would continue but finally gave up. "Well, would you mind sharing it with me?"

A pensive look crossed her face. "I look at it this way, Annie. If you're going to walk on thin ice, you might as well dance."

"Huh?"

"I mean," she continued, leaning against the wall while she explained, "that we all go through things that stress us out. But you know what the Bible says. What the enemy means for evil in our lives, God will use for good. He will. So you might as well start dancing now, even before you have all the answers. Why save the celebration for later?"

What was it with all of the dancing images God kept putting in front of me these days. First Judy Blevins, then my rose-in-the-teeth cha-cha dance with Warren — now Sheila. *Lord, are You trying to drive home a point? A little self-improvement choreography, perhaps?*

At this point, an older woman named Mrs. Powell entered the restroom, her face flushed. "I didn't think I'd make it 'til the end of the service," she explained with a cockeyed grin.

She went about her business, and I turned my attention to touching up my lipstick. When she left, Sheila got right back to *her* business, addressing my concerns.

"We all get stressed, Annie," she continued. "It's inevitable. And when you're menopausal —" She paused. She must have seen the look of pain in my eyes. "When you're *premenopausal,* the stresses just seem to pile up. They're exaggerated."

"I know." I let out a lingering sigh.

"And change brings about undue stress in a woman's life, but never so much as when she's going through changes in her own body."

I stared at my reflection in the mirror and groaned. "Did you have to go there?"

"I did." She stood next to me, and we both stared at our reflections in the mirror. "We have no choice but to go there."

"I'm getting old, Sheila." I stared at the crow's-feet around my eyes and my gray roots.

"That's not necessarily a bad thing."

"Gee, thanks. That was the part where you were supposed to disagree with me."

She laughed and then gave me a mock stunned look. "Why would I want to do that? Growing older is nothing to be

263

ashamed of. And nothing to worry about. I daresay, we're at the best age of all."

She said "we" as if "we" were both the same age. I had to stifle a giggle, knowing her to be several years older than me.

"That scripture I sent," Sheila spoke to my face in the mirror, "do you remember what it said?"

At the moment, I couldn't even remember my own name. "Something about calling out to God when you're stressed?"

"Well, that and more," she said. "The scripture I felt led to send you that day — and one of these days maybe I'll tell you the story of how God spoke to me — is from Psalm 18 and it goes like this: 'In my distress I called to the Lord; I cried to my God for help. From his temple he heard my voice; my cry came before him, into his ears.' That means you have to call out to Him when you're stressed. Don't pretend it's not happening. Don't try to act like you have it all together. You were never meant to carry everyone on your own."

"I know —"

"And I'm not just talking about this little investigation of yours," she went on. "I mean you have to cry out to Him about everything that's stressing you out. Your changing body. Your daughters growing up.

The weddings. The distrust that's crept up between you and Warren. Everything."

Emotion kicked in. "How do I do that? Warren and I have had our arguments through the years, but nothing like this. We don't trust each other anymore. And I truly can't see a solution. If the marriage falls apart —"

A little girl with pigtails bounced into the bathroom and we fell silent. A world of possibilities ran through my mind, none of them good.

"Annie, you're letting your imagination run away with you," Sheila consoled, after the child had left. "Calm down, take a deep breath. Your marriage isn't falling apart. You and Warren are just at an impasse right now. Eventually one of you will make a move. But in the meantime, you have to call out to God and know that He's heard you. Then you have to trust Him to put all of the pieces back together. If you go trying to do it on your own, well —"

"Say no more."

I glanced down at my watch. Ten fifteen. Oh no! Had I really spent more than an hour in the ladies' room and missed most of the service?

Yes, sure enough, the music began on the other side of the wall, signaling the altar call. Soon a flood of women would race through the restroom door for a respite before the Sunday school hour.

But with a minute or two of lead time, I opted to turn the ladies' room into my own personal prayer closet. An altar was simply a place where you met with God, right? Shouldn't matter where, should it?

"Will you pray with me, Sheila?" I implored. "I really, really need it."

She nodded and took me by the hand. "I thought you'd never ask." Right then and there we began to do business with the Lord over my struggles of the past couple of days. Sheila prayed that I would have wisdom and godly discernment. She offered up a plea for truth to reveal itself. I amened along with her as she closed out with a lilt in her voice.

Truly, by the time we finished, I felt as if I'd really been in the presence of the Lord. In fact, I wasn't sure when I'd heard a better sermon or experienced His presence in a stronger way.

Funny. God really does meet you right where you are. Even if it's in the ladies' room of the Clarksborough Community Church.

CHAPTER 20

My aversion to Tuesdays ended, ironically, on a Tuesday.

After nearly three days of avoiding me, Warren finally sat me down for "the talk." Though I'd tried to prepare for it since our Saturday afternoon encounter, I'm not sure I'd readied myself for his opening line.

"Annie, you trust me, don't you?"

"Um, I —" I stared across the dinner table at him and shrugged.

"Have I ever given you any reason not to?" He gave me a lingering gaze. "Before all of this mess, anyway?"

"No. Never." *Nothing I can prove, anyway.*

"Okay. So I'm a trustworthy guy. That much we've established." He paused, which set my nerves on edge. His gaze shifted to the table. He took his fork and played with his mashed potatoes, avoiding my eyes. "I knew I'd have to tell you where I got the money for the weddings," he said, finally.

"I've known it all along."

"Just like I knew I'd have to eventually tell you about using the credit card to sign up for those classes."

"Something like that." He looked up and sighed. "I should have just told you that day at the bank. I knew you were fishing around for answers, and I owed you one." He fell silent a moment, then continued on. "You know how money-conscious I am. I can't help it. I've always been really —"

Tight? Frugal?

"Careful. I had to be, in the early days."

"After I made such a mess of our finances, you mean?"

"No." He shook his head. "I never blamed you for that. But I've always felt the need for financial security. So, as you know, these past few years I've been socking away money for our retirement. I didn't want to have to worry about anything during our later years."

Here comes the part where he tells me he cashed in an IRA. I knew I should have checked into that.

"See, I hated to touch the money I'd set aside," he explained. "I didn't want to deal with penalties and taxes for early withdrawal . . . too much to handle psychologically."

"Okay, so — ?"

"Well," he said, his face lighting up, "with Richard's help, I came up with a better plan. At least I think it's better. Certainly better than borrowing from ourselves."

Richard? A better plan? "Honey, what in the world did you do? I'm swallowing my fingernails over here." Truly, I had gnawed them down to nubs, at least a couple of them.

"I took out a home equity loan," he exclaimed proudly.

"You did what?" A host of things raced through my mind, not the least of which was the fact that we'd only — finally — paid off our mortgage six months ago.

"Richard and I talked at length about my options," he explained. "I knew we'd probably need about twenty-five thousand dollars to cover both weddings, or at least somewhere in that neighborhood. And with Richard having expertise as a loan officer . . ."

Oh, good grief. Of course. Richard was the one who handled the loans for Clark County Savings and Loan customers. I'd filed that information in the back of my mind ages ago.

"So you're saying we have a new mortgage

payment?" I asked. "Why haven't I seen a bill?"

"I asked them to send it to the bank," he explained. "To buy myself time to work up the courage to tell you." He leaned forward, putting his elbows on the table. "I guess I'm just a coward at heart, and a little prideful. I'd bragged so much about paying off the house. It was such a huge relief. I didn't know how you'd feel about starting over again."

"Wow. And it must have killed you to do this, didn't it?" My eyes stung as they watered over. "But you're not a coward. I haven't exactly been accessible lately. And I can see where you'd be nervous about telling me."

"To be honest, the day I handed you the envelope, you didn't ask me right away where I got the money. I had prepared myself psychologically to tell you then, if you asked. And like I said, I should have told you that day at the bank. Don't know why I couldn't seem to get the words out."

"Oh my goodness."

I could see the tension in his face ease. "If it helps, Richard got us a really great rate. And we'll pay it off in five years, plenty of time before I actually retire. Besides, this new mortgage payment is just a drop in the bucket compared to our last one, so I can still set aside some money every month for the future." Warren leaned back in his chair and crossed his arms, a look of satisfaction on his face. "See, it's a win-win situation."

"Wow." Still, one question remained. "Why didn't you just deposit the money into our checking account?" I asked. "Why the envelope stuffed with *cash?*"

"I knew you could check our balance through online banking," he admitted, "and I didn't want you to see what I'd done until I was ready to hand the money off to you. You should've seen the look on Richard's face when I asked for it in cash."

"I'll bet."

"And besides . . ." Warren's face lit up. "I figured if I made the deposit into the checking account, the money would get all mixed up with our bill-paying money. That would've been a mess. This way, everything could be separated out."

"Right." I paused as I gazed at him with admiring eyes. "Honey," I said finally, "I totally trust you." *Is this really me speaking those words?* "You know far more about our finances than I do. You know what we can afford and what we can't. I think you're brilliant to come up with a plan like this."

"Really?"

"Yes, really." And I meant it. "You're a banker, for heaven's sake. Who would know more about paying for something of this magnitude than a banker?"

"I hated the idea of going into retirement still owing anyone money."

"Right." Made perfect sense to me. In fact, a lot of things made sense to me now, at least they appeared to. "So, let me ask you a question," I ventured. "Is this why Richard started avoiding me a few weeks ago?"

Warren sighed and glanced at the floor. "Probably." He looked back up into my eyes with a bit of a sheepish grin. "I'm sure it put him in an awkward position that I asked him to keep it a secret. But I apologized to him — just today, in fact. Felt like I needed to do that. With all he's going through, he doesn't need anything more to deal with."

Good grief. Had I ever taken that ball and run with it.

"Your cryptic phone call a few weeks ago," I started, "the one I overheard —"

"Richard," he mumbled. "Should've told you on Saturday. Sorry."

Good grief again.

"And the note in your pocket?"

He let out an exaggerated sigh. "Richard wrote it. I guess he was proud of the fact that we managed to pull one over on you."

I thought back to Sheila and her uncanny timing on that e-mail. The Lord had known all along my husband had nothing to do with this. I had stressed needlessly. Over nothing. If only I'd been able to apply the wisdom from that verse a little earlier, I could have saved myself several hours of anxiety.

"Are you mad at me?" Warren's brow wrinkled as he asked the question, and I felt compelled to rise from my chair and meet him at his, where I promptly pushed the curl back from his forehead and planted a kiss in its place.

"Are you kidding?" I whispered into his ear. "I was going to ask you the same thing. I suspected you of a crime, Warren. *A crime.*" A shudder ran down my spine. "That's just . . . crazy."

He drew me onto his lap and planted kisses along my upper arm. "Yeah, well, that's why I knew I had to work up the courage to tell you. It was one thing to withhold information from you, another to have you thinking I'd robbed the bank."

At this point, my sleuthing know-how kicked in. I gave him my most knowledgeable face. "It's not considered robbery unless there's bodily injury or death involved.

We're talking burglary here."

"Ah. Burglary."

"And," I went on to explain, "in the state of Pennsylvania, burglary is considered a second-degree felony. Learned that from my research. So, up 'til now, I've thought of you as a burglar, not a bank robber. I suspected you of being a burglar, I mean."

He leaned his head against my arm. "Wow. Well, that's good to know. What else have you learned?"

"Hmm." I rested against him. "I guess I've just discovered that my suspect list has pretty much been cut in half now. This revelation only leaves Nikki Rogers and the Mullins family in the line-up." I shook my head, unable to think clearly. "Though, for the life of me, I don't know where to begin. I'll have to pray about it."

"Well," he said, offering up a smile, "at least now we can work together to figure things out. You won't be on your own anymore. I can join you. You track the Mullins family, I'll keep an eye out for strange behavior from Nikki."

"Sounds good," I agreed. "But I guess I should also tell you that I haven't exactly been working on my own. Sheila has known for the past couple of weeks."

He chuckled. "Should've known. I guess

that explains the hour and a half you two spent in the ladies' room on Sunday morning."

"Um, yeah." I went on to tell him how I'd used the stall as a would-be confessional, and his lips curled up in the cutest grin I'd ever seen.

"You're a gem among gems, Annie Peterson."

"Why thank you, kind sir. I'll take that as a compliment."

"I mean it." His countenance grew more serious. "And our daughters are the spitting image of their mother, for which I'm truly thankful."

"I hope they don't turn out as nutty as I have." I looked up with a grin.

"But Annie, seriously, I'd do anything for those girls. If they'd asked for the moon, I would've tried to get it for them. I love them so much, and I want their weddings to be . . . memorable."

Wow. I would've responded, but I couldn't push down the lump in my throat long enough to accomplish it.

Warren gazed into my eyes with some of the deepest emotion I'd ever seen from him. "And I wanted this for you, too. I know our wedding wasn't all you'd hoped it would be. We didn't have anything fancy."

"I didn't need fancy," I whispered. "I had everything I needed. I had you."

"Still," he said, "I know you, Annie. You want to give the girls some of the things we didn't have when we were young, some of the things our parents couldn't afford."

I swallowed back my tears and nodded. "Brandi has such lofty ideas," I admitted. "But I know her heart. She's not going to spend money for the sake of spending money. She wants this to be lovely for everyone who's coming. And Candy —" I couldn't help but smile. "She's more frugal. Like you. But her ideas are just as lovely. She knows how and where to spend the money to make it count. I can absolutely assure you, their weddings will be as different as night and day."

"Just like they are."

"Yes, but both ceremonies will be equally as precious and just as godly."

"Just like they are." His hoarse whisper brought a little more moisture to my already-damp lashes. He changed gears with his next words. "Do you remember what I told you the morning Sheila sang?"

"Remind me."

"On the way home," he said. "I told you how blessed I felt. What great kids I have."

"Yes, I remember."

"Here's what I think — that a father who loves his children has to be prepared to kill the fatted calf every now and again, to celebrate their victories with them."

I laughed as the image of a fatted calf registered, particularly in light of the homecoming feast I'd recently prepared for my son and his friends. "You crack me up," I said. "But I totally get it. And I'm so proud of you, Warren. You are the best dad in the world."

"For a bank robber, you mean?"

"Burglar," I corrected. "Burglar."

We stared at each other in silence for a moment, then I started to giggle. Must've been contagious, because Warren joined me in short order. Devin walked in on the tail end of our laughing spell, a relieved look on his face as he saw the two of us wrapped in each other's arms.

"So, you two are talking again?"

"Yep!" I spurted, after releasing my husband from a much-needed lip-lock. "We're talking. Everything is fine."

"Awesome." He reached to grab a chicken leg from the platter on the table. "I'm starved."

"Get changed before you eat." I pointed to his workout clothes. My heart was warmed by the fact that at least our son was getting some benefit from our family's expensive gym membership.

"Why?"

"Devin —"

"Okay, okay." He sprinted from the room, chicken leg still in hand. I looked at Warren once more and asked the inevitable question, though I could have guessed his answer.

"Ready for some ice cream?"

"Mmm-hmm. A nice, big bowl."

I sprang from his lap and headed toward the freezer. "Of course."

He followed directly behind me and pinched me on my backside as he answered, "Well, get to it, then."

"Hey, you," I sputtered. "Watch that."

"I am." He winked as he examined my ever-widening rear end.

I turned away as I felt a blush coming on but couldn't hide for long. The man of my dreams stepped right alongside me as I filled our bowls with the familiar gooey delight. He talked incessantly. In fact, I couldn't remember when I'd ever heard him open up and share so freely. At one point, he took me into his arms and planted a tender kiss on my forehead. I responded by pressing a bowl of Moo-lenium Crunch into his waiting hands.

Who cared if our waistbands expanded a little? We had each other and we had the truth. What else did we need?

Chapter 21

"What do you think?" I asked Warren bright and early Wednesday morning. "Should I finish my Internet courses or just forget the whole thing?"

"Are you kidding?" He gave me an incredulous look. "I paid $150.00 for those courses. You're finishing them."

"Aye-aye, Cap'n." I offered him a salute then headed off to the office to face the computer head-on.

If I had to be completely honest with myself, I'd say all of this e-knowledge really wasn't doing much good. Most of the things I'd learned, investigation-wise, had either come as a direct result of my own failures or through some miraculous intervention of the Lord.

Still, if He could speak through a donkey, as He'd done in Old Testament days, surely He could teach me a thing or two through the World Wide Web.

If I could get through my stack of e-mails to find the current lesson, that was. I fended off nearly a dozen forwards, then breezed through an e-mail from a client, requesting a bid on a new editing project. I responded with a low bid, probably feeling generous because of the happy circumstances of the past twenty-four hours. Hopefully, I wouldn't regret it later.

I read one letter from my mother in Mississippi, a funny note about floral arranging from Nadine in Savannah, and a couple of prayer requests from Linda Jones, the head of our "E-Prayer Chain" at church. I stopped cold when I got to the one about Judy Blevins. Apparently she had taken a turn for the worse in the night. The doctors didn't give her much longer. I should go up there and visit her. As soon as possible. In my mind's eye, I could almost see her dancing now.

I paused to pray right on the spot. No point in beating around the bush. I poured out my heart, asked the Almighty for His perfect will in the matter. I prayed for her healing, yes, but I also prayed that the Lord would have His way in all of this. And I prayed for Richard, as I'd never prayed before. Regardless of the outcome, he would need God's strength. Finally, a sense of peace washed over me. I rested easy in the fact that God remained in control.

My prayer time put me in the right mindset to read my devotional, which I did next.

I opened the Web site to find one of my all-time favorite scriptures from Isaiah, chapter one: "Come now, let us reason together," says the Lord. "Though your sins are like scarlet, they shall be as white as snow; though they are red as crimson, they shall be like wool."

These words had always struck me as a little unusual. I knew what it meant to have my sins forgiven, but what did it mean to reason with God? When Warren and I "reasoned" things out, an argument usually ensued. Was I supposed to argue with the King of creation? Surely not.

Instead of chewing on the words, I took the matter straight to the One who would know the answer. I asked Him. I put it out there, much as a child would put out a request before a parent. In short, I spent time with Him. Seemed like I'd been doing a lot of that lately, but then again, I had a lot of things to "reason out."

At this point, I sought the Lord regarding my thought life and asked for forgiveness for the little things I'd let creep in, until now unnoticed. Then I asked for His thoughts to be my thoughts, something I didn't recall ever asking for before.

I would need His way of thinking if I were to pursue this investigation one step further. I didn't want to waste a moment on any more vain imaginations.

After spending some time with the Lord, I turned my attention to the latest lesson from www.investigativeskills.com. To my great delight, the title of lesson eight resonated with me. I almost laughed aloud when I read the words: *"A Good Investigator Employs Critical-Thinking Skills."*

Well, if that didn't beat all.

The lesson went on to explain the difference between everyday thinking and critical thinking. It discussed the various dimensions of proper reasoning: everything from avoiding oversimplification (*Yep, I've been guilty of that*) to thoroughly evaluating all available criteria (*Haven't done enough of that*).

I must've oohed and aahed a bit as Warren passed by the door, because he entered the office with a look of intrigue on his face.

"Learning a lot?"

"Yes, actually. I think this is the most fascinating one yet." I pointed to the screen. "See all this stuff about situation comparison and argument analysis? I've never heard of any of this before. It's a whole new way for me to approach the investigation, and life in general, for that matter."

"Sounds vaguely familiar." He rubbed at his chin as he continued to read the screen. "I think I remember learning some of this in my philosophy class back in college. This kind of stuff hurts my brain."

"No kidding," I admitted. "It's all a little deep for me, too, but I guess that's the point, to go deeper. To analyze. To explore all of the options reasonably, right?" A chuckle escaped the back of my throat as reality hit. "I'm already wide. I might as well be deep, too." We both broke into a rousing rendition of the children's song "Deep and Wide," laughter eventually filling the room.

Afterward, Warren leaned down and kissed me on my cheek. "I'm all for exploring options," he said, "but right now the only option I'm exploring is the one that says I'm going to lose my job if I show up late."

I glanced at my watch and gasped when I saw the time. "You're never late."

"I know." His eyebrows elevated mischievously. "But someone kept me up until the wee hours of the morning."

I felt my cheeks warm and shooed him away. "Better get a move on." I blew the fellow of my dreams a kiss as he left the room, then, with a song in my heart, turned back to the computer, deep in thought. Pun intended.

With all of this information in hand, I forged ahead with the investigation. I couldn't rest on my laurels, after all. By process of elimination, I'd rid myself of two suspects over the past twenty-four hours. Of the ones that remained, I'd have to say Nikki raised the most questions in my mind. Yes, if I really analyzed the situation, I'd have to say that something about her just didn't feel right to me.

I took the time to analyze the situation in its entirety. For the first time ever, it struck me that no money had disappeared beyond the initial twenty-five thousand dollars. I was also stumped by the idea that no other businesses in our area had been affected. Those two things certainly gave me reason to suspect an insider like Nikki all the more.

But why stop at twenty-five thousand? If she really had a thirst for expensive things, wouldn't she continue on in her quest to obtain more?

I'd just leaned back in the chair to rest when the phone rang. I answered it right away, once I saw the caller ID.

"Annie." Warren's voice sounded hushed,

strained. "I've got another clue to add to your list." *Mental note: Exonerated husband links arms with supersleuthing wife to solve the crime of the century. Details to follow.*

I responded with a "Really?" almost afraid to hear what he had to say. My poor husband. I'd pulled him into this investigation, whether he wanted to be involved or not. "What's happening?"

"I know you're not going to believe this," Warren whispered, "but the police are here again, questioning Nikki Rogers."

"No way." My heart thump-thumped against my chest wall.

"Has to be more than a coincidence, don't you think?" Warren asked, intrigue lacing his voice.

"Mmm-hmm." A thousand thoughts ran through my mind at once, not the least of which was the car Nikki had just purchased. Maybe the guys from the sheriff's office were on to her, at last. Maybe they wanted to confront her with new evidence.

I lowered my voice. "Keep me posted."

"Why are *you* whispering, Annie?"

"I don't know. I mean —" I raised my voice. "I don't know."

We hung up and I tried to return to the lesson but found it difficult, what with these heavy-duty thoughts filling every corner of my head like they did. I did pause as I read something quite profound: "A conclusion is simply the place where you got tired of thinking." Wow. Deep stuff. And how true. I prayed I would never get tired of thinking.

I read on through the lesson, amazed to see some suggestions for how to increase critical-thinking skills. "Crossword puzzles? Who woulda thunk it? And game playing?"

Yes, lo and behold, if game playing didn't top the list.

Games? I loved games.

Within minutes I'd put together a plan for a game night, to provide myself an opportunity to increase my critical-thinking skills. The sooner, the better.

I opened my calendar and glanced through it. Tomorrow night would work just fine. Warren and the kids could join me, and maybe I'd ask someone else, as well.

Nikki Rogers.

Yes, surely Nikki would be great at game playing. Unless my imagination had gotten the better of me, I'd have to say she'd been playing a few already. Like hide-and-seek from the Clark County Sheriff's Office. And truth-or-dare with the fine folks of Clarksborough.

Funny, every time I thought of Nikki, especially in that security guard uniform, an uneasiness fell over me. *What is it, Lord? Is this the one, or have I completely misjudged her?* Inviting her to the house would give me an opportunity to see her out of uniform, to watch her in a more comfortable environment.

Yes, we'd have her over for dinner and games. I'd suggest she bring her daughter along, as well. Might be fun for all of us to get to know one another. That way, if my suspicions were wrong, we'd have an opportunity to reach out to them both.

I waited about half an hour to give the police time to question Nikki. Then I telephoned the bank and asked to speak to her.

"H–Hello?" Her quivering voice let me know she hadn't quite recovered from her visit with sheriff's deputies.

"Nikki. Annie Peterson here."

"Oh, Annie." She suddenly became awash in emotion. "I'm so glad you called. What an awesome coincidence. I need prayer. I really do."

So I see.

"What's up?" I almost felt like a traitor asking the question but didn't really have the information in full, anyway.

She sighed. "It's awful. Those guys from the sheriff's office wanted to question me about my whereabouts on the night of the crime. Can you believe that? They didn't come out and call me a suspect or anything, but they questioned me like one."

"What did you tell them?"

"I told them I'd spent the night out-of-town, at my mother's place in Lancaster, but they didn't believe me."

"You should give them your mother's number," I suggested. "That way they could call and ask her themselves."

"I did," she said with a sniffle. "And they called her right after. But that didn't really solve anything. My mom and stepdad had gone away for a couple of days for her birthday," she explained.

"Ah." *Likely story.*

"She wanted me to drive out to Perkasie to puppy-sit her poodle while they were away. But I should've just stayed put in my own place." Nikki broke down again. "Everything about it was a mistake. I had to get up super-early the next morning to get back to Clarksborough. Amber was late for school, and I was about five minutes late getting to the bank."

"You were late for work?" Another new piece of evidence.

"Well, just a few minutes," she explained. "But I'm not the only one with the key. Warren and Richard were already here. We just hadn't opened for customers yet. I explained that to the deputies, but they acted like they didn't believe me." She lowered her voice. "Why would they suspect me, of all people? I'm a single mom, not a bank robber."

Burglar. And if you really were a security guard, you'd know the difference.

"I never took a thing that didn't belong to me," she went on. "Never."

"Well, maybe I can offer you a little diversion," I interrupted. I went on to extend a dinner and game-playing invitation — for Nikki and her daughter. Nikki sounded a little surprised to receive the offer but accepted at once.

"You're so sweet," she gushed. "No one has offered us an invitation like this since we moved to Clarksborough. Thank you so much for thinking of us."

A wave of guilt washed through me. *I'm thinking of you more than you know.* "We're happy to have you."

"Would you like me to bring anything?" she asked.

"Nope. Just bring yourself and Amber. And come prepared to have good food and a good time."

I could hear the excitement in her voice and felt a little bad. For a moment. When I remembered her new sports car, the private school tuition, and today's visit from the Clark County sheriff's deputies, my seared conscience eased a little.

We ended the conversation on a happy note. As I hung up, I reasoned things out — with myself and the Lord. That's what great investigators did, after all.

What would it hurt, really, to have Nikki over for a few games? If she turned out to be the perpetrator, my critical-thinking skills would surely reveal it. If not, perhaps we'd end up being great friends.

I rubbed at my head, my brain now hurting from all of the thinking I'd done. The melody to "Deep and Wide" played through my mind once more and eventually worked its way down to my lips.

Somewhere between the ice cream and the Internet lessons, I'd managed to move out in both directions at once.

Chapter 22

The following evening, just two hours after I arrived home from visiting Judy Blevins, my guests began to arrive. Candy and Garrett were the first in the door. My daughter proudly handed me a scrumptious-looking cheesecake. "I baked it myself."

"Wow." I'd been married twenty-seven years and still hadn't conquered the art of baking a "real" cheesecake. The kind from a box, sure. But the real McCoy?

I gave my daughter an admiring whistle. "You go, girl." That Garrett was going to be one lucky fellow.

Brandi and Scott came in next. She opened a bag from our local supercenter and pulled out a variety of things: French bread (to go with my homemade lasagna), lettuce, cucumbers, tomatoes, baby carrots, a red onion, and a head of broccoli.

"Mmm." Looked great. We went to work,

piecing together the most colorful salad in town.

At 7:00 p.m. sharp, the doorbell rang and I answered it with a smile.

"Welcome!" I let out an "ooh" as my gaze fell on Nikki in a lovely deep red sweater and trendy jeans. That security guard outfit did her no justice at all. She was quite a beauty. She'd pulled her hair back in a ponytail and looked considerably younger. To be honest, it took a moment to register. She was probably no older than my own daughters. Somehow, that put a whole new spin on things.

"Good evening, Annie!" Nikki handed me a plateful of brownies, which I accepted with a smile.

"You didn't have to do that."

"I know." The edges of her lips curled up in a playful grin. "But I wanted to. And Amber helped me bake them. She loves working with me in the kitchen."

For the first time, I glanced down at the youngster to her right. A precious child with blond curls and eyes bluer than my Dutch china stared up at me.

"You like helping your mom?" I asked.

Amber nodded, then shifted her focus to the ground.

"She's a little shy," Nikki explained.

"Well, come on in, ladies. Didn't mean to leave you standing out in the cold." I ushered them into the house, then reached to close the door. As I did so, my gaze fell on the car in the driveway.

The car.

Yep, the one and only "Sports Car Extraordinaire," to be precise. Sitting right there, in my driveway. I must've paused a bit too long, because Nikki interrupted my thoughts.

"Oh," She glanced out the door alongside me. "Do you like my car? I just bought it."

"It's very nice." I gave it another once-over before shutting the door. *I'd imagine a burglar could make a clean getaway in a car like that.*

"Remind me later," she said with a twinkle in her eye, "and I'll tell you how I got it. It's a miracle, really."

Yep. A twenty-thousand-dollar miracle, in fact.

Nikki and Amber followed on my heels to the kitchen, where I introduced her to my girls. My daughters, who had never known a stranger, took to her right away. Their conversations, as always, layered one on top of the other.

Less than five minutes later, I called everyone to the table. I'm not one to be prideful about such things, but we had quite a spread: two kinds of lasagna, a huge salad, and mozzarella-filled French bread. My stomach rumbled in anticipation.

"Wow." Warren looked over the beautiful feast the girls and I had prepared. "Looks amazing, Annie."

"Thank you." I reached up to give him a peck on the cheek and noticed Nikki's gaze follow me. *What's up with that?*

We took our places and Warren offered to pray over the food. As was our custom, we each reached out to grab the hand of the person on either side of us. Amber sat directly to my right. I took her little fist in my own and gave it a tender squeeze. She looked up at me with a bashful smile, jumbo-jet-length eyelashes batting over those saucer-wide blue eyes.

Warren prayed a deep, heartfelt prayer, and then the chaos began.

Let's just say I've never seen so much food consumed in such short order. And with so many of us gathered around the table, the conversation rose to a near-dangerous decibel level. But no one seemed to mind. In fact, the smiles on every face let me know a good time was being had by all.

I glanced at Nikki several times throughout the meal. Truly, she beamed. The young mother seemed in her element, a fact that surprised me a little. I'm not sure what I'd expected — for her to be uncomfortable in a "normal" family setting, perhaps?

No, there she sat, chattering away about everything from fashion to food to the upcoming Get Out to Vote rally.

It floored me.

After swallowing down more food than should have been allowed by law, we cleared the table and pulled out several games. I'd deliberately chosen to start with Clue, a personal favorite.

I opted for Mrs. Peacock. Warren took Colonel Mustard. And Nikki, who played with an inquisitive Amber at her side, chose Miss Scarlet.

You would *pick her, wouldn't you?*

Brandi, Candy, and Scott dove in as well, settling for Mrs. White, Professor Plum, and Mr. Green, respectively. Devin and Garret opted not to play, choosing instead to watch the sports channel on TV.

Not that any of our lovebirds were really focused on the game.

You know, I've noticed a lot of kissing goes on when you have two engaged couples in the house. Truly, at least a half dozen times during the game, I looked up to find Brandi and Scott smooching or Candy and Garret making goo-goo eyes across the room at one another.

I also noticed Nikki's reaction. I just thought I'd seen her nervous back at the bank. Her reaction to all of this romance let me know she carried some heavy-duty issues where men were concerned. Heavy-duty.

What secrets aren't you telling, girlie?

We played on and on, interrupting each other every now and again to tell a funny story or nibble on cheesecake.

At one point, the game nearly slowed to a halt. Clearly frustrated, Brandi popped out with something funny. "Scott, if you don't hurry up and make a move, I'm going to think you're the suspect."

We all laughed, but at the same time a chill gripped me. If only my daughters knew a potential burglar sat at our very table, they might not find the comment so funny.

"Give me a minute. I'm thinking." Scott's knotted brow left nothing to the imagination.

"That explains the look of pain on your face," Devin hollered out from across the room.

We all laughed again, but Scott had the last laugh. He won the game, fair and square. Mrs. Peacock. In the library. With the wrench.

Bingo.

"See," he bragged. "Told you I was thinking." My future son-in-law took his game playing quite seriously.

Shortly thereafter, we settled down in the living room with cups of hot coffee in our hands. Amber's cup contained cocoa, topped with a couple of big marshmallows. After a bit of chit-chat, the room filled with a delicious silence.

To my surprise, Nikki was the one who broke it. "You know," she said, "I remember nights like this when I was a kid. My mom and my uncle would teach my brother and me how to play cards or some board game, and then we'd all drink hot chocolate after." She paused, and her expression changed. "Of course, my dad was never there. He was . . ." Her voice kind of drifted away.

"I'm sorry, honey." I reached over to pat her hand.

As I did, the voice of the Holy Spirit filled my ear and nearly sent my heart into knots. *She's just a girl, Annie. A girl who never had a father. Point her toward her real Father and leave the rest to Me.*

Ouch.

My Bible verse bounced around between my ears again. *" 'Come now, let us reason together,' " says the Lord. " 'Though your sins are like scarlet, they shall be as white as snow; though they are red as crimson, they shall be like wool.' "*

A reminder, perhaps, that Nikki Rogers was no different than any of the rest of us? That she and my girls shared the same hopes and dreams? That her sins, whatever they were, were no greater than any of ours?

I thought back to the missing twenty-five thousand dollars and tried to remain focused on my job as an investigator. Sitting next to me was a prime suspect, possibly *the suspect*.

As I stared at the lovely young woman who now giggled at one of Devin's goofy jokes, the Lord spoke the same words to my heart again: *She's just a girl in need of a Father.*

I let my gaze shift to the little girl who sat beside her. Amber. Another fatherless child. For whatever reason, my heart suddenly grew quite heavy.

I stared across the room at Warren, who also laughed at his son's joke, his face alight with merriment. *Thank You, Lord. My children are so blessed.* Oh, if only it could be so for every child.

I thought of Jake, a young man in search of a father's love.

My thoughts shifted to Nikki, a woman angry because of a deadbeat dad.

I reflected on Amber, a child who — unless God intervened — would never know the warmth of a daddy's arms.

And, with today's visit to the hospital still fresh on my mind, I was reminded of Judy Blevins, who would soon dance into her Father's arms, a smile as broad as the Atlantic on her face.

The image was too much to take. I had to excuse myself to the restroom.

Seemed like I'd been spending a lot of time in bathrooms lately. But this time, I didn't cry. No, by the time I arrived, I'd managed to push back the emotion and focus on the one thing that would lift my spirits, not cause me to crumble, as I had so many times in the past.

I reasoned things out with the Almighty. In short, I gave Him a piece of my mind. And, in exchange, He gave me a piece of His.

I saw in a flash His brokenheartedness over those who'd been betrayed and His desire to see them restored. I took note of His love for the single mothers and their children. And I marveled at His unbelievable mercy for all of the dads who'd strayed far from His plan for their lives.

More than anything, though, I saw His desire to see all of us come to know Him in the way that Judy had. At this point, the Lord gave me a clear resolve to reach out to Nikki Rogers — even if she had taken the twenty-five thousand dollars — and point her in the right direction. He encouraged me to continue on in my quest to pinpoint the thief. And He challenged me to spend more time reasoning things out with Him.

"Go ahead and dish it out, Annie Peterson," I'm pretty sure I heard Him say. *"I'm a big God. I can take it."*

CHAPTER 23

I was awakened on the morning of the Get Out to Vote rally by a phone call. I'd known all along it would come, but the news still came as a shock nonetheless.

Apparently, in the middle of the night, sometime around 3:00 a.m., Judy Blevins had danced her way into the arms of her heavenly Father, just as she'd told me she would.

Though I'd expected it, I still found myself awestruck by the reality. The image of a little girl spinning across the living room filled my mind. Twirling skirts, child-like voice raised in glee, I could envision it all. *Oh, Father! Is that what she's doing right now, at this very moment?*

My heart sang for her. But at the same time, it broke for Richard. The poor man had already lost so much. How would he make it through this, as well?

One thing was certain. He would need his

church family. We would draw close to him and offer love and support in every conceivable way. This much I knew to be true. And I prayed he would respond by returning — in his own time, of course — to our midst.

I woke Warren to give him the news. He sat up in bed and raked his fingers through his messy hair, taking it in. His response startled me.

"I didn't think it would really happen," he whispered.

I didn't tell him I'd known all along it would. Instead, I just settled into his embrace as he reached out for me. We leaned against one another in the bed, and I let him do the talking.

"Annie, I don't know what I'd ever do if I lost you." His voice broke, which caused a lump to rise in my throat.

Wow. He'd spent some time thinking about this.

"I feel the same way," I whispered. "But I know God would get us through it. And I know He'll walk Richard through it, too."

"What can we do for him?" Warren looked at me. "He doesn't seem to want help from anyone."

"Maybe that will change now," I offered. "Maybe this is the best time to reach out to him. He's got no children, no relatives living nearby. He's going to need the people at the church more than ever. And if we're there for him, regardless of his absence over the past few weeks, he'll have to see how much we love him." I paused. "And how much we loved Judy."

"Right."

We sat in silence for a few minutes, each of us lost in thought. I finally rose from the bed, knowing the day would not wait on me.

"I wish we could just cancel this rally," I said. "My heart's just not in it now."

"Oh, I don't know." Warren loosened his embrace and then rose from the bed. "Judy was so patriotic. She loved the Get Out to Vote rallies. Probably more than any of us."

"You're right," I said with a smile. "I'd forgotten. She was the one who always took the stage and led us in the national anthem. And she would want us to be there today, with bells on."

We dressed, albeit slower than usual, for the annual event. Warren chose a deep red sweater over jeans, and I donned a bright red shirt, with a navy blazer, coupled with jeans. For effect, I wore a white belt.

The rally started at noon in the Clark County Park. Warren and I arrived early to help set up. Even at such an hour, people swarmed in with their red, white, and blue hats; flags, like kites, waved in the breeze; and children ran amuck.

I rubbed away the chill on my arms with outstretched palms. "When did it get so cold out?" I pulled a white wool scarf tighter around my neck, all the while wondering if the temperature had really dropped or if the news about Judy had left a permanent chill.

Warren headed off to the platform area, where he would soon open the event in prayer. I looked around at all of our friends and loved ones, and my heart swelled. In spite of so many in attendance, it just wouldn't be the same without Judy and Richard here. They'd always played such a critical role in the event.

The smell of barbecue filled the air. I looked across the picnic area to find Janetta Mullins and her family hard at work, preparing food for the masses. She wore a white chef's hat with an American flag on the band, and the sunlight picked up the sparkles in her white and silver sweater. I made my way through the crowd over to her. Though I hated to think about the investigation today, of all days, I knew I should probably try to get to the bottom of the cash deposit issue. If I could.

"Hi, Mullins family," I said with a smile.

"How are you doing today?"

Jake looked up with a smile. "Busy, but good."

"Here, try a piece of this, Annie." Janetta handed me a tiny piece of brisket, which I promptly popped into my mouth.

"Man, that's good." I licked the sauce from my fingers and looked over at her with an admiring smile. "Is there anything you Mullinses can't do?"

"Well, we're not very good at getting our mom married off," Kristina offered.

For some reason, that got all of us laughing. Well, all but Janetta, who swatted at the air with the back of her hand.

"I'm the last person on God's green earth who wants a man in her life, trust me. And I'm so old and set in my ways, I wouldn't even know what to do with a man if I had one, anyway."

I had to laugh aloud. "Girl, I'm sure you'd figure it out."

Jake shook his head and his gaze shifted back to the barbecue pit. *Is he embarrassed?*

Sheila walked up, her face more serious than usual. She took me by the arm and whispered, "Did you hear about Judy?"

I nodded and turned to face her. "I did. Has anyone talked to Richard?"

She shook her head. "Orin tried, but Richard didn't answer his cell. I'm just worried because I know he doesn't have family nearby. I think maybe Judy has a sister in Pittsburgh, but I don't know how close they were."

"Are you talking about Richard Blevins?" Jake looked over, wide-eyed.

"Yes," Sheila and I answered.

"What happened?" The young man looked genuinely concerned.

I felt the edges of my lips curl down as I responded. "His wife passed away in the night."

Janetta very nearly dropped the metal tongs from her hands at the news.

"Oh, that's awful. She was such a nice lady."

We all chimed in with a round of dittos.

"I've really missed working with her this year at the rally," Janetta added. "I always looked forward to seeing her." She shook her head. "It's such a shame."

"It is sad," I agreed, "but I've no doubt in my mind where she is right now." I went on to tell them — all of them — about Judy's dancing story. Janetta Mullins, softhearted soul that she was turning out to be, swiped away a few tears. "Well, if that doesn't beat all."

Sheila threw in a couple of stories about

Judy from years gone by and had us all chuckling within no time. Somewhere in the midst of the laughter, Janetta came up with a plan.

"Here's what we'll do," she interjected. "The kids and I will go by the Blevinses' house on the way home and take Richard some of this barbecue."

"Great idea." Sheila and I chimed in with a few more ideas for how we'd care for Richard over the coming days, then she headed off to locate her husband.

Jake, who'd been pretty quiet until now, spoke up. "I think Mr. Blevins would probably like it if I visited him, but I'd like to wait 'til the crowd thins a little."

"Oh?"

He nodded. "Yeah, he was so great to me when I was in jail. Came to see me every day."

If I'd had false teeth, I would've dropped them. "W–What?"

"Didn't miss a day," Jake said with a nod. "He came on his way to work every morning. They even let him bring in breakfast once or twice. Donuts. He also brought a Bible and talked to me about God. All sorts of stuff, really. Did you know he lost a son once?"

Janetta joined in. "I couldn't figure it out

at first, but he took a real interest in Jake. Said he wanted to make sure they were treating him okay and even gave me the name of an attorney he trusted."

"Whoa." In a flash, I could see it all — Richard Blevins, sitting shoulder to shoulder with a young man who could've been his own son, offering counsel and moral support.

"He was a blessing to our whole family, actually," Janetta went on. "Really stepped in and helped when we needed it most. In fact, he's the reason we came back to the church."

Okay, that made no sense to me at all. Richard Blevins was sending people to the very church he'd stepped away from?

Almost as if she could read my mind, Janetta went on to add, "He'll be back soon. You watch and see. I doubt he could stay away from that Sunday school class for long. He loves you guys so much."

Kristina's face broadened in a smile. "Right. Remember that story he told us?" She went on to share a story of something that had happened in the Sunday school classroom years ago — something, ironically, involving Sheila.

"I remember the day that happened," I said with a smile. "Sheila knows how to make people laugh, for sure. But if I recall, Richard was pretty embarrassed that morning."

At this point, I felt a tiny hand slip into my own and looked down to see Amber standing next to me. Without saying a word, her little palm spoke volumes.

"Well, hello pretty girl." I flashed a motherly — or would it be grandmotherly? — smile.

Her face beamed as she looked up at me. "Hi."

That was the most I'd heard out of her since we'd met on Thursday night. I looked up to see Nikki approaching with a striking woman, about my age, at her side.

"I see she found you," Nikki said with a smile. "All morning long we heard about you. Mrs. Peterson this. Mrs. Peterson that. This daughter of mine seems to think you hung the moon."

I felt my cheeks warm as I responded, "I think she's pretty special, too." Oh, if only the little doll to my right knew I suspected her mother of stealing money from the bank.

Nikki took a moment to introduce me to her mother.

"Carol Rogers." The lovely blond stuck out her hand, and I grabbed it for a warm handshake.

"Annie Peterson." I made the rounds, introducing Carol to the crowd before me. Within minutes, everyone chattered merrily.

A suspicious flush came over Jake's cheeks as he glanced over at Nikki. *Well, look at that.* She smiled his direction and they began to talk about the barbecue. Carol, Janetta, and I chatted about the weather and the ample assortment of red, white, and blue attire on attendees. At some point along the way, Amber took off for the swings, and we watched her with a smile.

"Seems like just yesterday my girls were that age." I sighed.

A sigh escaped Carol's lips. "Where does the time go?"

Janetta chuckled. "Well, if either of you figure it out, let me know. I'd like to reverse the clock, for sure. Nobody ever told me my body was going to take on a mind of its own when I turned fifty."

We all erupted in laughter and Sheila's "menopause antennae" must've gone off from across the park, because she appeared at my side in mere seconds. We introduced her to Carol, and before you knew it, Sheila was on a roll.

"I have a hot flash for you," she said with a grin. "Menopause is cool."

Janetta, who'd taken to fanning herself

311

with the Get Out to Vote program in her hand, shook her head in disagreement. "That one's going to be a hard sell."

"No, really," Sheila explained. "When you're going through menopause, you can eat all the chocolate you want, and no one questions you."

"You can put on a few pounds," I interjected, "and folks hardly notice."

"Yeah, but what about the bad stuff?" Janetta queried. "I saw this great infomercial for wrinkle cream — promised it would get rid of all your wrinkles — and I almost bought some."

"Why didn't you?" Jake, who'd been fairly silent until now, popped up.

Janetta shrugged. "Figured my whole face'd disappear."

Every woman within twenty feet lost it in laughter. And as we went on, talking about this stage of life we found ourselves in, I couldn't help but think of Judy Blevins, and how beautifully she would've fit right in with all of us. I also wondered about the spiritual depth she would've brought to our gathering.

In the middle of one of Sheila's one-liners, my husband took the microphone and asked everyone to stand for the opening prayer. I glanced up at the stage, warmed by the sight of him with his red, white, and blue hat, which he removed as he began the invocation. His words flowed, as always, like honey over my soul.

He wrapped up and passed off the microphone to Sheila, who had apparently bounded from my side the minute she realized the program had started. I wasn't sure why she felt the need to take the stage . . . until the music for the national anthem began. *Oh my. Don't tell me . . .*

She lit in, hand to her heart. All around, folks joined in, singing their hearts out. Katie Stolzfus now stood next to Nikki, with one arm slipped around the younger woman's waist and the other hand over her heart. She released it every few seconds to dab tears from her eyes. At about midway through the song, several of my husband's coworkers from the bank grouped together, blending their voices in harmony. Mayor Hennessey looked over the whole of us like a proud papa. And I . . . well, I couldn't help but brush away a few tears myself.

On and on Sheila sang, her eyes lifted heavenward. And I had to wonder if, somewhere up in heaven, Judy Blevins wasn't dancing along.

CHAPTER 24

Sheila always said life was like a roll of toilet paper . . . the closer you got to the end, the faster it went. That's kind of how I felt about this little investigation of mine; it seemed to be taking on a mind of its own, barreling forward in some yet-unknown direction.

With Warren and Richard off the hook, I'd hoped to focus on Nikki and the Mullinses, narrowing down my list one way or the other. But the information I'd acquired over the past several hours made me think I'd need to purchase new running shoes if I wanted to keep up.

The Get Out to Vote rally ended midafternoon, just about the time a light rain started. We stuck around to help clean up, Warren focusing on the stage area and I on the food pavilion. Janetta, who looked exhausted, worked like the dickens to gather up the remains of the food, then announced she was on her way to the Blevins home, along with Kristina, to hand deliver the goodies. I asked her to give Richard our love, which she agreed to do.

After tidying up the park, several of us piled into booths at the diner for coffee, apple pie, and a spirited political debate. Seemed like the rally always concluded this way, though not necessarily with these players.

I ended up in a booth with Amber, Nikki, and Carol. My daughters sat just across the way with their respective fiancés. My husband had opted to take a booth with Devin and Jake, and other friends and church-goers filled the rest of the diner to capacity. Every now and again, Sheila's laughter rang out above the crowd, bringing a smile to my lips. *How does she do it, Lord?*

I tried to focus on the folks at my table, attempted to give them my undivided attention. It was tough, especially with the frenzied look on Shawna's *don't-call-me-honey* face as she tried to wait on all of us. She also definitely looked uncomfortable waiting on Nikki. *Interesting.*

But not everyone in the place made her uncomfortable. I took note of Shawna's occasional sideways flirtatious glances at Jake, and I also took note of Jake's more frequent glances at Nikki, who sat to my left. *Even more interesting.*

We talked for some time about the rally, then the conversation shifted a bit as Sheila started a rousing chorus of "Happy Birthday" for someone on the other side of the room. As soon as the song ended, Amber looked up at her grandmother with a smile. "It was your birthday, too!"

"That was weeks ago, honey." Carol smiled and reached over to squeeze her granddaughter's hand. "Remember?"

"I remember. We went to your house."

My antennae went up right away. *That's right.* Nikki did say she went to her mother's place in Perkasie on the night before the money's disappearance — for her mother's birthday.

"You were a very good puppy-sitter," Carol said with a smile. "But next time you come, Grandma wants to stay with you. I miss you when I go away like that."

"I miss you, too." Amber nuzzled against her, face alight with joy.

Carol turned to me to explain. "My husband took me on a weekend getaway for my birthday, and Nikki and Amber took care of my poodle for me. He's quite a handful."

"We didn't mind, really," Nikki said. "Amber would do anything for her grandmother. Those two are like two peas in a pod," Nikki said, nodding in her mother and daughter's direction. "I'm almost jealous."

"Oh, pooh." Her mother waved a hand in the air. "You know I've always adored you. And I couldn't be prouder. You've turned out to be a beautiful young woman."

"After those crazy teen years, you mean." Nikki's gaze traveled to the table.

"Oh well." Her mother reached across to take her hand. "What's done is done. And you've made a fine life for you and Amber. I'm very proud."

Nikki's bashful smile warmed my heart. *Have I jumped the gun? Is she really suspect material?*

"And of course," Carol added, "I'm tickled to death that Charlie was able to get you such a good job, though I wish it was a little closer to home."

"Uncle Charlie!" Amber let out a squeal. "He's going to take me to Disney World for my birthday."

"Yes, he is." Nikki smiled in her daughter's direction. "Your uncle is too generous."

Ah. So her uncle really did help her get the job at the security company.

Nikki turned to face me. "Oh! That reminds me. I was going to tell you about the car, what a miracle it was." She paused for a second. "Well, a mixed blessing, really."

"Oh yes." I couldn't wait to hear. This would surely put my investigation back on track.

Nikki went on to share a fascinating tale. "I've told you about my dad," she started, "how he skipped out on us when I was little."

I noticed the look of pain as it registered on Carol's face.

Nikki forged ahead. "I saw him off and on when I was a kid, and I think he sent a little child support every now and again."

" 'Little' being the key word," Carol interjected.

"Anyway . . ." Nikki's brow wrinkled as she continued. "By the time I was in my teens, I'd pretty much given up on him. And I think I only saw him once or twice after Amber was born. Not that it really mattered to me at that point. I was used to not seeing him. But a couple of months ago —" Her eyes began to cloud over. "A few months ago, I got word that he was really sick. He was in a hospital in Philadelphia. I'm not sure what possessed me to do it, but I went to see him. I took Amber with me."

"I wasn't sure it was such a good idea," Carol threw in. "But she's a grown woman now and has to make her own decisions."

I nodded, then leaned forward to hear the rest.

"It was kind of weird," Nikki said with a shrug. "He was a lot different than the last time I'd seen him. Not just physically. That, too. But he was . . . I don't know . . . almost religious."

Carol interrupted once again. "The man always could talk a good game. So when I heard about this conversion of his, I told Nikki not to get her hopes up. He wasn't the kind to make amends. Never had been."

"Ah." What else could I say?

"Anyway . . ." Nikki drew in a deep breath. "The hospital called me a couple of weeks later to tell me that he had died in his sleep."

"Oh, I'm sorry."

Nikki shrugged. "I felt bad, but like I said, I hardly knew the man. That's why, when an attorney called a few days after that, I didn't know what to make of it."

"Attorney?"

Carol nodded, her eyes misting over. "Turns out he'd had money all along. And I guess he must've had some regrets for not taking care of Nikki better as a child, because he named her as the sole beneficiary in his will."

Oh, my. Oh, my.

"It felt funny, taking money from someone I didn't really love in the way a daughter should love her father," Nikki explained with a hint of a shrug. "But he obviously wanted me to have it."

"Of course," I interjected. "And you had every right to take it, especially with a daughter to raise."

"That's what I told her," Carol said with a nod.

"Well, Amber certainly benefited, what with the new school and all." Nikki glanced around the diner with a winsome look on her face. "And I needed a break from the second job. I hated to leave Noah and Shawna in the lurch, but Amber needed me in the evenings, and, to be honest, I was just exhausted from working both places in the same day."

Certainly couldn't fault her there. "And the car . . . ?" I asked.

"Oh." Nikki broke into a broad smile. "I'd wanted a car like that for ages. It was just a dream, you know? I never thought I'd live to see the day when I'd actually drive one. But I saw an ad in the *Gazette,* and it was a reasonable price for a car of that caliber, so I bought it on impulse."

Carol shook her head. "I told her to get an SUV," she explained. "But kids these days —"

"I know, I know." Nikki giggled. "It was probably not the wisest decision I've ever made, but there will be plenty of time for mom-mobiles later."

"I love our new car," Amber interjected.

I leaned back against the booth and looked at the women who sat around me. Somehow, my case against Nikki appeared to have unraveled right in front of me. Her uncle really had helped her get the job — albeit with a shady company — and she really was in Perkasie on the night in question. What other proof did I need?

A sigh escaped my lips. So . . . Nikki Rogers hadn't stolen the money after all. The news should have had me overjoyed. Instead, I found myself a little depressed.

I returned home after a long day of socializing with only one thing on my mind. I had to read my next lesson. The ninth title, *"A Good Investigator Returns to the Scene of the Crime,"* resonated with me, especially in light of today's revelations. I must eventually go back to the night in question one more time, revisit the night deposit box, and consider all of the facts. Just the facts.

I thought about Jake, who had talked with my husband as if they were old friends. Every now and again, he had looked my way

321

and smiled. A chill ran down my back as reality set in. Like it or not, I had to consider the possibility that the fine officers at Clark County Sheriff's Office had pinpointed the right man all along.

And like it or not, I had to consider the possibility that I'd pretty much wasted the last several weeks of my life chasing rabbits.

CHAPTER 25

They buried Judy Blevins on a Tuesday. I'm not sure why that registered so strongly with me, but it did. Richard decided to hold the ceremony at the church, with Pastor Miller leading it.

"It's how she would have wanted it," Richard shared privately with Warren.

We all agreed. And those of us who had known and loved Richard for years were thrilled to welcome him home again. He sat near the front of the sanctuary with Judy's sister — a healthier, slightly older version of Judy — seated at his side. Brenda. I'd met her the day before, in Richard's living room. To her right sat her husband and three grown children, with their respective spouses.

The woman's face appeared a bit strained. I'm not sure I saw her cry, but I did notice Richard break down several times as the service progressed.

I found it difficult to keep my emotions in check, as well. As Pastor Miller replayed scenes of Judy's life, I realized what an impact she'd made, both in our congregation and our little community. And though she'd never experienced the blessing of raising a child of her own beyond the tender age of four, she'd poured out her life for the children of the church, working in the elementary department for over twenty years.

Somehow, thinking about Judy working with children got me distracted. I allowed my thoughts to roll back to the story Richard had told about losing his son. And I found myself looking across the sanctuary at Jake Mullins, who sat with the rest of his family in the pew behind Richard. A couple of times, I noted, Richard turned around to glance at the young man, a woeful expression on his face. The two had clearly made a connection.

All in all, the funeral was everything I thought it would be and everything I hoped mine would someday be. Funny in places, poignant in others, and deeply spiritual, pointing would-be seekers toward the God Judy Blevins had loved with her whole heart.

For his text, Pastor Miller chose one of my favorite scriptures from the third chapter of Hebrews: " 'Encourage one another daily, as long as it is called Today,' " he read aloud, " 'so that none of you may be hardened by sin's deceitfulness. We have come to share in Christ if we hold firmly till the end the confidence we had at first.' "

I tucked away, in the recesses of my mind, a reminder to encourage my husband and children before day's end. While it was still today. I would count the moments, not let one slip by, unaccounted for.

Near the end of the service, a slideshow with photos of Judy at various stages in her life was presented. I did pretty well until a childhood photo of a little girl in a frilly dress popped up on the screen. I could just see those skirts twirling now, as she danced across the clouds. The image brought a lump to my throat and a bittersweet smile to my lips.

The service came to a close and folks made their way to the front to visit with Richard. I noticed the Mullins family paused longer than most. Something about all of that still intrigued me, though this probably wasn't the time or the place to wonder about such things.

Warren and I finally found ourselves standing directly in front of Richard. His tear-stained eyes registered more pain than

I'd ever seen in a man before. If ever he needed us, it was now. I reached out to embrace him, and he thanked me at once for being such a good friend to Judy.

I didn't feel like a good friend. In fact, a wave of guilt swept over me as I contemplated the facts. I'd been so busy over the past few weeks trying to incriminate all of my friends and neighbors that I hadn't taken the proper time to visit with her as I should have.

I couldn't ponder this for long because the line kept pushing me forward. Warren took my place and gave Richard a bear hug as I moved along to shake hands with Judy's sister and her family.

I gave Brenda a little nod and said, "Your sister was a beautiful woman of God. She taught me so much."

The woman's eyes, red-rimmed, filled with tears as I gave her hands a squeeze. "Yes," she whispered. "I just wish I'd spent more time with her while I had her."

I had to agree. And Brenda's words reminded me of Pastor Miller's sermon — about making the moments count. I vowed, once again, to do that with my own family.

After moving on to greet the others, I turned my attention to helping Sheila in the kitchen. Several of the ladies from the church had brought food items. At Richard's request, all Sunday school class members would join the family for a meal together in the church's fellowship hall after the graveside service.

I opted to remain at the church and not follow the caravan to nearby Clarksborough Cemetery. Though torn about it, I knew some of us would need to stay behind to make preparations for the return of the others.

Ironically, Janetta Mullins found her way to the kitchen, as well.

"You need some help?" she offered.

"Sure." I pointed to a couple of casserole dishes in need of warming, and she donned a pair of oven mitts.

"Jakey and Kristina went on to the cemetery," she explained, "but I just couldn't. I know it sounds weird, but cemeteries bother me. Ever since my mom's funeral —" She paused and put the casseroles in the oven. "I don't know," she went on. "It just tears me up to see that part."

"I understand," I told her. And I did. My grandmother's funeral had left a lasting impression on me as a youngster.

Instead of dwelling on all that, we focused on the task at hand. As the three of us worked side by side in the kitchen, we found ourselves with ample opportunity to talk. Our conversation, naturally, started with the funeral service, which, we all agreed, had been quite touching. We went on to discuss a plan of action for caring for Richard over the next few weeks, including the daily delivery of meals, as well as cards and letters from the Sunday school class.

Sheila, who looked especially somber in her black on black skirt and blouse, headed out into the fellowship hall, where she worked feverishly to wrap silverware and set out paper plates and napkins. After that, she placed centerpieces on the tables.

Janetta remained with me in the kitchen, where we both set about slicing several loaves of homemade bread she'd brought. I took a little nibble and voiced my opinion right away.

"You know," I said, "I don't know if I've ever just come out and told you this, Janetta, but you're a wonderful cook. I'm a little envious."

I saw her cheeks redden, which did my heart good.

"Thank you," she said with a bashful smile. "I've certainly been at it long enough. I love coming up with recipes, putting my own spin on things."

"Well, it shows."

"Thanks. But I'll tell you a little secret." She gestured to the large stove in the church kitchen. "It's amazing what commercial appliances will do for you. Having them has totally changed my life . . . and my cooking. I can do things now that I only dreamed of doing before."

"Oh?"

She told me about a commercial refrigerator she'd purchased last summer, then went on to sing the praises of her latest oven, "perfect for baking wedding cakes and prime rib alike," she boasted.

Almost made me wish I spent more time in my own kitchen.

Almost.

The fellowship hall soon filled with hungry guests, and I shifted gears to the task at hand. My husband and daughters slipped into the kitchen to see if I needed any help. I assured them all was well and sent them to spend time with Richard.

Sheila, Janetta, and I worked alongside a couple of the other ladies to feed the crew. I watched out of the corner of my eye as Jake and Richard chatted. Except for an occasional swipe of the eye with the back of his hand, Richard appeared to be doing well — as long as people kept him distracted.

I did catch him alone in the hallway at

one point, leaning against the wall.

"Just catching my breath," he explained. He reached up to run his fingers across his bald spot, and I couldn't help but notice the trembling in his hand.

I nodded and reached up to give him a hug. "I know you're probably hearing this from everyone," I whispered, "but I just want you to know we're here if you need us."

He nodded, then pulled back and looked into my eyes with a fatherly-type smile. "Judy loved you so much. And it meant the world that you brought her that little ballerina."

"Really? She told you about it?"

"Told me?" He broke into a broad smile. "She made me put it on the mantel at the house and —" His voice broke, and the tears started. With the wave of a hand, he attempted to offer an apology for his meltdown, but I felt it unnecessary.

"It's okay, Richard." I gripped his trembling hands until he composed himself. "I understand."

"S–She told me to think of her dancing every time I saw it."

I couldn't speak. The mountainous lump in my throat wouldn't let me.

Richard brushed the moisture from his

cheeks. "It's sitting on my mantel right now. I'll never move it."

With emotions running high, I dismissed myself to return to the kitchen, under the guise of wanting to help Sheila and the others. In reality, I needed time to absorb all of the information I'd acquired that morning.

After the crowd thinned, I finally took a seat at one of the tables and nibbled at some of the now-dried-out casseroles. Nothing appealed to me. I tossed my plate in the trash can and eased my way down the now-empty hallway toward the sanctuary, where I sat on the back pew for a little quiet reflection.

It didn't last long. Within minutes my family gathered round me, full of questions.

"Mom —" Brandi sat and then leaned her head against my shoulder. "I just wanted to tell you how much I love you."

"I love you too, honey." I kissed her hair, then nuzzled close.

Candy took a seat on the other side of me and took hold of my hand. "We don't tell you enough how much we appreciate you, Mom."

"We do, you know," Brandi interjected. "You're awesome, and sometimes we take advantage of that. We count on you for too much."

"No," I argued, "I need to be included. You'll never know how much." I offered up a shrug.

"It's just that —" Candy's eyes filled as she continued on, "we don't know what we'd ever do if anything happened to you, Mom. It's scary to think about."

"Then let's don't think about it," I whispered. In truth, I didn't want to think about funerals. Or investigations. Or commercial appliances.

I simply wanted time to reflect on what was right in front of me. As I leaned back against the pew with a daughter in each arm, Pastor Miller's words washed over me afresh: *" 'Encourage one another daily, as long as it is called Today.' "*

I had every intention of doing just that.

CHAPTER 26

The early bird might get the worm, but it's the second mouse that gets the cheese. I made it my goal to be that second mouse.

With lesson nine's title about returning to the scene of the crime firmly implanted in my brain, I headed off to the bank for another look at the night deposit box. I opted to go well after sunset, several hours after the funeral ended, because I wanted to put myself in exactly the same situation Jake would have found himself in on the night the money disappeared.

My darling husband, God bless him, wouldn't let me go alone. When I explained that I needed to spend some time looking over the night deposit box in detail, he appeased me by waiting in the car with the headlights on so that I could see.

In order to search for intricacies, I also carried along a flashlight and a magnifying glass. I'd tucked my "Just the Facts" notebook under my arm, in case I needed a quick place to jot down any clues.

I tried to envision what I must look like, stealing across the parking lot. Er . . . sneaking. *Stealing* just felt like the wrong word. Still, I felt a bit like a television detective, which, for some reason, got me tickled. *Mental note: Next time wear husband's trench coat for the full effect.*

Tiptoeing over to the box, I tried to think about what things were like on the night in question. Had Jake watched in the shadows as his sister dropped off the cash deposit? Had he then inched his way toward the box he'd already rigged? Did he know how much money to expect? Had Kristina, out of sympathy, perhaps, worked with him? Did Janetta somehow play a role, perhaps to bring attention to the family business? Had the whole event been staged? Were they secretly laughing at the rest of us as they counted out their cash and brought in new, sympathetic customers?

I examined the box with great care, looking for . . . well, I didn't really have a clue what I was looking for. Signs of tampering? Bends? Breaks?

I did take note of a few scratches on the upper right section of the box but nothing that smelled like trouble. In fact, nothing seemed out of the ordinary at all, nothing whatsoever. Well, unless you counted the part about the middle-aged woman with a paunchy middle who prowled around in the late hours of the night in search of a villain who didn't want to be found.

Defeated, I went back to the car and took my seat beside Warren with a sigh.

"Nothing jumped out at you?" he queried.

"No. Nothing but the cold, hard facts."

"What do you mean?"

Another sigh on my part set the stage for my next words. "I mean, it's a cold, hard fact that I'm not a very good investigator."

"Oh, Annie —"

"No, seriously," I explained. "I've wasted your money with those courses. I thought you were the burglar. I was wrong."

"Thankfully."

"Yes. And, as much as I hate to think about it, I suspected Richard, too."

"Right."

"Then, I was sure it was Nikki Rogers." I sighed. "But I think I can safely say she's off the hook now. She's got witnesses and an alibi."

Warren chuckled. "Alibi? You're even talking like an investigator now."

I tossed my notebook onto the floor, then leaned back against the seat and closed my eyes. "I just feel ridiculous. Everything points back to the Mullins family, and that means the police were probably right all along. When I think of the way I drilled Officer O'Henry that day at the jail —"

"Whoa," Warren interrupted. "You talked to the police?"

"Yeah. Guess I forgot to tell you that part."

"When did this happen?"

"The day after I ate apple pie with Jake Mullins."

"You ate apple pie with Jake Mullins?"

"Yeah." I sighed again, as much for effect as anything. "Did I forget to tell you that part, too?"

"Um, yeah." He gave me the funniest look. "Annie, you've got the best heart in town, but you live dangerously close to the edge. Have I ever mentioned that?"

"Yeah."

"Problem is," he said, "I don't know how close to the edge you can afford to live right now with two weddings to plan and Devin so thick into the football season. Do you think, maybe, you're reaching the point where you might want to just let this thing go? Let the police figure it out?"

"I don't know, honey." I leaned my head on his shoulder and thought about it. "Maybe." I'd have to pray about that.

At that moment, the parking lot filled with lights. Flashing lights, actually. Red, flashing lights.

"Oh no." Warren slapped himself in the head. "Now what have we done?"

I looked out the window to find a patrol car, light bar lit up like our subdivision at Christmastime. A rap on Warren's window caught our attention. He rolled it down, and Michael O'Henry leaned in, a look of chagrin on his face.

"Do you folks mind if I ask what you're doing here?"

"I, um — I work here . . ." Warren tried.

O'Henry shook his head, frustrated. "I know that, Warren. But you don't work here at this time of night. And why in the world are your headlights pointed at the night deposit box? Do you realize what that looks like?"

A wave of fear shot through me as I realized how things looked. Had we just put ourselves at the top of the suspect list with this goofy move on my part?

"Michael," I interrupted, "you know me. I'm just trying to get to the bottom of this crime. I want to solve this thing as much as you do."

"Yes, I know." He leaned in a bit farther. "But I told you that we're on the job.

There's not a thing you can think of that we haven't already considered."

He hadn't lost his touch with that stare. *Very effective.*

"I'd suggest you folks get a move on before I think up some reason to put you both in the back of my patrol car and take you in for questioning." A hint of a smile caused his lips to curl upward, but I sensed a little shiver go up my spine, regardless. A sign from above that I should let this thing go, perhaps?

"Have a pleasant evening, Michael." Warren waited until O'Henry backed away, then rolled up his window.

I fought to regain my composure but nerves made it difficult. Two different things caused the trembling in my hands. Fear topped the list, naturally. But anger played a role, too. *"There's not a thing you can think of that we haven't already considered."* His words frustrated me to no end. He had no clue as to my thoughts. In fact, he'd never once given me the time or the opportunity to share them with him in full. No, he had dismissed my attempts at crime solving altogether, a fact that truly bothered me.

It would be different if the police had actually made progress over the past few weeks, but they hadn't — at least from the outside looking in. They appeared to be taking their sweet time solving this crime, for sure. And if they really had their man with Jake Mullins, why was he still running around scot-free? Why hadn't they brought charges against him?

I leaned back against the seat and tried to relax as Warren made the drive home, but my thoughts now spun out of control. A thousand things ran through my mind, and pieces of the puzzle remained scattered all over the place.

"When all you have is a hammer, everything looks like a nail." I repeated Sheila's words aloud.

"What do you mean?" Warren asked.

"That's what Sheila says."

I considered, for the first time, that things weren't always what they appeared to be. Returning to the scene of the crime had somehow convinced me of that.

No, things were not always what they appeared to be — and in this case, two wrongs did not make a right.

But three lefts did.

I tapped my fingers on the armrest as my thoughts raced backward in time. I saw several things come into focus at once, and seeing them so clearly almost frightened me.

"I've been swinging at anything and everything," I whispered, "and ignoring the obvious."

Warren slowed the car to make the turn onto our street. "What's so obvious?"

Just the facts, ma'am. Before speaking a word, I offered up a quick prayer. The Lord's response of affirmation to my heart was swift and sure. So much so that it startled me. *Oh Lord, is this what it's like to hear Your voice?*

I waited until I felt sure I'd heard His answer before hesitantly sharing my thoughts with Warren. He seemed stunned to hear what I had to say but didn't interrupt me to give an opinion. Instead, he pulled the car into our driveway, then put it into PARK, where we sat together as I took him on a journey through my thought processes.

"Do I sound crazy?" I asked finally.

"No." I could hear his pained sigh, even in the darkness of the vehicle. "In fact, it sounds like you were headed in the right direction all along but just didn't go quite far enough."

"Do you really think so?"

"I think so." Warren turned off the car and opened his door. As he did, the car light overhead popped on, and I could read the concern in his eyes. "Looks like you're not supposed to give up," he said with a shrug. "To be honest, it sounds like you're really on to something here, Annie. Just keep following the scent. You're on the right trail."

"I am. I know I am."

We climbed from the car and made our way — hand in hand — across the very dark yard toward the front door. For some reason, the eerie black canvas of the night reminded me of something else Sheila had once said. What was it again?

Oh, yes. *"It's always darkest before the dawn. So if you're going to steal your neighbor's newspaper, that's the time to do it."*

The words hit me like a bolt of electricity. Whether she'd meant to do it or not, Sheila had given me the most critical piece of evidence yet.

CHAPTER 27

The following morning, I took a quick peek at my tenth and final www.investigativeskills.com lesson before heading off to the Mullins home. The title didn't surprise me. In fact, *"A Good Investigator Draws a Logical Conclusion"* made perfect sense and provided even more confirmation that the Lord was "in this," as it were.

I read over my Bible verse for the day, knowing it would somehow calm my troubled mind. Sure enough, I found the words from Matthew chapter seven to be just what the doctor ordered: " 'Ask and it will be given to you; seek and you will find; knock and the door will be opened to you. For everyone who asks receives; he who seeks finds; and to him who knocks, the door will be opened.' " The words brought courage to my heart when I needed it most.

I arrived at Clarksville Catering at 8:30 a.m., ready to chat with Janetta Mullins.

Ready to ask some hard questions. She looked a bit startled when I insisted upon coming inside, especially since I came with Sasha in hand.

"I'm not really company-ready." She gestured to her mismatched "This Little Piggy Stayed Home" t-shirt and blue stretch pants. "But come on in. You know you're always welcome, Annie."

I entered the home with my nerves still a bit raw. Sasha squirmed in my arms, and I asked if I could put her down.

"Of course." Janetta looked down with a smile. "Does she go out with you a lot?"

"Lately." I shrugged. "She has a . . . well, separation anxiety disorder."

"Wow. Never heard of that in a dog."

"Yeah, well —"

"Is there something you wanted to talk about?" Janetta pointed me toward a chair. "Something to do with the weddings?"

"Nope, not the weddings." I opted not to sit. *Too nervous for that, to be honest.*

"What's up, Annie?"

Might as well dive right in. "I've been trying to solve the mystery of who stole your money for weeks now."

Her face paled. "You've what?"

"Yes," I offered. "It started innocently. I wanted to prove to myself that Warren hadn't taken it."

"Are you kidding?" She looked flabbergasted. "You thought your husband stole the money?"

"Well, the idea crossed my mind. Let's just leave it at that."

She shook her head, and I could read the confusion in her eyes. "I'm assuming you got over that."

"Um, yeah. He didn't take it. But I'm pretty sure I know who did. In fact, I've got a hunch the one who did it is fighting a battle with guilt even as we speak." My astute observation skills took in the fact that her hands began to tremble at this point.

"Don't beat around the bush. Just tell me what you've come to say." Her lips pursed.

"I will," I began, "but I'd like to ask you some questions before I start."

She shrugged. "Go for it."

"First," I said, "one question about Jake, to relieve my mind."

"What's that?"

"Did he ever take a polygraph test?"

"Yes." She nodded, but her brow remained wrinkled.

"And did he pass it?"

Another nod. "With flying colors."

"Enough said." I paced the room for a moment, then turned to ask another question. "Would you mind showing me that new commercial oven you were talking about yesterday?"

"My oven?" She shrugged. "Sure. Come on."

I followed her into the kitchen with Sasha on my heels and stared at the double-decker beauty. "Wow. Nice."

"Yeah." She reached over to run her fingers along the handle. "I love it."

"I'd like to hear everything about it." I pulled out my notebook and thumbed through the pages. "Everything."

A look of confusion registered on her face. "O–kay. What do you want to know?"

"If you're up to it," I suggested, "just tell me the whole story of how and when and where you purchased it. Everything." I yanked an ink pen from my purse in preparation for taking notes. As I did, Sasha made herself at home under the kitchen table, sniffing at anything and everything that smelled like food. And in this home, that was pretty much everything.

Janetta dove in, telling me all about her "new baby" — starting with the cost.

I nearly swallowed my tongue as I wrote down the amount. Nine thousand dollars?

"Whoa, sister." I looked up from my scribbles and scratches. "I'd have to mortgage the house to pay for that." *Mental note: Forgetful wife can't seem to remember that her husband has already mortgaged the house to pay for two weddings.*

"Yeah, I know it's a lot," she explained. "But you'd have to understand how badly I wanted it. And needed it."

How badly?

"I didn't go into this decision haphazardly," she explained. "In fact, I'd hoped to make the purchase months before but had to wait until the price dropped before I could justify it."

"Ah." I continued to write as she spoke.

"I knew it would, eventually. I waited for weeks. *Weeks.* And it was finally low enough for me to consider — without losing sleep, I mean."

"I understand." I looked up to gauge her expression.

Her face lit into the broadest smile I'd ever seen. "I can't even tell you how many times I drove over to Lancaster and just stared at that stove, wishing, hoping —"

Lancaster. That answered the *where* question.

"I knew I'd make enough money from catering the conference in the Amish country to pay the down payment and still have plenty left over to cover my mortgage and other bills for the next few months."

"So you bought it after the conference?" I queried. "With money from the event, I mean?"

"Yes. I bought it the day after the conference ended. Well, technically I put a down payment on it that day. I'll be paying on it for months to come."

The day after the conference. That answered the *when* question.

She smiled. "I know it sounds silly now, but I was bent on catching it while the sale was on, or die trying. And I managed to do it, just in the nick of time. The sale ended that same day." She let out a chuckle. "You would've laughed, Annie. I know you would have."

"Oh?" I looked up from my notes and noticed the twinkle in her eye.

"I made the biggest fool of myself trying to get my paycheck cashed, then practically raced to the store with the money in my hand."

That answered the *how* question.

"I must've looked like some sort of menopausal maniac." Janetta shook her head with a woeful look on her face. "And all for the love of a stove. Is that the greediest thing you've ever heard?"

In light of what I now know to be true? No.

"Of course, I had no way of knowing the rest of my money would disappear within hours of paying the down payment. I sometimes think —" Her eyes misted over. "I sometimes think the Lord has punished me for my greed. If I hadn't been in such a hurry . . . if I hadn't insisted I had to have what I wanted when I wanted it, well —" She shrugged. "Who knows how different my life would be right now."

How different all our lives would be.

"Janetta, honey —" I reached out to squeeze her hands. "I have one more question, and then I'll tell you what I've come to say."

She nodded and I dove right in. "Did you let anyone at the bank know you'd be making a deposit that night?" Somehow I already felt I knew what she'd say but needed to hear the words as a confirmation.

She nodded. "I did. That's the part that's been driving me crazy, in fact. I felt so silly for carrying all of that cash and knew I wouldn't get it to the bank before the drive-through closed. The only other option was the night deposit, which wouldn't have been a problem if I'd been depositing a check. But I was so nervous about carrying cash that I called the bank to let them know in advance."

I knew it.

"See," she went on, her brow knitting as she spoke, "that's why it bothered me so much to hear the police say it was just a matter of my word against theirs."

"I understand." I offered up a sympathetic smile. "And I'm so sorry all of this has happened to you. I really am." At this point, Sasha began to jump up and down in an attempt to get my attention. I reached down to pick her up and cradled her in my arms.

"I'll tell you the truth . . ." Janetta's face grew quite serious. "After that twenty-five thousand dollars disappeared, I didn't know if I'd have the money to pay my mortgage and utility bills, let alone keep on paying for that crazy oven. In fact, if it hadn't been for the income from your daughters' weddings and the Get Out to Vote rally, I don't think I would've made it through this past month or so."

It warmed my heart to know our money had somehow eased the strain of her situation. But I sensed she had more to say.

"The thing that has stunned me most," she continued, "is how many people from the community have reached out to help us. They've all been so great: Pastor Miller, Sheila and her husband, Richard Blevins . . . He's been the most amazing of all."

Yep. Looks like I've hit a nail.

I took a deep breath before forging ahead with my facts, which could now be shared in full. "I have a story to tell you," I started. "And it starts on the morning after your daughter made the deposit." *"It's always darkest before the dawn . . ."* I could hear Sheila's words ringing loud and clear.

"Tell me, Annie," Janetta implored.

Just as I started to spill my guts, my cell phone rang out. Sasha whined a bit as I put her down to reach for it. When I recognized the number as Warren's, I offered up a quick apology to Janetta, then answered it right away.

"Honey," I whispered, "bad timing."

"No," he whispered back, "critical timing."

Yikes. "What's up?"

"I just thought you'd want to know," he spoke with strained voice, "that Richard was just in here to clear out his desk. He said he's going out of town for a few days on vacation. But something in his eyes told me otherwise. And after what you shared last night, I just thought you'd want to know."

I tried to still my mind before my thoughts took me captive. I had to formulate a plan and quickly. "Warren, here's what I'd like you to do. Wait about fifteen minutes and then call O'Henry at the sheriff's office. Tell him to meet me at Clarksborough Catering."

I couldn't help but notice Janetta's eyes widen.

"Why Clarksborough Catering?" Warren asked. "What are you thinking, Annie?"

I drew in a deep breath, hoping he wouldn't question my explanation. "I know Richard Blevins pretty well, and I don't think there's a chance in the world he's going to leave town without taking care of one little thing first."

Warren paused a moment before responding. "Are you saying what I think you're saying?"

"I am. So do me a favor and call the sheriff's office," I repeated, "but give Richard a few minutes to get here first. I want to talk to him."

"Annie, I don't like the sound of that."

"I know, but you have to trust me, Warren," I explained. "I don't feel I'm in harm's way, but it will make you feel better to pray. And Warren —"

"Yes, baby?"

"I think we can safely say I've gotten your money's worth."

CHAPTER 28

I don't think Janetta stopped shaking her head even for a moment as I presented my theory of how, when, and why Richard Blevins had stolen her money. She took it all in without uttering a word, though I did notice her eyes moistening a time or two when I gave her my take on what I felt had driven him to do such a thing.

"Oh, Annie," she whispered as I finished. "Do you really think so?"

With a slight nod, I responded, "I don't think so. I know so. And if Richard Blevins is the man I think he is, you will see for yourself, very soon."

I sensed the minutes ticking by and asked Janetta if we could pray together. She agreed, no questions asked. I took hold of her hands, right there in the kitchen, and I prayed in earnest. Prayed for Richard. Prayed for truth to prevail. Prayed for God to intervene. Prayed for safety.

The words to my Bible verse ribboned around my heart:

" '*Knock and the door will be opened to you . . .*' "Together, Janetta and I knocked at heaven's door, standing firm on the promise that God would indeed open it for us.

" '*Seek and you will find . . .*' "I'd been seeking the perpetrator of this crime long enough. I knew beyond a reasonable doubt that I'd found the person I'd been looking for all along.

" '*Ask and it will be given to you . . .*' "With that on my mind, I asked God to do the unthinkable — to bring the man who had committed this crime directly to us.

And that's exactly what He did.

Richard's car turned into the drive within minutes of our prayer, just as I'd expected. We watched him through the kitchen window — me with a tightened jaw and Janetta in stunned silence.

Only slightly complicating matters, Jake walked into the kitchen at that very moment, dressed in his boxers and t-shirt and rubbing the sleep from his eyes.

"W–What do we do now?" Janetta asked, eyes wide.

"Do about what?" Jake raked his fingers through his messy hair and looked at me kind of funny. "Hey, Mrs. Peterson." He opened the refrigerator door in an attempt to hide his sleeping attire. "You're here early. What's up?"

"Mmm-hmm." I continued to stare out the window. Richard sat in his car, not moving. I knew what I had to do. I turned to face Janetta. "Would you two mind waiting in the house? Give me about five minutes alone with Richard."

"Oh, Annie." Concern filled Janetta's eyes.

Jake gazed out the window, his face lighting up. "Is that Richard Blevins? What's he doing here?"

Janetta and I both just shook our heads and said, "Don't ask," in tandem.

Jake responded with a curious stare.

With a prayer on my lips, I left the house and boldly marched down the driveway toward the car. Somehow, Sasha must've slipped through the door, because she came bounding alongside me. I reached down to lift her into my arms and kept walking.

Richard never saw me coming. I found him with his head slumped over the steering wheel, back heaving up and down as he wept.

I hated to interrupt his privacy but decided to go ahead and tap on the window while I still had my courage intact. He looked up with tear-filled eyes, clearly stunned to find me standing there. I continued to stand in silence until he rolled down his window.

"A–Annie? What are you doing here?" He swiped at his face, as if to brush away both the pain and the guilt I'd found there.

"I think you know, Richard."

For a moment, a blank look crossed his face, and then understanding apparently set in. More silence passed before I asked if I could join him in the passenger seat.

"Are you sure you want to?" he asked. "You're not scared of me?"

I shook my head and offered up a hint of a smile. "No, Richard. I'm not scared of you." I walked around the car, opened the passenger door, and slid into the seat, placing Sasha in my lap. She gave Richard an inquisitive look and then began to sniff around the vehicle, overjoyed at the prospect of her new surroundings.

Richard looked directly into my eyes, which surprised me a little. "How did you know?"

I shrugged. "I wasn't sure until last night."

"Last night?"

"Yes." I gave a slight nod. "I've been trying to solve this thing from the beginning — for my own personal reasons. But last night I played back through all of the evidence in my mind one last time. All of it. And when I got to the part that involved you, the Lord triggered a memory. It was something you said on the day you came to my house that jumped out at me."

His gaze shifted down. "What was that?"

"Just a simple comment," I explained, "which is why I didn't think anything of it at the time. But last night, the Lord took me back to what you'd said — that you would do anything for Judy. And I remembered the look of desperation in your eyes as you said it."

He nodded, almost in slow motion. "Yes."

I reached out to grab his hand. "I believe you really would have done anything to save Judy's life."

"I would have. I — I tried to." I could see his Adam's apple bobbing up and down and knew tears would soon come. "There is a place in Philadelphia," he whispered. "A cancer treatment center that specializes in a natural approach — holistic. You know, Annie: vitamins, herbs, diet . . . that kind of thing."

"Right."

A look of desperation laced his words, the same desperation I'd seen in his eyes that day in my living room. "I researched for days. Weeks, even. And I really believe they could have cured her. I read so many testimonies from patients. At this center they take the toughest cases — people the medical community has given up on — and they offer them hope. We —" He wavered. "We needed hope. But she didn't want to go. I found a way to get her in the door, but she wouldn't move from one place to the next. She was —"

"Ready." In my mind's eye, I caught a glimpse of Judy, dancing with her Savior. "She was ready to go home, Richard."

"Yes." A gut-wrenching sob escaped from the back of his throat. "B–But I wasn't ready to let her go."

I pushed back the lump in my throat as I responded. "No one can fault you for trying to keep Judy here," I said, "only your methods."

"She never knew," he whispered. "I didn't tell her about taking the money. I would have been so ashamed if she'd figured it out. I'm already ashamed enough." He gave me a pensive look. "That's why I'm here."

"I know."

Sasha bounded from my lap down onto the floorboard and stuck her head under the seat, rooting around with a vengeance. "Sasha, don't be a nosy-poke." I reached down to grab her, but my hand brushed against something under the edge of the seat. I pulled up a large night deposit bag, zipped shut, with the Clark County Savings and Loan logo on the front of it.

That's two treats for you, Sasha.

"I came to give that back to Janetta," Richard whispered. "I promise. I was going to tell her. I was."

"You don't have to say anymore." I'd known it, probably even before Warren's phone call. "I believe you."

"Thank you." His words were hushed, strained.

In spite of the anxiety in his eyes, I worked up the courage to ask a question. "I'd like to ask you something, if it's okay."

He shrugged and leaned back against the seat. I could read the defeat in his eyes.

"I've spent a lot of time thinking about this," I explained, "and I just need to know. The power outage — it was just a co-incidence, right? Something you took advantage of?"

Richard rubbed at his temples. "It wasn't like that. Not at first, anyway. I'd been awake all night, tossing and turning, trying to figure out what to do. I got out of bed to sign on to the Internet around two thirty in the morning. I'd only been online about ten minutes when the power went down. I was frustrated, Annie, and so scared. I wanted to fix things, to make everything better for Judy."

"I understand."

"I got into my car and drove around, just trying to reason things out with God. Remember, I told you once I have a lot of head knowledge, but my faith is . . . lacking."

My nod must have given him the courage to continue. And if anyone understood reasoning things out with God, I did.

"The whole town was darker than I'd ever seen it, and that only made my mood even —"

"Darker?"

"Yes. I found myself in the back parking lot of the bank, just staring off into space. Everything was black. And I knew the cameras would be down."

"You also knew Janetta Mullins had made a large cash deposit."

Richard's brow wrinkled, and his gaze shifted to his hands, which now clutched the bag. "Yes. I'd overheard one of the tellers talking to her on the phone just before we closed on Monday afternoon. I could tell they were talking about a cash deposit, because the teller tried to encourage her to wait 'til morning and come in person. But I knew in my gut she would drop it off that night to get it over with."

"How did you know that?"

Richard shook his head. "I've been in this business a long time. When people — especially women — are carrying around a lot of cash like that, they get nervous. They want to get it deposited quickly. Otherwise, they worry that it might be —"

"Stolen?"

He sighed. "Anyway, I sat there in my car, staring at the back of the bank, just looking at that deposit box, and thinking about how the cameras were down." He shook his head. "And I kept thinking about that treatment center. I knew how much money it would take to get Judy in the door. And I knew our insurance wouldn't cover it — at least not much of it. At some point along the way, I think I just snapped. I jumped out of the car and went into the bank. I didn't have a flashlight. I didn't have anything. I was just stumbling around in the dark."

"It's always darkest before the dawn." Sheila's words rang out once again. Richard had reached his lowest point as he faced the darkness alone that night. His faith had wavered, and doubt had propelled him to do the unthinkable. In his case, he had given

up on the dawn altogether.

I tried to think of something to say, but no words would come. I focused my attention on the puppy in my lap, scratching her behind the ears as I dissected everything Richard had said. And done.

He turned to face me, the level of his voice escalating in both speed and intensity.

"I took the money, Annie. I left all of the other deposits there, but I took the cash, bag and all. I left the bank, went back home, and tried to sleep. But I couldn't. I felt sick inside. Sick. As badly as I wanted to see Judy get the help she needed, I couldn't keep it. I couldn't." His eyes grew wild as he continued. "This is the crazy part. I tried to return it. First thing in the morning. Showed up at the bank before anyone else. I even beat Nikki there, which was a first. I was going to put it right back where I found it."

"I think I'd already figured out that part, too."

He nodded. "I managed to get the money back inside the bank, but the electricity came back on just as I arrived. That meant the cameras kicked on. I tried to figure out what to do, but Warren showed up right after that, and everyone went to work like nothing had happened. Of course, they didn't know anything had. But I was terrified all day. Crazy thing is, no one even realized we were short the twenty-five thousand dollars until Janetta Mullins called that afternoon to make sure the deposit had been credited to her account."

"You could have told them right then and there. They would have understood."

He shook his head, eyes closed. "No. I reached a point where there was no turning back, especially after the police got involved."

As the word "police" was spoken, I remembered what I'd asked Warren to do and wondered if he'd already contacted O'Henry.

Mere seconds later, the piercing wail of a siren broke the stillness, and I looked up to discover flashing lights in the rearview mirror. Sasha awoke with a start and leaped into the backseat to see out the rear window. The barking began the moment she laid eyes on the patrol car. I'm not sure what unnerved me more — her incessant yapping or the look of sheer terror in Richard's eyes.

CHAPTER 29

I looked back — beyond Richard's dazed expression — to the Clark County sheriff's squad car in the driveway behind us. O'Henry's voice rang out over the loudspeaker, instructing us to stay put, not to move a muscle. I couldn't quite figure out what to do about Sasha, who continued to bark uncontrollably. I whistled for her to join me in the front seat, and she bounded over into my lap, tail going to town.

Somehow, in spite of the chaos, I managed to reach over and slip my hand into Richard's for a tight squeeze.

"What am I going to do, Annie?" he whispered.

I spoke the only words that came to mind. "The right thing."

He nodded and we sat in silence for what seemed like an eternity; though probably only a minute or two, in reality. During that time, two other patrol cars arrived, lining the long driveway almost to the street. As the officers approached from behind, I took advantage of the moment to give Richard one last bit of encouragement. My words were rushed but framed in love.

"This will be the hardest thing you've ever had to face, next to losing Judy," I spoke softly, "but you can do this. God will redeem this thing and turn it around for His glory if you let Him."

A silent nod from Richard would have to suffice. The police swarmed the car like flies on a slice of watermelon. Sasha never stopped barking for a second, which only set my nerves on edge all the more. Seconds later, I found myself in the cold morning air, leaning against a Clark County Sheriff's Office patrol car, being questioned by one of the officers. Thankfully I'd managed to calm my canine crime fighter down. She rested in my arms as I talked. Out of the corner of my eye, I caught a glimpse of Richard as he visited quietly with O'Henry, and I whispered a silent prayer for courage on his part.

Just then, Warren's car pulled up. Directly behind him came Sheila. The officer, sensing my sudden loss of attention, said he'd get back with me later if he had additional questions.

Warren bounded from the driver's seat. "Annie! Are you okay?"

"I'm fine." *Unless you count the part where my heart is broken for the man now seated in the backseat of the patrol car in handcuffs.* I pressed Sasha into my husband's arms, and he took her, no questions asked.

Off in the distance, I could see an officer talking with Janetta and Jake. They stood with expressions of shock on their faces all the while.

Seconds later, Sheila sprinted my way, panting as she arrived. I had to laugh as I saw what she was wearing over her clothes — the plastic cape from our local salon. Silver foil wraps lined the left side of her head. The right side, apparently, would have to wait until another day.

Sasha took one look at Sheila in that getup and went bananas. Barked like a maniac. Warren struggled to control her. He also struggled to control his laughter as he looked at Sheila. And who could blame him? She looked, for all the world, like a Martian. On the left side, anyway.

Sheila either didn't notice or didn't care. She sputtered and spewed like my dad's old '59 Chevy. "I — I was at Th–The Liberty Belle having my hair done," she exclaimed, "and I saw all the commotion. First it was

O'Henry with his lights on, then the other officers in their patrol cars. Then it was Warren pulling out of the bank like a man possessed. I figured something must've happened and came running."

She glanced at the patrol car, then clamped her hand over her mouth as her gaze fell on Richard Blevins in the backseat. "Oh, Annie."

"I know."

"Did you . . . I mean, did you have anything to do with this?"

Warren nodded as he finally got Sasha calmed down. "She had everything to do with this. She's a crime-fighting diva, this girl of mine." He gave me a wink.

As I looked over at Richard, who sat with tears in his eyes, I had to admit, I didn't feel like a "crime-fighting diva." I felt a bit more like a traitor.

Then Janetta Mullins sprinted across the lawn and wrapped her arms around me with a squeal of joy. "They told me about the money." She clasped her hands together like an excited schoolgirl. "Not a penny missing."

"Yep, I know."

"But oh, Annie . . . Richard Blevins." She cast a wistful gaze at the patrol car. "It's just so . . . sad. Who would've guessed it?"

"Obviously Annie would have." Sheila grinned, then patted me on the back.

Janetta looked Sheila's way with the most curious look on her face. I could see her fighting to control the laughter, which just got Warren tickled all over again.

"If you ever get tired of editing, maybe you could go into crime fighting full time." Sheila carried on, as if nothing were out of the ordinary.

"No, thank you. I'd be perfectly content if I never had to track down another suspect as long as I live."

Sheila nudged me. "Speaking of suspects —"

I glanced across the yard to see Jake approaching, now dressed in jeans and a t-shirt. I'd never seen him so focused. He asked O'Henry if he could speak to Richard, and the officer agreed. The whole group of us held our collective breath as the young man leaned into the backseat of the patrol car to have his say.

Lord, please . . .

Whatever transpired between the two men happened quietly, without drama.

Jake stood aright, turned on his heels, and walked back toward the house, not a word to anyone else.

"What do you think he told him?" I asked Janetta.

"I haven't got a clue."

That word sent a little shiver down my spine. To be perfectly honest, I'd be one happy woman if I never heard the word again. You could remove it from the dictionary, in fact. And you could take my Internet courses and toss them right out the window, too. My crime fighting days were behind me.

Janetta and Sheila moved on to talk with a couple of the officers. At that moment, a reporter from the *Clark County Gazette* arrived and, after an inquisitive stare at Sheila in her beauty shop attire, inquired about an interview with yours truly. O'Henry gave the okay, with the understanding that I couldn't divulge any information pertinent to the case. With that in mind, I offered up a few carefully selected lines for our local paper. *Just the facts, ma'am.*

Just about that time, the patrol car pulled away. Richard kept his head low, not looking at any of us as they headed off toward town. I didn't blame him. I began to put together a plan for how the fine folks of Clarksborough Community Church could reach out to him. Surely Warren would go along, if only I could find him.

I'd just turned to look for him when my daughters arrived on the scene.

Brandi sprinted from her car, face etched with concern. "Mom, what in the world happened?" she asked. "Everyone in town is talking. Something about the bank robbery?"

"Burglary," I corrected.

Candy joined us, grabbing ahold of my hand. "We just need to know if you're okay. You are, aren't you?"

I assured them both that everything was fine, but neither looked convinced. Sheila's radar went off, and she scurried over to join us, patting at the foil on her hair, cheeks flaming.

"I forgot about these crazy things," she said sheepishly. "Do you think anyone noticed I came from the beauty shop?"

My laughter rang out across the lawn. Leave it to Sheila to come up with a question like that. I could read the headline in the *Gazette* now: MARTIAN LANDS ON CLARKSBOROUGH CATERING PROPERTY. Story on page four.

Oh, it felt good to laugh. Awfully good.

Once I calmed down, I told my girls the truth — the whole truth, and nothing but the truth. I started by telling them about my Internet courses and about how I'd suspected their father of stealing the money to pay for their weddings.

Brandi clamped a hand over her mouth, clearly stunned. "Mom, you're kidding. You thought Dad took the money?"

"For us?" Candy chimed in.

I shrugged. "Hey, I'm on a learning curve. What can I say?" I went on to tell them about the many ups and downs of my journey, even the part where I'd tied the dog to the flagpole — all in the hopes of catching the perpetrator.

Brandi giggled, then sputtered, "This certainly sheds a lot of light on things. So this is why you've been acting so strange."

"Hey now —" I started.

"Yeah, no kidding," Candy chimed in. "I thought for a while there you just weren't interested in our wedding plans, that you were deliberately avoiding us."

"Are you kidding me?" I looked at them both with excitement mounting. "Now that this investigation is behind me, I can dive in headfirst. Talk to me about flowers. I'm your girl. Tell me about your bridal registry. I'm on board. Share your concerns about reception halls. I can take it."

As the girls came alive with their latest wedding stories, I glanced across the yard, finally locating Warren. He stood next to

Jake, deep in conversation. Sasha lay curled up in his arms, sound asleep. As I called his name, Warren looked up, and our eyes met from a distance. Even from so far away, I could read the love written there.

Epilogue

I think the 463 handwritten letters from the fine folks at Clarksborough Community Church must've made a difference. Three weeks before Christmas, the judge who'd been assigned to Richard Blevins's case gave him the lowest possible sentence. Two years in the county jail, with three days credit for every one day served. In essence, he would probably be released in about six to nine months, with community service to follow. And we — his friends and family — would be here to welcome him home with open arms when the moment arrived.

On the morning after the trial, I tried to settle back into my routine. I spent an enjoyable hour soaking in a bubble-filled tub and praying. *Mental note: This new almond bath gel is just the ticket. Closest thing to heaven I've smelled in years.*

After toweling off, I dressed in a green and red Christmas sweater and my most comfortable pair of jeans. Instead of reading my devotional on the Internet, I opted to sit next to the fireplace with my Bible in hand. I turned to the book of Psalms and browsed the pages. After reading through several verses, I paused as I came across one in chapter sixty-eight that jumped out at me: "God sets the lonely in families, he leads forth the prisoners with singing."

I thought back over the past few months, how the Lord had done just that. He had taken Nikki Rogers and made her a semipermanent fixture at our family gatherings. My girls had connected with her on such a deep level that she currently found herself a bridesmaid-to-be in two upcoming weddings. The smile on her face had broadened when she learned that Jake Mullins would be the one escorting her down the aisle. Yep. He'd become a regular, too. And Amber, now a bona fide chatterbox, had agreed to welcome guests and hand out programs at both ceremonies. Talk about a transformation!

I pondered the situation with Janetta Mullins and her children, how they'd been grafted into the Clarksborough Community Church with such ease — how she'd taken over the ministry that provided meals for shut-ins. *What a natural she is at that!* I thought back to the day she had first arrived in church, a prodigal in need of a home. Surely God had drawn her back — with a little help from Sheila and that lovely singing voice.

He leads forth the prisoners with singing . . .

I stumbled a bit when I thought about Richard Blevins — currently imprisoned at the county jail. I knew that God would one day set him free, not just from his current situation, but from many losses in his life, and the guilt that surely lingered after the past few months. I contemplated the grace and mercy of a young man like Jake Mullins, who had taken the time to visit with Richard every week, rain or shine.

Most of all, however, I thought about my own family — how the Lord had invigorated us for the tasks ahead and how He had given me the courage to release my daughters into the hands of their future husbands. I prayed they would be as happy as Warren and I had been.

With such contented thoughts in mind, I set about my daily tasks. Now that the investigation was safely behind me, I found myself focusing on the truly exciting things of life, like laundry, dishes, and grocery shopping. I met up with Sheila for lunch at the diner and had a great chat with Shawna, who'd taken to calling me "honey" — not out of sarcasm but affection. I wasn't surprised to hear she had reconciled with her family in Philadelphia, not after all of our heart-to-heart chats over the prior weeks, but it did sadden me to know she would be leaving our little town. I would miss her dearly.

After lunch I returned home to edit a manuscript for a new client — the one I'd agreed to do at a lower cost. I read through it, excited to find little to edit. God had blessed my generosity with His grace.

The hours passed quickly, quietly. I fully enjoyed every moment. Even Sasha seemed content to rest easily at my feet as I worked. Her behavior over the past few weeks had improved slightly, but I still pondered the veterinarian's suggestion to get a second dog. Maybe one of these days we'd find Sasha a suitable husband. And why not? We were all in the wedding mind-set, anyway.

That evening I cooked up a delicious chicken recipe Janetta had sent me via e-mail. Warren offered a host of compliments as I dished out his second helping. Even Devin chimed in with some flattering remarks. After dinner, Devin headed off to a friend's house to watch a movie, and I set about the task of loading the dishwasher.

I'd no sooner started than Warren's voice interrupted me. "Annie."

"Hmm?" I kept my focus on the dishes, not looking up.

He cleared his throat. Loudly. I looked across the room to find him leaning against the kitchen wall . . . with a red rose in his teeth.

"What in the world?"

He held his hands out to the side and did a little cha-cha, then extended his arms in my direction.

Ah, an invitation.

I quickly dried my hands and eased into my husband's embrace. He took the rose — real, not fake — and pressed it behind my ear, then slowly danced me around in a circle. After giving me a final spin, he closed out our choreography with a well-rehearsed dip.

For whatever reason, as he lifted me back up into his arms for one of the sweetest kisses of my life, I was reminded of my very first Internet lesson: *Just the facts, ma'am.*

I ran through them again in my mind, so that I would never forget.

Fact #1: I am the happiest, most blessed woman on the planet.

Fact #2: Refer to Fact #1.

As I gazed up into my husband's eyes, I

felt the inevitable question coming on. He gave me a wink as he asked: "Moo-lenium Crunch?"

"It's freezing out tonight," I argued. "Are you sure you still want ice cream?"

He nodded and reached for the bowls. Together, we filled them and headed off to the den, where we sat side by side on the sofa.

Well, we tried to sit side by side. Sasha somehow managed to squirm her way between us, head resting on Warren's knee. Yep, she definitely needed a companion.

We sat quietly — the three of us — enjoying the crackling of the logs in the fireplace as we ate our ice cream together. When we finished, I leaned my head against Warren's shoulder and rested, content for the simplicity of such a blissful night.

As it so often did, life interrupted. The telephone rang out, shattering the stillness. I looked at the caller ID and had to smile. Brandi. Warren must've guessed from my smile.

"One of the girls?"

When I nodded, he said, "Let me get it." He answered the phone and dove into a joyous conversation with our eldest daughter.

He eventually passed the phone off to me, and Brandi began to fill my ears with tales of wedding photographers and tuxedo rentals. I leaned back against the sofa and let her go on, enjoying the cadence of her voice as the words flowed.

Warren slid his arm around me, and I leaned against his shoulder, phone still pressed to my ear. Every now and again I got in a "Sounds great, honey," but mostly I just listened. Listened with all of my senses — another thing I'd learned from my crime-fighting days. We ended the call, and I thought about those words. *Crime-fighting days. Hmm.*

Much as I hated to admit it aloud, I had enjoyed the past several weeks. Figuring out who had stolen the money from the bank had been challenging, sure, but I'd had a blast doing it.

My excitement rose as I considered the possibilities. Maybe the Lord had more adventures in store for me. Maybe He wanted me to scale the highest mountains. Maybe He wanted me to swim the deepest seas.

Or maybe . . .

I glanced over at my husband, who now snored like a freight train, his head tilted back against the sofa, lips slightly parted. I pulled the flower from behind my ear and slipped it between his teeth with a giggle.

Maybe He just wanted me to take the time to smell the roses.

ABOUT THE AUTHOR

Janice A. Thompson is a Christian novelist who lives in the Houston area. She has authored eleven books and has several more in progress, including a line of contemporary humorous wedding mysteries for Barbour Publishing. Janice considers herself somewhat overqualified when it comes to writing about weddings. In 2004, her two oldest daughters both received proposals within weeks of each other. Janice coordinated both weddings — a lovely Valentine's ceremony in February for her daughter, Randi, and a festive summer gala the following June for daughter, Courtney. The weddings came off without a hitch! Janice has since coordinated weddings for friends and is thrilled to incorporate many of her adventures into her stories. She's also tickled to be able to include her canine companion, Sasha, in each of her "tails."

The employees of Thorndike Press hope you have enjoyed this Large Print book. All our Thorndike and Wheeler Large Print titles are designed for easy reading, and all our books are made to last. Other Thorndike Press Large Print books are available at your library, through selected bookstores, or directly from us.

For information about titles, please call:
(800) 223-1244

or visit our Web site at:
http://gale.cengage.com/thorndike

To share your comments, please write:
Publisher
Thorndike Press
295 Kennedy Memorial Drive
Waterville, ME 04901